THE
GIRL
WHO FELL
BENEATH
THE SEA

AXIE OH

HODDER

First published in Great Britain in 2022 by Hodder & Stoughton
An Hachette UK company

This paperback edition published in 2023

6

A CIP catalogue record for this title is available from the British Library

Hardback ISBN 978 1 529 39169 5
Trade Paperback ISBN 978 1 529 39170 1
eBook ISBN 978 1 529 39171 8
Paperback ISBN 978 1 529 39173 2

Printed and bound in Great Britain by Clays Ltd, Elcograf S.p.A.

Hodder & Stoughton policy is to use papers that are natural, renewable
and recyclable products and made from wood grown in sustainable
forests. The logging and manufacturing processes are expected to
conform to the environmental regulations of the country of origin.

Hodder & Stoughton Ltd
Carmelite House
50 Victoria Embankment
London EC4Y 0DZ

www.hodder.co.uk

For my mom,
who has always believed in me.

1

The myths of my people say only a true bride of the Sea God can bring an end to his insatiable wrath. When the otherworldly storms rise from the East Sea, lightning breaking the sky and waters ripping up the shore, a bride is chosen and given to the Sea God.

Or sacrificed, depending on the measure of your faith.

Every year the storms begin, and every year a girl is brought to the sea. I can't help wondering if Shim Cheong believes in the myth of the Sea God's bride. If she'll find comfort in it before the end.

Or perhaps she sees it as a beginning. There are many pathways destiny can take.

For instance, there's my own path—the literal path before me, stretching narrowly through the waterlogged rice fields. If I follow this path, it'll eventually lead me to the beach. If I turn around, the path will take me back to the village.

Which destiny belongs to me? Which destiny will I grasp on to with both hands?

Even if it were up to choice, it wouldn't really be mine to make. For though a large part of me longs for the safety of home, the pull of my heart is infinitely stronger. It tugs me toward the open sea and to the one person I love beyond destiny.

My brother Joon.

Lightning streaks through the storm clouds, splintering across a blackened sky. A half second later, a clap of thunder rumbles over the rice fields.

The path ends where the dirt meets the sand. I take off my soggy sandals and fling them over my shoulder. Through the torrent of rain, I catch sight of the boat, tossing and turning upon the waves. It's a small, hollowed-out vessel with a single mast, meant to carry eight or so men—and one Sea God's bride. Already it's a distance from the shore, and moving farther still.

Lifting my rain-soaked skirt, I sprint toward the raging sea.

I hear a shout from the boat the same moment I crash into the first wave. Immediately I'm pulled under. The freezing water steals my breath. I tumble beneath the water, spinning violently to the left, then the right. I fight to get my mouth above the surface, but the waves pour into and over me.

I'm not a weak swimmer, but I'm also not a strong one, and although I fight to swim, to reach the boat and *live*, it's so very hard. It might not be enough. I wish it didn't hurt so much—the waves, the salt, the sea.

"Mina!" Strong hands wrap around my arms, pulling me out of the water. I'm placed firmly on the boat's undulating deck. My brother stands before me, familiar features twisted in a scowl.

"What were you thinking?" Joon shouts over the howling wind. "You could have drowned!"

A massive wave crashes against the boat, and I lose my balance. Joon grabs my wrist to keep me from tumbling overboard.

"I followed you!" I shout, just as loudly. "You shouldn't be here. Warriors aren't supposed to accompany the Sea God's bride." Looking at my brother now, his rain-lashed face and defiant expression, I want to collapse into tears. I want to drag him to the shore and never look back. How could he risk his life like this? "If the god should know of your presence, you'll be killed!"

Joon flinches, his eyes flicking to the prow of the boat, where a slender figure stands, hair whipping sharply in the wind.

Shim Cheong.

"You don't understand," Joon says. "I couldn't . . . I couldn't let her face this alone."

The breaking of his voice confirms what I've suspected all along, what I'd hoped wasn't true. I curse under my breath, but Joon doesn't notice. His entire being is focused on *her*.

The elders say Shim Cheong was fashioned by the Goddess of Creation to be the Sea God's final bride, the one to ease all his sorrows and usher in a new era of peace in the kingdom. She has skin forged from the purest of pearls. She has hair stitched from the deepest night. She has lips colored by the blood of men.

Maybe this last detail is more bitterness than truth.

I remember the first time I saw Shim Cheong. I was standing with Joon beside the river. It was the night of the paper boat festival four summers ago, when I was twelve and Joon was fourteen.

It is tradition in the seaside villages to write wishes onto pieces of paper before folding them carefully into boats to set upon the river. The belief is that our paper boats will carry our wishes to our dead ancestors in the Spirit Realm, where they can bargain with the lesser gods to fulfill our dreams and desires.

"Shim Cheong might be the most beautiful girl in the village, but her face is a curse."

I looked up at the sound of Joon's voice, following his gaze to the bridge spanning the river, where a girl stood at its center.

With her face lit by moonlight, Shim Cheong seemed more goddess than girl. She held a paper boat of her own. It fell from her open palm onto the water. As I watched it drift down the river, I wondered what someone so beautiful could possibly wish for.

I didn't know then that Shim Cheong was already destined to be the Sea God's bride.

Now, standing on the boat in the pouring rain with thunder rattling my bones, I notice the way the men keep away from her. It's as if she's already been sacrificed, her otherworldly beauty separating her from the rest of us. She belongs to the Sea God. It's what the village has always known, ever since she came of age.

I wonder if it happens in a day, for your fate to change. Or if it takes longer for your life to be stolen from you.

I wonder if Joon sensed this loneliness in her. Because ever since Shim Cheong was twelve, she belonged to the Sea God, and while everyone might have seen her as someone who would one day leave, he was the only one who wanted her to stay.

"Mina." Joon tugs my arm. "You need to hide."

I watch as Joon anxiously searches the uncovered deck for a place for me to conceal myself. He might not care that he's broken one of the Sea God's three rules, but he worries for me.

The rules are simple: No warriors. No women, besides the Sea God's bride. No weapons. Joon broke the first rule by coming tonight. I broke the second.

And the third. My hand curls around the knife hidden beneath my short jacket, the blade that once belonged to my great-great-grandmother.

The boat must have reached the center of the storm, because the winds stop howling, the waves cease their crashing over the deck, and even the rain lessens its relentless battering.

It's dark in every direction, the clouds obscuring the moonlight. I move closer to the boat's edge and look over the side. The lightning flashes, and in the brightness, I see it. The fishermen see it, too, their screams swallowed by the night.

Beneath the boat moves a massive silver-blue dragon.

Its snakelike body circles the boat, the ridges of its scaled back breaking the surface of the water.

The flash of lightning dissipates. Darkness falls once more, and all that can be heard is the endless roll of the waves. I shiver, imagining all the awful fates that might await us, either through drowning or being devoured by the Sea God's servant.

The boat groans as the dragon slides right up against the hull.

What is the purpose of this? What was the Sea God thinking, sending his terrifying servant? Is he testing the courage of his bride?

I blink, realizing my anger has dispelled most of my fear. My gaze sweeps the boat. Shim Cheong still stands at the prow, but she's no longer alone.

"Joon!" I shout, my heart dropping.

Joon whips his head in my direction, abruptly releasing Shim Cheong's hand.

Behind them, the dragon rises silently out of the water, its long neck extending into the sky. Seawater falls off its dark blue scales, dropping like coins onto the boat's deck.

Its black, fathomless eyes are riveted on Shim Cheong.

This is the moment.

I don't know what's supposed to happen, but this is the moment we've all been waiting for, what Shim Cheong has been waiting for since the day she learned she was too beautiful to live. This is the moment when she loses everything. Most devastatingly, the boy she loves.

And in this moment, Shim Cheong hesitates.

She turns from the dragon, her eyes finding Joon's. She gives him a look I've never seen before—one of agony, fear, and such desperate longing it breaks my heart. Joon lets out a choked sound, takes one step toward her, and then another, until he's standing in front of her, his empty hands spread wide in protection.

And with just this, he's sealed his fate. The dragon will never let him go, not after this act of defiance. As if to prove my fears, the great beast lets out a deafening roar, bringing all the men left standing to their knees.

Except for Joon. My fierce, stubborn fool of a brother, who stands as if he can single-handedly protect his love from the Sea God's wrath.

An unbearable anger rises up within me, starting in my stomach and clawing up to choke me. The gods have *chosen* not to grant our wishes—our wishes from the paper boat festival, but also the small wishes we make every day. For peace, for fertility, for love. The gods have abandoned us. The god of gods, the Sea God, *wants* to take from the people who love him—take and take and never give.

The gods might not grant our wishes. But I could. For Joon. I could grant his wish.

I rush to the prow of the boat and leap onto the edge. "Take me instead!" I whip out my knife and make a deep slash across my palm, raising it up high above my head. "I will be the Sea God's bride. I pledge my life to him!"

My words are met with utter stillness from the dragon. And right away, I doubt everything. Why would the Sea God take me instead of Shim Cheong? I haven't her beauty or her elegance. I just have my own stubborn will, the one my grandmother always said would be the curse of me.

But then the dragon lowers its head, turning to the side so I can look straight into one of its black eyes. It's as deep and endless as the sea.

"Please," I whisper.

In this moment, I don't feel beautiful. Nor do I feel very brave, my hands trembling. But there's a warmth in my chest that nothing and no one can take from me. This is the strength I call upon now, because even if I am afraid, I know I've chosen this.

I am the maker of my own destiny.

"Mina!" my brother shouts. "No!"

The dragon lifts its body out of the water, dropping a length of its massive bulk between my brother and me, separating us. In the silence, surrounded completely by the dragon, I hesitate, wondering how much it can understand.

I grasp for the right words. The truth.

I take a breath, lifting my chin. "I am the Sea God's bride."

The dragon drags its body away from the boat, revealing an opening in the churning water.

Without looking back, I jump into the sea.

2

As I sink, the roar of the waves abruptly cuts off, and all is silent. Over and around me, the dragon's long, sinuous body circles, swirling a great whirlpool.

Together we fall through the sea.

Strange, but the urge to breathe never rises. My descent is almost . . . calm. Peaceful. This must be the dragon's doing. It's using its magic to keep me from drowning.

My throat tightens, and my heart pounds with relief—all the brides before me, they lived.

Down into the darkness we sink, until the sea above me is the sky, and we—the dragon and I—are like falling stars.

The dragon circles closer, and through its tightening coils I catch sight of one hooded eye, opened slightly to reveal a glittering pool of midnight. Time slows. The world stops. I reach out my hand. Droplets of blood leave the open wound to trail like gemstones across the distance between us.

The dragon blinks, once. A rift opens up below me.

I drop through it into darkness.

My grandmother often told me stories about the Spirit Realm, a place between heaven and earth filled with all kinds of wondrous beings—gods and spirits and mythical creatures. My grandmother said it was her own grandmother who used to tell her the stories. After all, not all storytellers are grandmothers, but all grandmothers are storytellers.

My grandmother and I would make the short walk through the rice fields and down to the beach, each carrying one side of a folded bamboo mat. We'd spread the mat on the pebbled sand and link arms as we sat side by side, dipping our toes into the cool water.

I remember the way the sea looked in the early morning. The sun peeked out from over the horizon and lit a golden pathway across the water. The briny air misted over our faces like salty kisses. I would lean closer to my grandmother, basking in her steady warmth.

She'd always start with stories first, those with beginnings and endings, but as the orange and purple hues of the early morning settled into the bright blue of afternoon, she would begin to ramble, her voice a soothing melody.

"The Spirit Realm is a vast and magical place, but the greatest of all its wonders is the Sea God's city. Some say the Sea God is a very old man. Some say he's a man in his prime, tall as a tree with a beard as black as slate. And others believe he might even be a dragon himself, made of wind and water. But whatever form the

Sea God takes, the gods and spirits of the realm obey him, for he is the god of gods, and ruler of them all."

My whole life, I've lived surrounded by gods. There are thousands of them—the god of the well at the center of our village, who sings through the croaking of the frogs; the goddess of the breeze that comes from the west as the moon rises; the god of the stream in our garden, to whom Joon and I used to leave offerings of mud cakes and lotus lily pies. The world is filled with small gods, for each part of nature has a guardian to watch over and protect it.

A strong sea wind swept over the water. My grandmother lifted her hand to her straw hat to keep it from being ripped away into the darkening sky. Even though it was still early in the day, clouds gathered overhead, thick with rain.

"Grandmother," I asked, "what makes the Sea God more powerful than the other gods?"

"Our sea is an embodiment of him," she said, "and he is the sea. He is powerful because the sea is powerful. And the sea is powerful . . ."

"Because he is," I finished for her. My grandmother liked to speak in circles.

A low groan of thunder rumbled across the sky. The pebbles at our feet skittered into the water and were washed away with the tide. Beyond the horizon, a storm brewed. Clouds of eddying dust and ice crystals swirled upward in a funnel of darkness. I gasped. A feeling of anticipation swept through my soul.

"It's beginning," my grandmother said. Quickly we stood and

rolled up the bamboo mat, then walked swiftly toward the dunes that separated the beach from the village. I slipped in the sand, but my grandmother grabbed my hand to steady me. As we reached the top, I looked back one last time.

The sea was in shadow. The clouds above blocked the sunlight. It looked otherworldly, so unlike the sea of the morning that, though I had sat by the water only a moment before, I suddenly missed it terribly. For the next few weeks, the storms would grow worse and worse, making it impossible to travel close to the shore without being swallowed by the waves. They would rage uncontrollably until the morning when the clouds would part overhead, allowing for a brief ray of sunlight to peek through, a sign that the time to sacrifice a bride had come.

"What makes the Sea God so angry?" I asked my grandmother, who had stopped to gaze out across the dark water. "Is it us?"

She turned to me then, strong emotion in her brown eyes. "The Sea God isn't angry, Mina. He's lost. He's waiting, in his palace far beyond this world, for someone brave enough to find him."

I sit up and gasp in a lungful of air. Last I remember, I was falling through the sea. Yet I'm no longer underwater. It's as if I've woken inside the belly of a cloud. A white fog covers the world, making it difficult to see past my knees.

Standing, I wince as my dress, dried and brittle with salt,

scrapes against my skin. From the folds of my skirt topples my great-great-grandmother's knife, clattering against the wooden floorboards. As I reach to pick it up, a flutter of color catches my eye.

Wrapped around my left palm, over the wound I cut to make my vow to the Sea God, is a ribbon.

A bright red ribbon of silk. One end circles my hand, but the other blooms from the center of my palm outward, leading into the mist.

A ribbon floating on air. I've never seen anything like it, yet I know what it must be.

The Red String of Fate.

According to my grandmother's stories, the Red String of Fate ties a person to her destiny. Some even believe that it ties you to the one person your heart desires most.

Joon, ever the romantic, believed this to be true. He said he knew when he met Cheong for the first time that his life would never be the same. That he felt, in the way his hand tugged in the direction of hers, the subtle pull of fate.

And yet, the Red String of Fate is invisible in the mortal world. The bright red ribbon before me is decidedly *not* invisible, which means . . .

I am no longer in the mortal world.

As if sensing my thoughts, the ribbon gives a firm tug. Someone—or some*thing*—is pulling me from the other side, from within the mist.

Fear attempts to grab hold of me, and I squash it with a stubborn shake of my head. The other brides endured this, and I must, too, if I am to be a worthy replacement for Shim Cheong. The dragon accepted me, but until I speak with the Sea God, I won't know whether my village is truly safe.

At least I am more prepared than most, armed as I am with my knife and my grandmother's stories.

The ribbon flutters in the air, beckoning me forward. I take a step, and the ribbon alights against my palm in a spark of stars. Tucking my knife inside my short jacket, I follow the ribbon into the white fog.

All around me the world is still and silent. I slide my bare feet against the smooth wooden slats of the floor. I reach out a hand, and my fingers brush something solid—a railing. I must be on a bridge. The path slopes at a shallow decline, giving way to cobblestoned streets.

Here the air is thicker, warmer, filled with an aroma of mouth-watering scents. Out of the fog looms a line of carts. The closest is stacked high with dumplings in bamboo steamers. Another cart holds salted fish, strung up by their tails. A third is spread with sweets—candied chestnuts and flat cakes of sugar and cinnamon. Every cart is abandoned. No peddlers in sight. I squint, trying to make out the darker shapes, but every shadow turns out to be just another cart, a chain of them, stretching onward into the mist.

Leaving the carts behind, I enter a long alleyway lined with restaurants. Smoke from cooking fires wafts through open doorways. A glimpse through the nearest one reveals a room laid out with tables spread with dishes of food ranging from small bowls of spices to large platters of roasted fowl and fish. Bright cushions are arranged haphazardly about the tables as if revelers had been sitting comfortably, enjoying their meals, only minutes before. At the entrance, pairs of neatly placed sandals and slippers are lined up all in a row. Patrons went into the restaurant, but they didn't come out.

I back away from the doorway. Carts without owners. Cooking fires without cooks. Shoes without people.

A city of ghosts.

There's a soft breath of laughter against my neck. I turn around abruptly, but there's no one there. Still, I feel as if there are eyes on me, unseen and watchful.

What sort of place is this? It's not like any of the stories my grandmother told of the Sea God's city—a place where spirits and lesser gods gather in joy and celebration. The fog covers the realm like a cloak, muffling sight and sound. I cross over short, arched bridges and down abandoned streets, everything around me colorless and dull but for the ribbon, achingly bright as it cuts through the fog.

How did the Sea God's brides feel, waking to a realm of fog with only a bright ribbon as a guide? There were many who came before me.

There was Soah, who had the loveliest eyes, framed by dark lashes that looked as if they were coated in a heavy layer of soot. There was Wol, who stood as tall as any man, with strong, handsome features and a laughing mouth. And there was Hyeri, who could swim the span of the Great River twice over, and who broke a hundred hearts when she left to wed the Sea God.

Soah. Wol. Hyeri. *Mina*.

15

My name sounds small beside theirs, these girls who always seemed larger than life. They traveled from far away to marry the Sea God, from villages closer to the capital—even *from* the capital in the case of Wol. They were girls who would never have ventured to our backwater village in any other life than the one that forced them to give up their own. These girls, these young women, they were all older than me, eighteen when they left to be brides. They walked the same path as I walk now. I wonder if they were nervous or afraid. Or if hope made fools of them all.

After what seems like hours of walking, I turn a corner and step out onto a wide boulevard. The fog is thinner here. For once, I can see where the ribbon leads. It flits down the length of the boulevard, floating up a grand sweep of stairs and vanishing through the open doors of a massive red-and-gold gate. With its ornate pillars and gilded roof, this can be none other than the entrance to the Sea God's palace.

I hurry forward. The ribbon begins to sparkle and hum, as if it can sense my nearness to the end.

I reach the stairs and take one step, then another. I'm about to pass through the threshold of the gate when a sound catches my ear. The soft chime of a bell, faint enough that if the world hadn't been blanketed in silence, I might not have heard it. The sound came from somewhere to my left, down the stairs and back into the labyrinth of streets.

My eldest brother, Sung, thinks all wind chimes sound the same. But I think he just doesn't have the patience to listen. The clanking of bronze baubles against seashells sounds different from the tapping of tin against copper bells. The wind, too, has vary-ing degrees of temperament. When it's angry, the chimes make a sharp, shrilling sound. When it's happy, the chimes clink together in a lively dance.

This sound, though, is different. Low. Melancholy.

I step back down the stairs. The ribbon doesn't resist but grows in length, trailing after me.

I can hear my grandmother's voice in my ear. *There are rules to the world of spirits, Mina. Choose carefully which ones you break.* There is a reason this city is veiled in mist. There is a reason I can only travel through it by way of a ribbon of fate. But the sound of the chime was close, and the truth is, I think I've *heard* it before.

The sound leads me to the doorway of a small shop off the boulevard. I brush aside the rough curtain and step inside, gasp-ing at the wondrous sight. The shop is filled with hundreds upon hundreds of wind chimes. They cover the walls and hang from the ceiling like teardrops. Some of the charms are round and small, made of seashells, acorns, and tin stars; others are large waterfalls of golden bells.

And yet, as within the white fog, there's no wind in the shop.

But I could have sworn I heard a sound. My eyes are drawn to the far wall, where a gap at the center displays a single wind chime. A star, a moon, and a copper bell are threaded on a thin bamboo string. It's a simple construction for a chime.

I recognize it immediately.

I carved the star from a piece of driftwood and the moon from a beautiful white seashell I'd found on the beach. The bell

I purchased from a traveling bell maker, pestering him as I rang each bell inside his cart, one after another. I wouldn't settle until I found the perfect sound.

I spent a week crafting the chime. I meant to hang it above my niece's cradle, so she could hear the wind.

But she was born too early. If she'd been born in the autumn, she would have lived. But as everyone knows, all children born during the storms never survive past the first breath.

Sung was heartbroken.

In a rage I've never felt before or since, I took the charm to the cliffs outside our village and pitched it over the edge. I watched as it fell and shattered upon the rocks. Last I saw the chime, it was in pieces as they were swept away into the sea.

All around me the chimes in the shop begin to jingle— somehow swaying in the windless air—until the shop is a clamor of cacophonous sounds.

Wind chimes ringing without wind mean there are spirits about.

I exit the shop, the sound of the chimes dampened to my ears. If there are spirits here, and they're invisible, watching, what do they see when they look at me?

I walk fast. The night is long, and the ribbon is a weight against my hand. Beyond the gate is one grand courtyard after another. I look at none of them. After the fifth, I'm running.

I step through a final gate, climb the stone steps, and enter the throne room of the Sea God, stopping only then to catch my breath.

Moonlight filters through breaks in the raftered ceiling, slant-ing broken light across a great hall. The twilight gloom of the fog is muted here, but still the eerie silence remains. No servants rush out to greet me. No guards move to block my path. The Red String of Fate ripples. Slowly it begins to shift from a bright, sparkling crimson to a deep bloodred. It leads me to the end of the hall, where a massive mural of the dragon chasing a pearl across the sky frames a throne on a dais.

Slumped over the throne, his face shadowed by a magnificent crown, is the Sea God. He's dressed in beautiful blue robes, stitched silver dragons climbing up the fabric. Around his left hand is the end of my ribbon.

I wait for the spark of recognition in my soul.

According to myth, the Red String of Fate ties a person to her destiny. Some even believe that it ties you to the one person your heart desires most.

Is the Sea God tied somehow to my destiny? Does my heart desire him most?

There's a sharp pain in my chest, but it's not love.

It's darker, hotter, and infinitely stronger.

I *hate* him.

I take a step. And then another. My hand that holds the ribbon goes to my chest and comes away with the knife.

What would the world be like without the Sea God? Would we still suffer the storms that rise out of nothing to wreck our boats and drown our fields? Would we still suffer the loss of our loved ones to famine and sickness, because the lesser gods can't *or won't* hear our prayers, fearful as they are of the Sea God's wrath?

"What would happen, if I were to kill you now?"

As the words echo in the vast hall, I realize these are the first words I've spoken aloud since arriving in the Sea God's realm.

And they're words of hate. My anger swells up like an unstoppable wave. "I would kill you now and sever the ties of our fate."

My words are reckless. Who am I to defy a god? But there's a terrible ache inside me that needs to know—

"Why do you curse us? Why do you look away when we cry and scream for your help? Why have you abandoned us?" I choke on these last words.

The figure on the throne doesn't answer. The magnificent crown he wears leans so far forward over his face that it shadows his eyes.

I take the last few steps to the dais. Reaching out, I remove the crown from the Sea God's head. It slips from my fingers to land with a thud against the silk carpet.

I lift my eyes to look upon the face of the god of all gods.

The Sea God is . . .

A boy. No older than myself.

His skin is smooth, unmarred. His hair flops against his forehead, curling around slender ears, one pierced through with a golden thorn. His eyelashes are noticeably long in the way they fall across his cheeks, dusky and misted. I watch as his mouth parts, letting out a soft sigh of breath.

He's . . . asleep.

My hand tightens around the handle of my knife. I don't know what I expected, but it's not *him*, a boy who appears so . . . human, he could be a neighbor or a friend. I watch as a tear slips down his face, catching on his lip before falling over his chin and sliding down his neck.

"Why are you crying?" I growl. "Do you think your tears will break my will?"

I can *feel* it breaking. I am not like Joon, who has a gentle heart. I can be stubborn and cruel. I can be bitter and resentful. I want to be all of those things now, because they keep me brave. They keep me *angry*. And don't I deserve to be angry, after all that he's done to my village, to my family?

But the expression on the Sea God's face matches Shim Cheong's on the boat. There's such loneliness there and a deep, unbearable sadness.

A traitorous thought slips into my mind, and I wonder . . .

Is it you that makes the world cry, or the world that makes you cry?

My legs give out beneath me, and I sink to the floor.

So much has happened in a night, from discovering Joon was missing to chasing him in the rain to jumping into the sea. By now Joon will have returned with Cheong to the village and told our family what I've done. I know my sister-in-law will weep, and my heart aches knowing that I've caused her further grief. My eldest brother will want to scour the sea in search of me, unable to accept that he can no longer protect me. As for my grandmother, she'll have faith that I've entered the Spirit Realm, that I'm on my way to meet the Sea God at this very moment.

"And what would the Sea God's bride do, once she's found him?" I stood with my grandmother in the small seaside temple. It was the first night of the storms, and the rain pattered on the clay tiles of the rooftop.

"She would show him her heart."

21

I frowned. "And how would she do that?"

"If you were to show the Sea God your heart, what would it look like?"

My eyes caught on the odd assortment of items left on the shrine, offerings from the children of the village—a seashell, a wind flower, a curiously shaped stone.

Reaching forward, I picked up the tail feather of a magpie.

"Brides don't often travel with gifts for the Sea God," my grandmother chided. "Use your voice."

"But I have nothing to say! End the storms. Protect my family. Watch over us all. He has done none of these things." Tears pricked the corners of my eyes.

My grandmother patted the rush mat, and I sank to my knees beside her. Gently, she took my hands in her own. "You remind me so much of myself when I was your age. After much loss, grief and disappointment were rooted deep in my heart. It was my own grandmother who took me to this very same shrine. She was a lot like you, incredibly fierce and devoted to those she loved."

It was not the first time my grandmother likened me to hers, and I instinctively reached for my knife, comforted by its weight against my chest.

"It was she who taught me the song that I'll pass on to you now."

In the Sea God's hall, I rise to my feet. The melody my grandmother used to sing to me, I sing it for the Sea God now.

> Beneath the sea, the dragon sleeps
> What is he dreaming of?

Beneath the sea, the dragon sleeps
When will he wake?

On a dragon's pearl,
your wish will leap.

On a dragon's pearl,
your wish will leap.

The echo of my voice fills the hall. Tears slip down my cheeks, and I brush them away with the back of my fist.

The myths of my people say only a true bride of the Sea God can bring an end to his insatiable wrath. I may not be the chosen bride, but is it too much to hope that a girl like me—a girl with nothing but herself to give—could be the Sea God's true bride?

I catch a subtle shift out of the corner of my eye. The Sea God's fingers twitch, the barest tremble of movement.

I reach out my hand toward his. The Red String of Fate, as if sensing the immensity of the moment, pulls taut, and I wonder, hope like the fluttering of a bird's wings, if my life's about to change.

A voice like steel cuts through the silence. "That's enough."

3

Three masked figures stand below the dais, positioned in a half circle like the arc of a crescent moon.

The space of the hall is cavernous, and yet I'd heard no sign of their approach. Clouds pass overhead, sealing off the light from the rafters and sweeping a curtain of darkness over the hall. It eludes two of the figures, those positioned nearest the throne, enveloping the third standing apart from the others. The last glimpse I have of him before he's consumed by darkness is the curve of a pale cheek.

"What's this?" The figure on the right flips a dagger into the air and catches it. "A magpie lost in a storm? Or is she another bride for the Sea God?" His low voice is muffled beneath the cloth mask. "Are you a bride or are you a bird?"

I lick my lips, tasting salt. "Are you a friend or are you a foe?"

"If I'm a friend . . . ?"

"Then I'm a bride."

"If I'm a foe . . . ?"

"Are you?"

"Perhaps I'm a foe who'd like to be a friend." He tilts his head, and a dark curl falls across his eyes. "And perhaps you're a bird who'd like to be a bride."

It's close enough to the truth that I wince. The elders of my village have a saying: *A magpie may dream it's a crane, but never will it be one.*

"I see," the figure on the left murmurs, black-clad like the first, with hair that reaches past his shoulders. His eyes—an odd, light brown—move from my half-unraveled braid to my rough cotton dress. "You were never meant to be the Sea God's bride."

Unlike the curly-haired youth, this young man holds no weapons, only—curiously—a wooden birdcage, slung over his shoulder by a rope. "The elders of your village select the bride a year before the ritual. She is always extraordinary, in either skill or beauty."

"Preferably both," the boy with the dagger interjects.

"It is not an honor bestowed upon the common, the weak, or the rash. So tell me, No One's Bride, who chose *you*?"

If the curly-haired youth wields a blade for a weapon, the cold-eyed stranger brandishes words. For all my many blessings—a loving family, courage, and health—I have neither beauty nor talent.

I can imagine how upon Joon and Cheong's return, the elders must have raged in disbelief and cursed my willfulness. But they weren't there, on the boat. They didn't feel the sharp spray of water, the heart-stopping fear when a loved one is in danger. I may be rash. Common, perhaps. But I am not weak.

"I chose myself."

The third figure at the back shifts his feet. Wary of him, I

notice the subtle movement. Strangely, so do my two interroga-
tors, though they face me with their backs to him. They tilt their
heads inward, waiting . . . for a signal? He doesn't speak, and they
ease back into position.

The first boy crosses his arms, tucking the dagger against the
side of his chest. "Don't you think it romantic, Kirin? A young,
ordinary magpie hopes to save her kind from a terrible dragon, and
so she agrees to marry him. In time, she discovers that he's caught
in a powerful enchantment, the root of his destructive nature. The
brave, clever magpie finds a way to break the curse, and in turn,
falls in love with the dragon, and he with her. Peace is restored to
the sky, land, and sea. A grand tale if ever I've heard one. I'll call it
'The Dragon and the Magpie.'"

"No, Namgi," the cool-eyed stranger—Kirin—drawls, "I don't
think it's romantic."

Namgi responds to Kirin with an insult, and Kirin follows
with his own rude rejoinder. This must be a routine of theirs,
because their exchange grows quite colorful.

I ignore them, concentrating instead on the story the first boy
just told. My grandmother always says to pay attention to stories,
for there are often truths hidden within.

"Is it a curse, then?" Namgi and Kirin cease their quarrel,
returning their attention to me. "The Sea God hasn't abandoned
his people. He's under a curse."

I have no control over how others might measure my worth,
but stories and myths I'm familiar with. Stories and myths are my
blood and breath.

And for this one I can already see a pattern forming, like a melody woven through myth. The dragon appears to deliver the Sea God's brides safely to this realm. The world is covered in mist, but the Red String of Fate guides them to the palace.

Yet, why have none of the brides succeeded in their task? It's almost as if the melody was cut short, as if, when they finally arrived to finish the story, an enemy arose to stop them.

The Sea God cries out. I gasp as an unfamiliar feeling grips my heart, like a knot cinching tight. The Red String of Fate heats in my hand. Behind me, a floorboard creaks. I twist around.

Namgi and Kirin have moved. They still hold the same positions, Namgi with his arms crossed over his chest, Kirin motionless with the birdcage, but they're closer by three steps.

I've been so concerned about defending who *I* am, a stranger in a strange world, but who are *they*? What sorts of men wear masks? Those who wish to remain unremembered. Thieves.

Assassins.

"It's time," Kirin says to Namgi.

Uncrossing his arms, Namgi brings the dagger to his side. "Sorry, Magpie. You shouldn't put so much faith in stories."

I still hold my knife. I take the defensive stance my grandmother taught me, blade angled against the threat. "Stay back."

There's another sharp twist, and I grit my teeth through the pain. I can't think clearly. Did they *kill* all the brides before me? My hand trembles. In a pinch, I might be clever with a knife, but I'm no warrior. Two against one, three including the figure still in shadows.

Kirin turns his face away, dismissing me. "You should have never come, No One's Bride."

Why is this happening? Is the Sea God . . . rejecting me? Because I am not Shim Cheong. Because I am not the Sea God's bride. All of this began with her. Joon risked his life because he couldn't accept losing her, and I risked mine because I couldn't accept losing him. And Shim Cheong . . . what couldn't she accept?

I can see her clearly as she stood on the boat, confronting her fate in the form of the dragon, rising up out of the sea. A fate she never asked for. A fate she refused.

On the throne, the boy-god thrashes from side to side. He's still asleep, his eyes squeezed shut. The Red String of Fate lashes out, searing me.

With a desperate leap, I reach for the Sea God. At the same time, there's a shout behind me. I ignore it, grabbing the Sea God's hand and gripping tight. The Red String of Fate disappears between our clasped palms, and then I'm abruptly pulled forward into a blinding light.

I'm met with a flurry of images, moving too quickly to make sense of—a cliff by the sea; a golden city burning in a valley; crimson robes on the ground, darkened with blood; and a colossal shadow.

I look up. The dragon descends from above, clutching a pearl in one giant talon, as if holding the moon.

Then I'm torn from the images, my hand ripped from the Sea God's. The third assassin grips my wrist, and it's as if I'm still in the Sea God's dreams, because I can almost believe I see the dragon reflected in his dark eyes.

Then he releases me, stepping back. I struggle to hold on to the images in the dream—or were they memories? The cliffs are familiar; they stretch all along the coast. The city must be the capital, though all the messengers who come through our village bring only news of the conqueror's triumphs, not of war or destruction. As for the robes, the Sea God's are silver and blue.

"Those images." I shake my head, trying to concentrate. "It felt like I was seeing them through the Sea God's eyes."

I'm surprised when the assassin responds. "They're from his nightmare. Every year he has the same one."

"Then there truly is a connection to the Sea God's bride. The power to lift the curse lies within her."

"You wanted to kill him, not so long ago."

I glance sharply at the assassin. He and the others must have been in the hall when I arrived, if they saw me raise my knife. Why didn't they stop me? I don't think they mean to harm the Sea God, otherwise they would have attacked him, vulnerable as he is in his sleep.

Like Namgi and Kirin, the third assassin is dressed in thin cotton robes, a blue so dark it appears black. Even with the mask, his youth is undeniable—smooth skin, a strong, lean body. He can't be much older than seventeen.

"Am I not allowed to be angry?" I say curtly. "My people have suffered much because of the Sea God's abandonment. Because of his neglect, the other gods have turned away from us."

I think of my grandmother, calling me to the shrine to pray. I think of the wind chime I made for my niece, dashed upon the rocks. And then another memory calls from deep within me, of a dark forest and a winding path.

I shake my head, willing away the images. "But that was

before I came here, where nothing is as I expected. Nor is *he* what I expected." On the throne, the Sea God sleeps, peaceful after the tumult only moments before. He is not the cruel and spiteful deity I envisioned, but a boy-god, asleep and crying in his dreams.

I didn't run to the beach to become the Sea God's bride but to save my brother. But I am here now, and if there's a chance I can save not only him, but everyone, then I have to try.

And maybe, when this is all over, I can go home. To my village. To my family. My heart yearns at the thought.

"If it is a curse that plagues him, then I will find a way to break it."

The Sea God lets out a gentle sigh. Between us, the Red String of Fate flutters, and a feeling like hope steals into my heart.

"You're just like all the other brides," the dark-eyed boy says softly. I turn to find that he's stepped back, his eyes downcast. "Humans tell myths to explain what they cannot understand."

He lifts his gaze, and his eyes are like the deepest part of the sea, cold and unknowable. I realize, *His eyes do more to hide his thoughts than his mask does to hide his face.*

"But I can explain it to you," he continues. "Your people suffer not because of any great will of the gods, but because of their own violent acts. They wage the wars that burn the forests and fields. They spill the blood that pollutes the rivers and streams. To blame the gods is to blame the land itself. Look upon your reflection to find your enemy."

His words ring out across the hall with a bone-chilling truth.

I feel as if I'm back in the sea, the icy water pulling me deeper and deeper.

"You will fail, like all the brides before you," he says.

No dragon to save me. No hope to hold on to, the world above winking out like a star.

"It is inevitable." He looks away. "It is your fate."

My fate?

The feeling of drowning ceases.

This fate was never mine to begin with. I claimed it for myself when I jumped into the sea. But even before then, I wasn't the one who changed the pattern of the story. It was Shim Cheong, who denied her fate when she wouldn't let go of Joon. At least, isn't that why she turned from the dragon? I brush away the thought. I might not understand Shim Cheong's motives, but I do know my own.

"You're right," I say. The boy's eyes flit back, narrowing as I speak. "I *am* like the other brides. I know what it is to love someone you would do anything to protect. Who are you to say what my fate is—if I am to fail, or if I am to succeed? My fate is not yours to decide. My fate belongs to *me*."

The boy watches me, a slight crease in his brow.

Namgi whistles low. "Never thought I'd see the great Lord Shin of Lotus House speechless before a Sea God's bride."

A nobleman. Somehow I'm not surprised. Though undoubtedly the youngest of the three, Kirin and Namgi seem to defer to him in all things.

"Lord Shin," Kirin says—low, urgently. "The fog lifts." His eyes are raised skyward, where moonlight breaches the rafters, bathing the hall in light.

Shin steps back. "Keep your fate, Sea God's Bride. It has

nothing to do with me." He reaches to his side and pulls a sword from its scabbard. The metallic glide is deafening in the silent hall.

"My name is Mina."

He pauses.

"I am not Sea God's Bride or No One's Bride or Magpie," I say. "I have a name. Chosen by my grandmother to give me cleverness and strength. I know who I am, and I know what I must do." I raise my great-great-grandmother's knife. "And I will not let you take my life."

Reaching up, Shin tugs at his mask. The cloth slips, pooling around his neck. "Mina," he says, and my traitorous heart skips a beat. "The Sea God's bride."

I swallow thickly. His voice without the mask is clear and warm. He has beautiful features—a straight nose and soft lips. With his sea-dark eyes, he's breathtaking.

"I won't take your life."

A painful hope blooms within me.

"Just your soul."

Wrapping his hand around my wrist, he twists. The knife clatters to the floor. With his other hand, he raises his sword and plunges it downward. I scream. The piercing sound abruptly cuts off as his sword connects with . . .

The ribbon.

He slices clean through the Red String of Fate.

I gape, watching the slow fall of the severed ribbon like two halves of a broken feather. How is this possible? For a brief second, all is silent and still. Then my scream rushes back, but the desperate sound bursts not from my mouth but from *outside* my body, in the air above. The scream swirls and coalesces, a mass of bright colors whirling together. The ribbon slips from my hand, rising, followed closely by the Sea God's half of the ribbon. Together they wrap around the scream, forming a dazzling sphere of light.

Shin steps forward, his hand outstretched.

There's a brilliant flash of color. In the aftermath, I blink away stars. And my ears pick up a wondrous sound, unexpected in this desolate hall—a bird's cheerful warbling.

Cradled in the center of Shin's palm, its wings folded snugly against its sides, is a beautiful magpie with red wing tips.

4

The magpie coos in the palm of Shin's hand. Unlike the black-and-white magpies that flit about my village, this magpie's wing tips shimmer a vibrant shade of red—the exact color of the Red String of Fate.

The magpie flutters its wings, and I feel a strange ache in my chest.

Kirin approaches, his long strides eating up the short distance. He lifts the wooden birdcage, and Shin gently places the magpie inside. The bird doesn't seem to mind its imprisonment, content to hop up and down the cylinder perch that spans the width of the small cage. As Kirin ties closed the door with a piece of bamboo string, Shin turns away, sliding his sword back into its scabbard.

I point to the birdcage. *"Where did that magpie come from?"*

No sound comes from my mouth.

"Where did that—"

Nothing. No sound. No *voice*.

I press my fingers to my throat; my pulse beats strong. *"What's going on?"* I can *feel* the words, the familiar vibrations. *"Why can't I hear myself?"*

"Your soul is a magpie."

I look to where Namgi grins at me on the bottommost step, having pulled the mask down from his face.

"What do you mean?"

He doesn't have to hear my words to read my expression. Sauntering over to Kirin, he bends down to peer into the cage. "When Shin severed the Red String of Fate, it took your soul. For you, your soul is tied to your voice. It's not unexpected with singers and storytellers."

My . . . soul?

He raps a knuckle against the wooden bars, causing the magpie inside to ruffle its red-tipped wings. "A temporary state of being. Nothing too serious. Imagine it like missing every third heartbeat."

I blanch, that in fact sounding *very* serious.

Kirin tugs the cage out of Namgi's grasp. "At the end of the month, come to the south gate of Lotus House." His voice is dull, as if he's said these same words many times before. "A servant will deliver your soul to you. We will not be responsible for what might happen should you fail to appear."

I struggle to understand. How different it is to believe in myths than it is to live inside one. If I *am* to trust their words, my soul is a magpie and somehow *outside* my body. Yet I feel no different than when I first woke to this world. Perhaps a bit salt stained and bone weary, but nothing compared to what I'd imagine losing a soul might feel like—one less heartbeat a minute, a chasm as wide as the world inside you.

"Lord Shin," Kirin calls out, "with your permission, Namgi and I will return to Lotus House."

Shin straightens from where he's been leaning to pick something up off the floor. "You have my thanks, Kirin. I'll join you shortly."

Kirin bows, followed closely by Namgi. They turn to leave. The magpie shrills a warning.

"Wait!" I shout, but as before, I make no sound.

They sprint from the hall, taking with them the magpie, *my soul*. Soon, they're gone.

"Tell them to come back!" I rush up the steps and grab on to Shin's arm. Through the thin fabric of his shirt, I can feel the warmth of his body, the jump of his muscle flexing in response. He turns, the glint of a blade in his right hand. I stumble back and lift my arm. When no attack follows, I look up. He watches me with one brow raised, proffering my knife out to me, handle first.

"After the trouble I went through to take your soul," he says mockingly, "you think I'd kill you now?"

His sardonic tone makes me bristle with anger. *"I didn't think it would matter. To someone like you, what is a body without a soul?"*

His eyes immediately move downward, and I grit my teeth to keep from blushing. After a few excruciating seconds, they move back to my face, apparently having found nothing of interest.

Once more, he extends the knife, and this time I grab it and step to the edge of the small dais, putting as much distance between us as possible.

"Keep that with you," he says. "A weapon forged in the human realm cuts sharp in the realm of the gods."

His advice is unnecessary. I would have kept the knife regardless, the only item I have left from my own world other than the dress I wear. The only connection I have to my family and loved ones.

Shin claims to have stolen my soul, but why then do I feel like this—a sharp ache deep inside at thoughts of my family? Where does the pain come from, if not my soul?

"My grandmother gave me this knife." I slide my thumb against the rough etching of a moon carved into the bone handle. *"It belonged to her own grandmother, whom she said I reminded her of."* I roll the knife to the side, revealing the scar underneath, where I bled to make an oath to the Sea God.

"The song from earlier . . . was it your grandmother who taught you the words?"

I slip the knife back into my short jacket. *"She taught me many songs, as well as folktales and myths. She said that through songs and stories I could learn about the world, and about the people who live in it."*

And about my own heart, but I don't tell him this.

Then a thought occurs. How are we having this conversation? As I've been speaking, I've made no sound. I narrow my eyes. Can he read my mind? I wait. His face remains decidedly blank.

"You can read lips."

"Yes."

"Why did you cut the Red String of Fate?"

"To protect the Sea God."

"From me?" I ask incredulously.

Shin's gaze moves to the boy-god on his throne, where throughout the commotion he's remained asleep. "The Spirit Realm cannot sustain a human bride. Your kind are weak, your bodies more susceptible to the dangers of this world. Anything could effectively kill you, if it so wanted. The Red String of Fate binds your soul to the Sea God. If you were to die, the Sea God might also suffer the same fate. To protect him, I severed your ties."

I try to make sense of his words. *"Before, what did Kirin mean when he said I could retrieve my soul at the end of the month?"* Shin doesn't respond, and I realize he doesn't know I've spoken, his gaze still upon the Sea God. I tug at his sleeve, and when he looks at me, I repeat my question.

"In a month's time, you'll have spent thirty days in the Spirit Realm. You will become a spirit then. As I said, human bodies are weak: Without a stronger tie to keep them grounded in this world, they—"

"You mean I'll die?"

"You'd have died anyway," he says, "in time."

"I'm sixteen years old. I'm supposed to have all the time in the world!"

He scowls. "Then you should have stayed where you belong."

"My world, the place where I belong, is being destroyed because of your world. If you won't be bothered to fix it, then I will!"

"How?"

"The Sea God—"

His eyes flash. "What about him? Oh right, your precious myth. You believe only a human bride can save him, that he will fall in love with her. That he will save her people because of his love for her."

"No." I grit my teeth. "I wouldn't be so naive."

"It's what your people believe. It's what every bride before you has believed."

"You can't possibly know that—every bride has her reasons. Maybe some are not as grand as you'd like them to be. To know because of their sacrifice, their family will be taken care of when they're gone, fed and clothed. To know they've done everything in their power to protect those whom they love most. To know that they tried when no one else could or even would!"

Shin's brow furrows; he's clearly frustrated. "Slow down. I can't catch everything you're saying."

"Who are you to judge their hopes? At least they have them. What do you have? A sword that cuts. Words filled with hate."

We're both breathing heavily. His gaze moves upward, from my mouth to my eyes. "For someone who can't speak," he says slowly, "you have a lot to say." There's a hint of something in his voice—respect? He looks as if he means to say more, but he turns away. "But it doesn't matter. In another life, you might have found a more welcome shore than this. As it is, the sea is dark and the Sea God sleeps, and the shore is too far to reach."

I've heard the cadence of these words before. They're a farewell.

"Wait!" I shout, but of course no sound comes out. I reach for him, only to grab empty air.

He sprints from the room, his steps soundless across the wooden floors. In the space of a breath, he's gone.

What just happened? The level-headed part of me *knows* that I can survive without my soul. After all, I'm living and breathing at this very moment. But a larger part *feels* that without the magpie, I am not wholly myself. I feel lighter without it, and not in a pleasant way. I feel as if a breeze could set me adrift, as insubstantial as a leaf on the wind.

The silence that felt thick before now feels empty without the familiar sound of my own breathing. Shivering, I wrap my arms around my body and turn to face the Sea God.

He's just as he was before, but for one difference. The hand that held the ribbon is bare, nothing to evidence that he and I were once connected. There is no color in the air between us, no Red String of Fate. If he were to wake now, would he even recognize me as his bride?

The Sea God lets out a soft sigh.

I take a step forward.

There's a thunderous crack of sound, and I'm flung backward. Digging my heels into the floor, I grapple for purchase, but it's as if solid wind has taken hold of me. The Sea God becomes a distant blur as an invisible force drags me from the hall, through one empty courtyard after another. Doors slam shut as I pass through each gateway, the sound of great planks of wood sliding into place behind me.

I'm released outside the Sea God's palace. Stumbling, I almost fall down the grand stairs. A loud groan signals the closing of the main gate. I scramble to my feet and throw my body against the doors as they shut with a resounding boom.

I pound my fists against thick wood. All I get for my efforts are bruised hands and a terrible ache in my chest. I slump to the ground, exhausted. My pulse throbs erratically, and I have to count my breaths to calm the wild beating of my heart.

I remain on the ground, dazed, for several minutes before I notice something has changed. The air is clear.

And then I hear it, a sound like laughter drifting through the wind. Slowly I get to my feet and turn. The mysterious fog has lifted, revealing the night.

Behind me, spread out like a painter's canvas, is the Sea God's city.

It's like nothing I've ever seen before—a labyrinth of buildings with curved rooftops and bowed bridges, scattered throughout like solid arcs of rainbow. Gold light shines from lanterns hung from three-story-high poles, like sails of ships caught on fire. There are more lanterns floating in the water, on the canal streets piercing through the city like branches of a magnificent, glowing tree.

Brightly colored fish swim along the breeze, as if the sky were an ocean. Whales like clouds float lazily overhead. And in the distance, the dragon slips through the air like a kite freed of the earth.

I've never seen anything more beautiful. I've never seen anything more terrifying.

The wonders of this city reveal an undeniable truth: I have entered a new world—a world of dragons, of gods with unfathomable powers, of assassins who move unseen through the shadows, where your voice can be transformed into a bird and then stolen, and where no one I love can ever reach me.

5

I'm too visible outside the palace where anyone—any*thing*—can see me. However much I might dislike Shin, his words were a warning: Humans are vulnerable in a world of gods.

I stumble down the steps, body sore from the rough sea tossing and the perhaps even rougher wind tossing. I slip into the nearest alley and hunker down in the recess of a doorway. A paper lantern creaks atop the cracked wooden frame, the small candle inside casting baleful shadows on the walls. I'm behind a fish shop; the smell of day-old catch is unmistakable. If there are people about, I see no sign of them, and soon it's impossible to see at all as tears begin to blur my vision.

I cry without sound, racking sobs that spread tremors throughout my body.

I know I need to be strong, like the heroines in my grandmother's stories. But I am frustrated. I am exhausted. And, if Shin's words are true, I am soulless. Strange, but it was easier to be brave when he was in front of me, when I was bolstered by my fury *at* him. It's harder to be brave when by myself, cold and alone.

What am I supposed to do now?

I pull my legs to my chest and press my face to my knees. Desperately, I try to think of one of my grandmother's many sayings, something wise to give me comfort and strength. But despair has its grip on me now, and it won't let go. Only once before have I felt like this, as if the world had jumped ahead and left me behind.

It was the night of the paper boat festival. I was excited because Joon said we would sail our boats down the river together, as we had every year since I was old enough to go. I was kneeling on the riverbank, writing the final flourish of my wish onto the paper when I heard Joon's voice.

"Shim Cheong might be the most beautiful girl in the village, but her face is a curse."

It was the beginning of their story, a story I would play no part in, at least not for a while.

I stood at one end of the bridge as Joon followed Shim Cheong over to the other side. I remember staring at my brother as he walked away, willing him to look back—just one small wave to prove that I was still in his thoughts, that he hadn't forgotten me. And when he didn't, it felt like a premonition that things would never be the same again.

I was twelve years old, and I could feel the hours of our child-hood slipping through my fingers like sand in the sea.

Later that night, my grandfather found me crying beside

the pond in our garden. He settled himself on the grassy bank, his eyes on the blurry reflection of the moon on the water. The ducks appeared as if they were swimming across its pearly face. Neither of us said a word for a time. My grandfather understood the comfort there is in shared silence.

When I was ready to listen, he said, "In all my lifetime, I've never seen more wonderful creatures than ducks." He paused to chuckle at the baffled expression on my face. "When ducks are born, they imprint on the first thing they see, usually their mother, and they will follow her quite determinedly until adulthood. Did you know this?"

I shook my head, unable to speak. There were still tears in my throat.

"You were born into this world an orphan." His eyes were on the water, and I knew he was thinking of his daughter—my mother. "You were crying and crying, and your eyes were closed tight, and nothing seemed to comfort you. I was afraid you'd drown in your own tears. Even your grandmother was lost as to how to help you. But then Joon, who had been waiting in the garden, came quietly into the house. He was so little himself, not yet three summers old. He insisted on holding you. Your grandmother placed you gently in his arms, and when you opened your eyes and looked into his for the first time, the smile that lit your face was the most wondrous thing I'd ever seen. Like sunlight after a storm."

"Grandfather," I said, tilting my head to look up at him, "are you saying I'm a duck?"

Grandfather brought his rough hands to my eyes, wiping the tears from my face. "I'm saying, Mina, that Joon has loved you your entire life. Since the day you were born. He will always love you. It is his forever gift to you."

I shook my head. "Then why did he leave me behind?"

"Because he knows that you love him enough to let him go."

In the damp, cold alley of the Sea God's city, I squeeze my eyes shut. *Grandfather.* He always knew the right words to say to make everything better.

He's been gone for so long. *Grandfather, I miss you. More than anything, I wish you were here now.*

"Lookit!" a young boy's anxious voice shouts from close by. "There's a girl crying behind the fish shop. What should we do, Mask?"

A girl's voice answers—much calmer than the boy's and slightly muffled. "Wait for her to use up all her tears, of course. Once she's finished crying for herself, she won't start again. This one has a strong spirit."

I lift my face from my knees, gasping, when I'm met with the most peculiar of sights.

A girl around my height stands before me, her head tilted to the side, the whole of her face covered by a wooden mask. Grooves in the wood show wrinkles, while the cheeks and forehead are painted with red circles. It's the face of a grandmother, the mouth etched in a downward grimace.

"How can you tell, Mask? She doesn't look like she's going to stop anytime soon."

I turn and almost touch noses with a small boy crouched beside me. Perhaps eight or nine, he wears loose hemp trousers and a thin jacket with wooden buttons. He has unruly hair, one long cowlick popping up at the side of his head like a flower. On his back, he carries what appears to be a cloth knapsack.

"Not even Miki cries nearly as much as she does," he says, his brow puckering.

This statement is followed by a noise like bubbles rising out of the ocean.

The boy's fingers fly to his shoulder, loosening the strings of his knapsack. He shuffles the bag around to reveal an infant tucked inside.

"Ay, Miki," the boy laughs, lifting the tiny girl out of the knapsack. "Smile for the baby."

He holds the infant out before me. She can't be more than a year old. She has rosy cheeks and a short haircut very much like the boy's, except hers is neatly combed to the side. From the way she's dressed in a soft cotton dress, sewn with small pink flowers, I know she's very much loved. Miki and I blink at each other. Whether it's magic, or whether it's Miki's infectious smile, my tears stop flowing altogether. Miki giggles, reaching her small hands out toward me.

"No, no, Miki," the boy scolds, pushing the knapsack wide and tucking the baby gently back inside. "You stay with me, now." He pats Miki on her head before moving the knapsack to his back once more.

I look to the masked girl. The expression carved onto the

wood of her mask has changed, from a frowning grandmother to a smiling grandmother. "That's better," she says. "Tears are fine every now and then, but it's never a good thing to waste water."

"Who—who are you?" I say. Or try to say. Like before, I make no sound.

She surprises me by answering. "We are spirits." Her voice has a soft muffled quality to it, coming as it does from behind her covered face. "I'm Mask," she says, pointing to herself, "and this is Dai and Miki." She waves to them offhandedly, and Dai gives me a wide grin. "We saw you in the alley making a silent racket, and we came to investigate."

Dai looks from Mask to me. "How is it that you know what she's saying, Mask? Can you hear her?"

"Of course I can't hear her!" Mask says, exasperated. "Her voice is a magpie, after all. I'm just using my wits. What do you think a human girl like her, caught alone in an alley in the middle of the Sea God's city, would ask? Who are you? What are you? Why are you here? What do you want? I've answered all of these questions. Nod, girl, if I'm right in answering at least the one you asked."

I nod.

Dai claps his hands. "Ask the girl her name, Mask! She's very pretty."

"How would you know if she's pretty or not? You're just a little boy!"

I ignore their bickering and latch onto Mask's words. *Her voice is a magpie.*

I wave my hands in the air to grab their attention. Placing my thumbs together, I move my fingers up and down, mimicking the flight of a bird's wings.

"I've got it!" Dai snaps his fingers. "I know what she's trying to say."

I nod my encouragement.

"She wants to fly. Like a bird. Should we take her to the highest waterfall, Mask? We could push her off. Then she could fly!"

I gape.

"No, that's not what she's saying!" Mask cackles. "I knew your bloodline was inferior!"

"Take it back, Mask! Say you're sorry."

I lean upward on my knees and wave my hands, trying to keep the two of them focused. *How did you know my voice is a magpie? Did you see what happened to me? Do you know where they've taken my voice?*

Mask and Dai give me blank looks. Or at least Dai looks at me blankly. Mask's grandmother mask remains showing its beatific smile.

"Uh," Dai says, scratching the bridge of his nose. "Do you know what she said just then?"

Mask shakes her head. "We're not mind readers," she says kindly. "Neither are we skilled lip readers. Treat us as if we couldn't hear you even if you were able to speak."

"Magpie," I say, mouthing the word. Again, I lift my hands, making the shape of the bird, this time bringing it down in a

dramatic swoop through the air. It's more like the flight of a falcon than a magpie, but at this point, I'm past worrying over the details.

Dai points to my hands. "That looks like a falcon."

"Ah!" Mask exclaims. "I see now. Magpie, right? We saw Lord Kirin and that wily thief Namgi got your soul, trapped as a magpie in a cage. You need it back, otherwise the Sea God won't recognize you as his bride."

My eyes widen. *You know I'm his bride?*

She must gather an impression of what I'm asking, because she answers, "What else could you be? The only humans allowed to enter the Spirit Realm are the Sea God's brides— the only humans that are *whole* humans, not the *spirits* of humans." She points between herself and Miki and Dai. "Like us."

She tilts her head to the side. "You're not dead, are you?"

Even if I had a voice, I'd be speechless.

"Every human has a soul," she explains. "When they die, they leave their bodies in the world above, while their souls travel down the river. Spirits are the souls of humans who've pulled themselves from the river, too stubborn to move on to another life. We linger here in the Spirit Realm, wreaking havoc and growing fat on ancestral rites." She pats her belly, and Miki giggles.

I stare wide-eyed at them. If what Mask says is true, then *they are dead*.

"Let's help her, Mask," Dai says, wincing as Miki bites down on his shoulder. "I can get her into Lotus House. That's where Kirin and Namgi will be heading. We'll just tell whoever's in charge that she's looking for a job." He pats my head gently. "You're so quiet. They'd be sure to hire you."

"Unless they find out you're a human and not a spirit." Mask laughs. "Then they'd want to eat you!"

I blanch. She must be jesting.

Mask holds out her hand, and I take it. She pulls me to my feet, turning me so that she can brush the dirt off the back of my dress. We are of the same height, she and I.

With her profile to me, I study her freely. The mask she wears ties around the back of her head with thick strings. Her warm brown hair is styled in a long braid, signifying her status as an unmarried maiden. That and the youthful curve of her neck suggest she's around my age.

"Let's go!" Dai says, Miki giggling from her place on his back. Mask straightens to join him. I hesitate. I am not usually a mistrustful person, but my run-in with Shin and the others has made me wary. Still, I feel a strange affinity to these spirits, so friendly and filled with life—even if they *are* dead.

My eldest brother, Sung, says trust is earned, that to give someone your trust is to give them the knife to wound you. But Joon would counter that trust is faith, that to trust someone is to believe in the goodness of people and in the world that shapes them.

I'm too raw to believe in anyone right now, but I do believe in myself, in my heart that tells me they are good, in my mind that tells me they are the help I need to find the magpie and take back my soul.

"Are you coming?" Dai shouts from over his shoulder. I hurry to catch up, following Mask, Dai, and Miki out of the alley and into the heart of the Sea God's city.

6

We emerge from the alley onto a wide boulevard. Immediately I'm overwhelmed. I've never been outside my small village, where at most twenty or thirty villagers will gather on market days—perhaps as many as fifty during a festival. Here in the Sea God's city there are hundreds, *thousands* of people dressed in vibrant jewel-tone colors, as if the city were a great reef and the people its coral.

Magnificent buildings with tiered roofs line the streets, stacked up almost on top of one another, as far as the eye can see. Shining lanterns hang from the buildings' many eaves, illuminating the shadows of figures moving behind papered windows. Gigantic, ghostly carp drift serenely over the rooftops, while luminous golden fish dart in and around the lanterns.

A door slides open up the street, spilling light and laughter. A young woman expertly balancing a tea tray above her head disappears into the crowd.

There's a whistle and crack of sound. I look up. A firework

explodes, illuminating the night and scattering a school of minnows.

"Watch where you're going!"

Mask pulls me back in time to avoid being trampled by a young boy pushing a cart of anemone.

"You watch where *you're* going!" Dai shouts back, raising a fist. "She's a Sea God's bride, you know."

"Sure she is," the boy throws over his shoulder. "And I'm the Sea God!"

This earns a smattering of snickers from those within hearing distance.

The cobblestoned streets are paved in mosaics of sea creatures. We follow a chain of blue and gray dolphins down one street to an avenue of red crabs, and finally to a great central square depicting a large jade turtle.

The square is filled with people. Groups of girls crouch in circles tossing and catching stones. Old men sit at low tables arguing loudly over board games.

They all must be spirits, yet they appear as Miki and Dai do—healthy, *alive*.

Mask turns from the square, leading us down a cramped side street lined with food carts.

We pass carts stacked high with rice cakes and others with salted fish strung up by their tails. More carts are spread with roasted chestnuts and sweet potatoes dipped in sugar. Dai dodges out of the way of an oncoming cart, pressing his back against another packed with dumplings in bamboo steamers. As he steps away, Miki reaches out and grabs a dumpling off the cart.

"Ay, Miki!" Dai yelps. "Leave the thieving to the thieves!"

Reaching into his pocket, he produces a short rope strung with metal coins of tin and copper. He unknots a small tin coin and flicks it to the cart's owner, who catches it neatly from the air. "We'll take four, please!"

He accepts the dumplings and presents one to each of us in turn. Curious, I watch Mask out of the corner of my eye to see if she'll remove her mask to eat, but she hands hers to Miki. The little girl devours the dumpling in an impressive three mouthfuls.

Delicious steam escapes from my own dumpling. I follow Miki's example and practically inhale it. The combination of the soft, fluffy outside and the salty leek and pork inside is exquisite. After we've licked our fingers clean, Miki and I band together to fling beseeching looks at Dai. He sighs loudly, unstringing another coin from his money rope.

I take my time with the second dumpling, savoring each delectable bite.

The food cart alley opens up onto another bustling street, at the end of which lies a grand-looking bridge situated over a smooth-flowing river. Lanterns float lazily on its current in red, green, and white. There are boats moored to the riverbank, while others travel downstream, oared by ferrymen in feathered hats.

The bridge must be a major crossing point. It's overflowing with people, carts, mules, and even an ox, a garland of flowers strung between its horns. Children around Dai's age climb on top of the railings, making their way across the thin beams. Mask's hand shoots out, grabbing Dai's shoulder before he can join them.

Halfway across the bridge, the rumble of drums beats the air. A procession moves slowly through the packed crowd. Along with everyone else, we're pushed to the edge to make room.

A group of soldiers passes by, armed with spears. They surround four bearers carrying a large, ornately decorated box. Two bearers on either side lift the box on poles balanced across their broad shoulders.

I've heard of carrying-boxes like these, common in the capital, used to transport noblewomen across short distances. The palanquin's thick walls shield its occupant from prying eyes.

Excited whispers follow the procession. I lean forward, curious to know who sits inside the gilded box.

"Shiki's bride."

I turn to see Mask following the movement of the palanquin. She nods, indicating the guards' black-and-red uniforms. "Those are the colors of his house."

I tug on her sleeve, and then pat my lips to draw her gaze. *"Shiki?"*

"A death god."

My eyes dart to the golden box. The person inside is the bride of a death god. *"She must be very beautiful. What is she the goddess of?"*

"A goddess, did you say? She's no more a goddess than you or me. Just a girl. A former Sea God's bride."

A Sea God's bride. I whip my head in the direction of the procession.

A warm, sun-colored hand sweeps the drapes of the box

aside, and I catch a glimpse of a round, sweet face before a guard blocks my view.

Hyeri.

A year ago, the Sea God's bride had been a girl from the next village over. Year after year, the brides arrive from all over with caravans that stretch for miles and miles. Sometimes they come from small towns, sometimes from large cities, some even from the capital itself. But Hyeri arrived in the night, with just a sack of belongings slung over her shoulder, her hair in a simple braid down her back.

She'd stayed with our chief elder and his family for three nights before there was a knock at my family's door. She needed someone to help prepare her for her wedding ceremony.

It was strange, sitting in a room with a girl I'd never met before, helping her dress in the colors of a bride—bright colors signifying love, happiness, and fertility—when, come morning, she would be drowning, and the dress would do nothing but pull her beneath the waves.

"You could run." The words were out of my mouth before I could stop them.

Hyeri turned to me, her lips painted pink with the crushed petals of azaleas. Her eyes were darkened with coal from the smoldered hearth. "Where would I run to?"

"Don't you have someone who would look after you? Family to protect you?"

Hyeri shook her head slowly. "Just my sister, and she's been gone these past five years."

"Gone?" I leaned forward, encouraged, thinking Hyeri could go wherever her sister had gone. To the capital, maybe. To somewhere safe. "Gone where?"

Hyeri turned away. The open window of the room looked out toward the rice fields and, beyond them, the sea. In the darkness, you couldn't see it, but you could hear it—the tireless wind blowing the warm air across the room. You could feel it—the salt on your skin, pooling in a thick layer. Like ashes.

Hyeri's voice was quiet. "I was always better at swimming. Much better than my sister, who feared the water. Tomorrow, when they throw me into the sea, I'm just going to swim. I'm going to swim and swim until I can't any longer."

"But your sister—"

"Five years now. They say every bride of the Sea God is the same. But they're wrong. Why can't they see?"

Her voice turned urgent then. She grabbed my wrists and pulled me closer, her eyes fever bright. "Some brides are chosen, but then there are those who *choose* to be brides."

Dropping my wrists, she closed her eyes. "They wonder why someone would choose to give up her own life. They could never understand."

"They?" I asked. "The villagers?"

She nodded. "There are the girls who choose to be brides because they want to bring wealth to their family, since the bridal price paid by the village is steep. There are the girls who choose to be brides because they want the glory of being one of those beautiful few, tragically sacrificed. There are even the girls who truly believe that all of this is real, and that they won't drown, but will be saved by the Sea God."

Hyeri opened her eyes, her gaze finding the window and the night beyond. "Then there are the girls like my sister, who want to be the Sea God's bride because it hurts too much to be themselves."

I moved closer to Hyeri then, taking her cold hands in my own.

"All this makeup will wash away in the water," Hyeri said, choking back a laugh. "And until then, I'll look like I have ink for tears."

"I'll wipe it off." I reached for a cloth, dipped it into a bowl of water, and dabbed it beneath her eyes.

"You're a kind girl, Mina. I may seem confident, but I'm very afraid. I want to live. Is there any way a person can die, yet still live?"

At the time, I didn't have an answer for her. It was the night, and she would soon leave to be sacrificed in the morning. And for a year, I couldn't understand why she'd *choose* to be a Sea God's bride.

Not until that moment when I stood at the prow of the boat, my anger like a storm in my soul, and jumped into the sea.

"You cry too much." Dai looks up at me, hands cupped beneath my chin to catch the tears slipping down my face.

"Do I?" I say, laughing. A beaming happiness floats within me, that Hyeri should be here now, alive and well. I point to the slowly moving procession. *"Tell me more. Tell me anything."*

"You want to know about Shiki's bride?"

I nod emphatically.

"I don't know much about her." He pauses. "Shiki, on the other hand . . ."

"Yes?" I smile at him encouragingly.

"He's a coldhearted bastard!"

"Watch your language," Mask chides. "Shiki isn't so bad. Just a little on the serious side. And even if he were a *little* bad, rumors hint that the death god adores his new bride. The wedding was a grand celebration."

I widen my eyes, making exaggerated movements between her and the moving caravan. *"What was it like?"*

"I wasn't invited!" Mask says. "Only the most important people in the city were invited. The lords of Tiger House and Crane House. The Great Spirit. Every lesser god with a shrine to his name." Mask scratches her wooden cheek. "Now that I think about it, lots of people were invited."

"Just not us!" Dai shouts.

"The Sea God, of course, but seeing as he hasn't left his palace in a hundred years, that was a waste of an invitation! Oh, and Lord Shin, I suppose. Though I doubt he made an appearance. All things considered."

"They had a huge fight," Dai explains to me. "Do you know what the fight was about?" he asks, turning to Mask.

"What fights that matter are always about."

"Food?" Dai suggests.

I think of the local warlords who fight over the land back home. *"Power?"*

Mask's expression remains benign, and yet I sense hostility emanating from her. "Who raised you both? Did they teach you nothing? *Love* is what drove them apart, and love is what will bring them together—if they're not too stubborn to forgive each other!"

"Shin was in love with Hyeri, too?" Dai asks.

Mask throws her hands up in the air, clearly frustrated. Pivoting, she walks into the crowd that has dispersed around Hyeri's retreating caravan. We hurry to catch up.

What did Shin and Shiki fight over, if not their love of Hyeri? What hurt have they caused one another that must be forgiven? Having met Shin, I don't find it difficult to believe he's involved in a feud—with a god, no less. The dark-eyed boy was so infuriating—he stole my voice! He might not realize it, or care, but he's in a feud with *me*.

We reach the other end of the bridge. "There it is!" Dai shouts. "Lotus House!"

A massive stone wall takes up an entire block of street. The tops of great trees line the perimeter, obscuring what lies on the other side. The only entrance is a wide gate manned by guards dressed in black. At the moment, they're allowing individuals through one by one, matching names to an official-looking scroll.

I swallow thickly, faced with the impossibility of my task. Not only do I have to lie my way past those walls *without a voice*, but then somehow locate a small bird and figure out how to restore it to its original form.

I've been fortunate to meet Mask, Dai, and Miki, but soon

they will leave, and I'll be on my own once more—with only a knife and my grandmother's stories.

Mask places a warm hand on my shoulder. "I thought you were brave! No need to look so fearful. You are a Sea God's bride, are you not? You have a purpose, and you won't give up until you've seen it carried through to the end, or at least tried your very hardest. Or have you already tried your hardest?"

I shake my head.

"Good!" She steers me away from the gate, rounding a corner to where Dai waits outside a small side door facing a much less-traveled back road. He unstraps his knapsack, giving Miki a kiss before handing her over to Mask. "Leave it to me," he says.

Confidently, he approaches the door and raps loudly against the wooden frame.

I rush to follow, coming up behind him just as the door cracks open. A girl around my age peers out at us, with a wide, frowning mouth; sharp, intelligent eyes; and long brown hair pinned up in a messy bun. Flyaway hairs curl around a familiar, heart-shaped face.

I gasp. *"Nari?"*

7

When I was growing up, there was a girl in my village whom I admired above all others, in part because I was so afraid of her. A friend of Joon's, she was two years older than me and bright as the day, with a reckless heart. Joon had a gentle nature, and because he was big for his age, he would often get teased by the other children.

It was Nari who would stick up for him. When she intervened in the bullies' attacks, they would listen. When she condemned their cruel words, they would beg her forgiveness. To have Nari's good opinion was to have the sun's light upon you. Or I imagined that's what it must have felt like; she never paid much attention to me. Last I'd seen her was a year ago when she'd jumped into the storm-flooded river to retrieve the boats that had torn away from the dock. The river surged, taking the boats—and Nari—away with it to the sea. I never thought I'd see her again. Yet here she is before me, smiling and in tears.

"Mina, it can't be." Pulling me across the threshold, she enfolds me in a strong embrace, smelling like wildflowers and the sturdy reeds that grow beside the river. "If you're here, that means . . . that means you're dead!"

Ah, of course she would think that. The only way to enter the Spirit Realm is by dying or being spirited away by the dragon. And she, like everyone in my village, had always known Shim Cheong was meant to be this year's bride.

"I'm alive. It's just that—" I sigh. She can't hear me.

"And Joon! Your poor brother. To lose you and Cheong in the same night. He must be devastated. Tell me, how did it happen? Did you drown during the storm? Was it a raiding party from the north?"

"You've got it all wrong!" a loud, indignant voice interrupts. "She's not dead! She's a Sea God's bride."

Releasing me, Nari turns to where Dai stands outside the door. He's alone; Mask and Miki have disappeared.

"Who's the boy, Mina?" Nari asks with a frown. "Has he been bothering you? Say the word and I'll get rid of him." She reaches for a long pole with a curved blade leaning up against the wall. I hadn't noticed before, but she's wearing the same black robes and armored vest as the guards outside the main gate.

"I'm Mina's friend," Dai shouts. "Unlike you, accusing her of being dead when she's clearly a Sea God's bride."

Nari's eyes widen. "A bride? But . . . what year is it? One hundred years since the emperor disappeared. They were going to sacrifice Shim Cheong, if I remember correctly. And brides are always eighteen. You must be sixteen now, the same age I was when I died. Mina, why aren't you saying anything?"

"I can't speak."

"She can't speak," Dai says. "Her voice was stolen and transformed into a bird!"

I would think this of all explanations would be hard to believe.

"Ah," Nari says. "That makes sense. Last year there was a huge upset after Lord Shin cut Hyeri's Red String of Fate and her soul turned into a minnow. Her lover, the death god Shiki, demanded its return. When Lord Shin refused, they had a great battle, right here in this very house."

Dai tilts his head to the side. "Who won?"

"It's not certain. Those who witnessed the fight believe Lord Shin had the advantage, and would have won, had Hyeri not intervened at the last minute."

Which means Shin *lost*. I feel a smug satisfaction at this bit of knowledge.

"One final question remains." Dai leans forward conspiratorially. "Would you ever go against the wishes of your lord?"

"Of course not." Nari grips her pole firmly. "I am a loyal servant of Lotus House."

Dai grabs my arm. "Let's go, Mina."

"Wait!" Nari reaches out, catching my sleeve. "If you truly are the Sea God's bride, then that means you've come here to retrieve your soul." She frowns, her brows furrowed in thought. "I remember you, Mina. I remember the way you used to follow Joon and me around, onto the beaches and down the forest paths. I have to admit, I found you bothersome. I never was one for patience. I always wanted to race ahead."

She pauses, her dark eyes thoughtful. "Not like Joon. I used to wonder to myself, *Is this what it's like to have a younger sibling?* I wouldn't know, being an only child myself. Because Joon, knowing you followed, always walked a little slower."

I feel a tightness in my chest.

"He loved you, Mina. And I loved him as a true friend. I have a new life here, one that I plan on keeping for as long as I can, but I *will* help you—for you and for your brother. You can trust me."

This time, she holds out her hand, and I take it. Dai grins from where he watches the exchange by the doorway. "What was the plan to get her inside?" Nari asks him now.

"I thought she could pose as a servant."

Nari steps back to get a closer look at me, then nods, satisfied. "That should work."

"Wonderful! I leave her in your capable hands." Dai pushes me through the doorway. "I wish you luck, Mina!"

He takes off down the street, calling over his shoulder, "When we meet again, I look forward to hearing your voice!"

I lean my head out the door and wave until he's disappeared around the corner. Stepping back inside, I look about to see that we're standing in a small cobblestoned courtyard. An open gate to the right reveals a pathway leading deeper into the house's grounds. In the middle of the courtyard is a cherry tree with white and pink blossoms. From its elegant branches dangle paper charms, a few swaying, others spinning slowly in the light wind.

"This is the servants' courtyard," Nari says, coming up beside me after closing the door. "We should go unnoticed here for a time." She gestures for me to sit upon a stone carved in the likeness of a turtle. Then she walks over to the tree, grabs a shallow tin bucket, and places it near my feet. I peer inside to see the bucket is filled with rainwater. "Wash up and I'll find you some slippers."

Immediately I comply, sinking my feet in the warm water and scrubbing off the dirt and soot from the streets. Nari returns, handing me an apron—I tie it around my waist—as well as a white piece of cloth. This I secure around my nose and mouth to conceal my face.

"Illness is rare in the Spirit Realm," she explains, "but anyone might wish to hide their face after a night of heavy drinking." Last, Nari hands me a pair of sturdy slippers. After I slide them on, she looks me over. I must make a passable servant, because she nods, turning and gesturing for me to follow her out the eastern gate.

From the servants' courtyard, we step onto a wide dirt path. On either side are large cookhouses, the savory scents of soy sauce and rice wine wafting through the windows. A door to the left slides open, and we press our backs to the nearest wall, watching as servants dressed in light blue uniforms emerge, each carrying a tray of covered dishes. We count our breaths as they pass, then quietly slip down a grassy road lined with large earthenware pots, emerging close to the outer wall.

"It's called a house," Nari explains as we climb a small hill scattered with flowering pear trees, "but it's actually a large residence encompassing several buildings with gardens, fields, and lakes in between them. If we get separated, you're to look for a pavilion northeast of where we are now. It sits atop a small pond and can only be accessed by boat, or a bridge on the south side. That should be where they're keeping your soul. The area isn't crowded, and should be even less so tonight, with most of the activity centered around the main pavilion."

As we crest the hill that overlooks the grounds of Lotus House, I stop to catch my breath.

A magnificent lake lies below, spanning almost the full length of the grounds. Lotus flowers bloom across the dark water to the center of the lake, where a shining pavilion sits upon a small island. Tonight, it appears to be the gathering place for a celebration. Figures dressed in bright colors move among the great stone columns, and sounds of music and laughter drift from the upper-floor balconies. There are two bridges leading to the pavilion. On the western bridge, I spot at least four covered palanquins carried on the shoulders of liveried bearers, while the torches on the eastern bridge are unlit.

I wonder why they've come tonight. I remember how earlier the guards at the gate were only allowing through select individuals.

"They're here to act as witnesses," Nari says, following my gaze. "Every year all the great houses of the realm gather to ensure the tie between the Sea God and his bride is broken. While the Sea God remains asleep, there are some in the city who'd take control for themselves." She nods toward two of the larger processions entering through the gate, one arrayed entirely in red and gold, the other in silver and blue. "The lords of Tiger House and Crane House, to name the leaders of two of the more ambitious houses. By severing the tie that would make the Sea God mortal through his connection with you, Lord Shin keeps the Sea

God invulnerable to attack, and the great lords under control, at least for another year."

She turns from the lake. "Enough lingering. Come, Mina. We're close."

So Shin *was* telling the truth, back in the Sea God's hall. He severed the Red String of Fate to protect the Sea God from those who might seek to replace the god in power. In anyone else, such a show of loyalty would be considered honorable. My chest tightens with an unwelcome sensation at the thought of the dark-eyed lord.

Turning from the lake, I climb down the opposite side of the hill, where Nari has already disappeared into a copse of trees. I find her crouched down behind a low bush, peering over the edge at a clearing.

"The pond is just on the other side of this building." She nods toward a large open-wall pagoda, spilling light onto the wet grass. I can see the shapes of people inside, seated around low tables. From the sounds of laughter and porcelain cups clinking together, they must be drinking.

I look past the pagoda to the trees; somewhere beyond them lies the pond, the pavilion, and my voice.

"We have the advantage of darkness," Nari says. "You go first. They'll take little notice of a servant. Are you ready?"

I check the back of my mask to make sure it's secure around my mouth, then step onto the path. We might be in full view of the pagoda, but it's dark out, and the people inside are more interested in their entertainment. A musician taps a rhythmic beat on a drum as a clown in a bridal mask—a mask painted white with bright red circles on its cheeks—tumbles in and around the tables, as if caught in the swell of a great wave.

I hurry past the pagoda toward the shadows of the forest on the other side. The trees loom up before me, a dense thicket with a small path trailing into darkness. My steps falter at the sight of it, but then I take a deep breath, grabbing my skirt to run.

"Wait!"

I recognize the voice. An image flashes through my mind from only a few hours earlier. Curly hair. A crooked smile. *Are you a bride or are you a bird?*

Namgi.

8

I bring my fingers to my face to ensure the mask covers my nose and mouth and gauge the distance between myself and the tree line. Namgi's footsteps crunch as he approaches; a pebble skitters ahead of him, tapping the heel of my slipper.

"We've gone through all the wine-spirits," he says, his low, rough voice slurred. Clearly he thinks I'm a servant. "A pitcher or two more should—"

His cheerful tone falters. "Why are you going that way? There is nothing for you over there."

I can't respond—I have no voice! And even if I did, what would I say? I bow slightly, casting my eyes to the ground. His shadow is almost upon mine. Inwardly, I curse.

"Lord Namgi!" Nari calls out in a loud, confident voice. "Let the girl alone. She has her own tasks to complete without the burden of completing yours."

There's a short pause as I neither move nor breathe. Then Namgi chuckles, his voice receding as he turns to Nari. "Your barbed tongue never disappoints."

"You can go, girl," Nari says in that same assured manner. "Never mind his lordship's drunken ramblings."

I seize the opening Nari provided and walk away with purpose.

"Am I drunk?" I can hear Namgi's voice as I slip between the trees. "I can never tell. The world looks the same to me drunk as it does sober."

"Let's test this theory," Nari quips. "Shall we wager on a game of cards?"

Leaving the pagoda behind, I travel deeper into the forest, the heady triumph of my escape dimming the farther I walk, the path before me dark and winding. Unlike at the servants' quarters or the pavilion beside the lake, the trees here are numerous; their thick canopies block out the moonlight. An eerie silence hangs over the forest, and I'm tempted to turn back, if only to hear the sounds of voices again.

When I was a child, I lost my way in the great forest that lies beyond our village. I had been following Joon and Nari when, glimpsing a fox, I wandered off the path. I roamed for hours, finally taking shelter in the roots of a large camphor tree. I sat, curled up with my knees to my chest, and sobbed heartily, afraid I would be lost in the forest forever—or worse, eaten by a demon.

I don't remember how I eventually got out of the forest, whether I was found or whether I discovered a way out myself. I must have been five or six years old, and yet the memory is hidden from me, veiled in mist, as if my mind were protecting me from some greater hurt. All I remember is the fear.

A light appears out of the darkness, winking through the

trees. With relief, I follow it until I reach the edge of the forest. The pavilion is just as Nari described it, on an island at the center of a pond, accessible only by a narrow wooden bridge. The winking light comes from a lantern held by a single figure making his slow way across the bridge. Immediately I recognize the bearer of the lantern. The Goddess of Fortune laughs at me tonight.

I step behind a tree as Kirin draws near. I almost startle when a second figure appears to melt from the darkness to join him—a woman, dressed in the same armor as Nari.

She bows. "My lord."

Kirin acknowledges her with an elegant dip of his head. "Have you any news to report?"

"The guests have all been searched. Nothing of note was discovered but for a few body weapons among the priestesses of Fox House, which we allowed them to keep per Lord Shin's orders. Most of the guests grumbled but submitted themselves to be searched. The lords of Tiger House and Crane House, however, proved . . . difficult. They protested loudly and accused Lotus House of dishonoring its guests."

At this, Kirin growls, "Such insolence should not be allowed. Lord Shin is too forgiving."

When the guard doesn't respond in kind, Kirin demands, "What is it? You look as if you wish to speak."

She hesitates, then says, "There have been rumors circulating among the guests that the Sea God's power is waning, and so is Lord Shin's. Less than a year ago, he was defeated by Shiki, their friendship broken irreparably. Without such a staunch and powerful ally, many believe Lord Shin's role as guardian of this city is at an end. And the Sea God, without Lord Shin to protect him . . ."

The guard's voice fades as she and Kirin move away from the tree. Keeping low to the ground, I follow, curious to hear more of their conversation. When I catch up, however, it's only to find Kirin voicing his dismissal.

"Tell the others to keep their eyes open. I wouldn't put it past Crane or Tiger to stir up trouble tonight."

She bows, stepping backward. "Yes, my lord." She leaves just as she arrived, appearing to blend into the darkness. Soon she's a blur of movement at the corner of my eye.

Alone now, Kirin sighs, turning his gaze toward the pond. A lone heron sweeps over the water, the tip of its wing brushing the surface. "Protecting the Sea God is too much a burden to bear, even for you, Shin."

I step back and a branch snaps beneath my foot. Immediately Kirin's head turns, and I duck, wincing at my clumsiness. Through a gap in the foliage, I watch as Kirin peers into the forest. For a moment his eyes seem almost to glow a bright, burning silver, and then a squirrel leaps from the underbrush, skittering up the trunk of a tree. When I look back, Kirin's eyes are brown once more.

Slowly he moves down the same path the guard took, toward the lake. When he's safely out of sight, I step out from the trees and make my way across the bridge.

That unwelcome feeling from earlier steals back into my heart, that perhaps I misjudged Shin. I don't yet have a complete understanding of the troubles of this realm, but they remind me of home, where because of a weak and spineless ruler, warlords squabble over land and shed blood because of petty grievances. It must be the same here. In the Sea God's absence, the inhabitants of this realm, sensing a weakness, would try to upset the balance of power in their favor.

Then there's Shin, who alone strives to hold back the tide. Like the people in my village. Like myself.

I shake my head, willing away the direction of my thoughts. Regardless if I feel sympathy for him, I have my own challenges, beginning with taking back my soul.

The pavilion is shrouded in darkness. If Nari hadn't been so certain the magpie was being held here, I might have searched in a place more heavily guarded, not one that appears abandoned. I pull open the door, and the moonlight behind me floods across dark wood. On either side of a narrow hall are rooms, the shadows of clouds moving across the thick paper walls.

Just as I'm closing the door behind me, another slides open down the hall. I throw myself into a corner, hunkering in the shadows. Two figures dressed in black slip across the corridor. I only glimpse them for a moment—one thickset, a sword at his waist, the other skinny, weasel-like, carrying a large crossbow strung across his shoulder—before they disappear through the opposite door. Thieves?

Ironic, that they should steal from Shin, who stole from *me*. In all the stories, magpies warn of thieves.

Not tonight.

To my right, stairs lead upward. I climb them quickly, careful not to make a sound. At the top is another narrow hall, this one shorter than the one below. Only a single door is set in the wall.

Inside, a sound stirs, like restless wings. The magpie! I slide open the door, step inside, and shut it behind me.

Eagerly I sweep my gaze over the room, only for my heart to sink. The magpie isn't here. The source of the noise is a cool breeze rustling against the paper of the window. The room is sparsely furnished. A low shelf sits beneath the window opposite the door. Against the wall to the right is a worn cabinet, and to the left, the only other object in the room is a folding paper screen.

The magpie must be in one of the rooms below. But how to avoid the thieves?

I reach for my knife, gripping the handle. There's a noise in the hall outside. Footsteps approaching. I rush to the screen and slip behind it, crouching low just as the door slides open.

9

A figure enters the room, holding a candle. The light of the flame casts his silhouette onto the paper screen. The intruder's shadow matches neither of the men I saw below. It's oddly shaped—a strange protrusion erupts from its back.

Suddenly, the shadow lengthens, the unmistakable stretch of wings unfurling, like those of a heavenly being. Or a demon. I press my back against the wall. Then a sound breaks the silence. A magpie's gentle warble.

Shin.

Soundlessly he moves across the room, sliding the birdcage from his shoulder and placing it on the low shelf. How the Goddess of Fortune plays tricks with me tonight! First Namgi, then Kirin, and now Shin.

And the magpie. So close, I feel an echoing thump in my chest with every beat of its wings.

Shin's shadow moves back across the room. He's leaving without the magpie! My heart races with impending triumph.

But then he stops, as if he noticed something. I rack my brain for what might have caught his attention. I didn't touch any of the furniture after entering the room. Did my footprints leave marks upon the floor?

Lifting the candle, he blows out the flame. The scents of smoke and plum blossoms fill the balmy air.

My heart beats rapidly in my chest. The silence stretches interminably. When I can't bear it any longer, I peer around the screen. He's gone. The room is as empty as before.

No, there's one difference: The birdcage now sits on the low shelf. The magpie shuffles its wings, excited by my presence. This isn't the time to hesitate. Quickly I bound across the room, reaching for the cage.

"I thought I sensed a thief."

I twist around. Shin leans against the frame of the doorway. His dark hair, slightly damp, is swept back from his face. He must have come from the bathhouse. He's changed from when I last saw him, wearing black silk robes, the collar edged with lotus flowers embroidered in silver thread. His sword is strapped to his waist.

"I'm impressed," he says, watching me through half-lidded eyes. "You are blessed with luck to have made it this far."

"Funny, I feel like luck has escaped me all night."

He frowns. "I can't see your lips from here. I don't know what you're saying."

"Just because you can't hear the words doesn't mean they're not being said."

He straightens and steps past the threshold. "I don't think a bride has ever given me as much trouble as you have."

"What about Hyeri? From what I hear, you lost a match to her intended. Did it hurt your pride, to be thwarted by a human?"

His eyes narrow. "You're still speaking."

"It's your own fault that you can't hear me. Anyhow, it's better this way. If you knew what I was saying, you would not be pleased."

He approaches from across the room, stepping into the moonlight before me. I feel a tick of annoyance, reminded again of the differences in our height. My eyes are level with the intricate threadwork of lotus flowers on his collar. We stand so close, I can see the pulse beating steadily in his neck. I can smell the fresh scent of his robes, a blend of lavender, mint, and sandalwood.

"Speak your offenses," he says, "now that I can see you clearly."

He's so close to me, I feel my cheeks releasing a telltale blush. I grit my teeth and lift my chin. *"You are the real thief here."*

There's a pause as he puzzles out the words from my lips. Then he says, speaking so softly I have to strain to hear him, "I should have known that you wouldn't give up so easily." His eyes flit over my shoulder to the birdcage.

I know what happens next. I'll be thrown out of Lotus House, as I was at the palace, all chances of retrieving my soul lost. Stepping forward, I draw his gaze back to me.

"Let me help you," I say.

I can admit now that I had misjudged him at our first meeting. His actions, while misguided, were in service to the Sea God. If I can somehow convince him that my actions are also in service to the god, he could be an ally to me—a strong one, if the vastness of his house and the loyalty of his people are any indication.

His eyes move from my lips to my eyes. "There is nothing you can do that can help me."

I take a breath. *"You were right about sensing thieves."* I watch him watch my lips, his frown deepening as he sees what I have to say. *"I saw two enter one of the rooms below. One is large, bear-like. The other is short, but . . . more dangerous, I think. Perhaps they want to hurt you for something you stole from them. Just like I want to hurt you for what you've stolen from me."* I can't help adding this last bit.

"Why should I trust what you have to say?"

Outside in the hall, there's a creak.

"Because I want your help in return."

His eyes leave my lips to hold my gaze.

Soft, almost silent footsteps draw near, belonging to many more people than the two I'd seen below.

I take my turn to read his lips.

Hide, he mouths, nodding toward the paper screen. I move back into my previous position, crouching low.

The door crashes open.

Feet pound against the floor as opponents rush through, circling the room. I scramble back as the screen moves, pushed from the other side. My knees knock against the paper. A heavy silence descends over the room, thick with tension.

Then there's the slow glide of steel as Shin draws his sword. A shout goes up, and the gang of thieves surges forward. The whole room erupts into chaos. Steel clashes against steel. Low grunts and cries of pain fill the air. I grip my knife, unsure whether to remain hidden or join the fight. I can't differentiate Shin's voice from the rest, if he's wounded, if he needs my help. Something large topples over, banging against the floor—the cabinet. A spray of blood splatters across the paper screen, like ink on canvas.

The magpie lets out a cry of distress. Standing, I step from behind the screen.

The floor is littered with the bodies of a dozen or so men. Only two intruders remain standing. They face off with Shin, including the bearlike man from earlier.

"Lord Shin!" he calls out, one hand pressing down a wound at his shoulder. "You serve a weak and thankless master. Lend your strength to our lord and you will be rewarded."

Shin stands by the window, his sword at his side. Even after so unequal a fight, he appears composed, his back straight and face expressionless. Then I notice the blood trickling down his wrist. He's hurt. "And whom," he says, his voice low, "do you serve?"

The bear looks to answer, but his comrade hisses, "Don't be fooled! He would have us reveal our master, only to kill us immediately after. Keep to the task we were given. The bird is our prize."

I frown. Why are they after my soul?

Shin's eyes flicker to where I stand, though neither of the men takes notice. With a roar, the bearlike man charges forward. Shin bends backward, and the sword skims above his throat. Moving with impossible speed, he grabs the shoulder of the other thief, stabbing him through the stomach; he slumps to the floor. The bear man, clearly stunned, drops his sword and rushes toward the door.

As he passes the threshold, moonlight glints off something in the far corner, cloaked in shadows. The weasel-like man with the crossbow. In the chaos, I'd forgotten about him.

He nocks a bolt, aiming its silver tip at Shin's chest.

I don't hesitate. I sprint across the room. Everything happens in a moment. I collide with Shin. The bolt from the crossbow whizzes over our heads, splintering the window. Thwarted, the weasel-like thief flees the room. As Shin and I fall together, we knock against the low shelf. The birdcage wobbles at the lip of the edge, then drops.

Time seems to stand still as it falls, fracturing upon impact with the floor and releasing the bird. The magpie flaps its red-tipped wings, letting out a shrill, piercing sound, before bursting in an explosion of light.

I flinch at its radiance. The darkness after the light is blinding, and the silence after the bird's call is deafening.

Until I hear it.

My breath. Heavy and rasping.

Until I see it.

Spread between my hand and Shin's is a bright red ribbon.

The Red String of Fate.

Our eyes meet.

"Oh no," I say.

My voice comes out as clear as a chime.

10

Neither Shin nor I move as we stare at the Red String of Fate suspended between us. Shin's the first to react. He reaches for his sword, plunging it downward. It passes *through* the string and lodges in the wooden floorboards. His gaze meets mine, a troubled look in his eyes. I try next, taking my knife and slicing in an upward motion. The Red String of Fate remains intact, almost cheerfully so—a bright, shimmering bond of light.

"How could this have happened?" Shin says, but his words are more to himself than to me.

I scramble to my feet, stepping onto the wooden splinters of the birdcage. "You said the magpie was my soul . . . Perhaps, when returning to me, it got tangled up with yours." It's the only explanation I can think of.

Shin shakes his head. "It's not possible."

I hold out my hand to where he still sits on the floor.

He raises a brow, his expression skeptical. "What are you doing?"

"Maybe if our hands touch, the Red String of Fate will come full circle and disappear. Our souls will return to us."

He frowns. "That sounds . . . unlikely."

I tap my foot. "We should try everything we can. When I reached out to the Sea God, for a moment it *did* disappear. That is, unless you're afraid?"

As I intended, his expression changes, and I smile, feeling a bit smug. But then, as he moves to take my hand, I have a sudden thought—like I was with the Sea God, could I be drawn into his memories? Could he be drawn into mine?

A paper boat ripped in half. My sister-in-law in tears. My grandmother screaming my name as I ran and ran and ran . . .

He takes my hand in his strong grip. His skin is dry and warm.

Nothing happens. I see now the foolishness of my plan. Blushing, I move to extricate myself, but he doesn't let go. I frown. "What are you—"

He yanks me forward, and I nearly fall to the floor. He moves quickly, shifting over me to catch my head with his other hand. For a moment I blink up at the ceiling, stunned. Then slowly he interlocks our fingers, increasing the pressure of his palm against my own. The Red String of Fate flares, as if we hold a burning star between us. I look up to see the light of the string, and my own startled face, reflected in his dark eyes.

"Well," he drawls deliberately, "has your soul returned to you?"

And though I know he's mocking me, my heart still stutters in my chest. He releases my hand just as Namgi dashes into the room, sword drawn.

"Shin!" he shouts. "I heard a commotion . . ." He trails off, his eyes alighting on Shin and me on the floor. He lowers his sword. "This is unexpected."

Shin ignores him, rising to his feet. The Red String of Fate lengthens as he moves across the room, crouching to inspect one of the fallen thieves. "Their uniforms don't bear insignia."

"Who would dare attack Lotus House?" Namgi says loudly. "Tell me, and I will go and hunt them down, tear them limb from limb. Destroy their homes, their sons, their goats, if they have them—"

I interrupt his tirade. "Where were you a few minutes ago? Not drinking to excess, I hope."

"Ah." Namgi points at me. "You've got your voice back."

Suddenly, Shin looks up from where he's been crouching. "Namgi, do you not see it?"

Namgi cocks his head to the side. "See what?"

The ribbon floats in the air—red and glittering. Unmistakable.

I turn to Shin. "What does it mean that he cannot see it?"

Shin grimaces. "Nothing good."

Behind us there's a crackle and a pop of sound. The bodies of the thieves begin to fade, smoke swirling off them. After a few minutes, all that's left are piles of empty clothing and discarded weapons. Even the blood on the paper screen has vanished.

"Where did they go?" I ask.

"They've returned to the River of Souls," Shin says. "Their second life has ended."

"Their last life," Namgi adds. "No more coming back for them."

I shudder. I'm not unfamiliar with death, but seeing it never gets easier.

Shin wrenches his sword from the floor and sheathes it. "We'd better hurry to the main pavilion. It's almost midnight."

He looks toward the broken window, where the night seems to pulse. I notice a new scent in the air, like sulfur.

"What about her?" Namgi says, throwing a glance in my direction.

"She comes with us."

This earns an eyebrow raise from Namgi, but he doesn't question Shin.

We leave the pavilion. Outside, the once balmy summer night is now hot and dry.

Trailing Shin, Namgi sweeps back his wide sleeves to reveal wiry arms tattooed with intricate markings. "What are you going to do about the soul?" he asks, glancing at me. "Everyone will expect some evidence that you've taken it."

"I'll think of something," Shin says, then proceeds to lengthen his stride.

Instead of the forest, we follow the path Kirin traveled earlier over a green field. I look up, expecting to see stars, but the sky is filled with dark, ominous clouds. A fire must be burning somewhere, because I can smell the smoke.

Namgi slows to a walk beside me. His hand is on the hilt of his sword, his eyes on the sky. He wears a grim, worried expression.

"What you said earlier," I say. "What did you mean by my soul being used as evidence?"

"Ah, it's part of the yearly ritual. Why all these opportunistic spirits are in our house, drinking all our good liquor. They've come to bear witness that the Red String of Fate has been cut, ensuring some semblance of peace, at least until next year. The evidence is the soul of the bride—your soul. Though now that it's gone, I don't know what we'll do." Namgi scratches his chin with his knife, appearing unconcerned.

"How long has this ritual been going on for?" I ask.

"No one knows for sure. But if you're the one hundredth bride, it stands to reason for as long as that. Things get a bit hazy in the Sea God's realm, where spirits and gods can live indefinitely. One day is much like the next. One century, too, for that matter.

"Shin has *always* protected the Sea God. He's the head of Lotus House, and his duty is to serve him. Nothing drives Shin like his sense of duty."

If he protects the Sea God, then should he not help the brides in breaking the curse? But I swallow my question for now.

Shin leads us across the unlit eastern bridge I saw earlier with Nari, toward the pavilion on the lake. The bright interior is filled with people reclining on silk cushions as they pick from tables laden with fruit and colorful rice cakes. I spot what must be the lords of Tiger and Crane Houses, judging by the miniature courts they've set up on either side of the pavilion.

The music stops at our arrival. Kirin approaches, his light, enigmatic eyes sweeping over me before settling on Shin.

"They're here," he says.

At first I think he means the lords of Tiger and Crane Houses, but then I notice that every person in the pavilion has their gaze trained on the sky over the lake.

A storm appears to be rolling in, bringing with it that sulfuric stench from before, but now it's more pronounced. Inside the pavilion, guests lift silken cloths to their mouths. The heat grows unbearable, dry and thick. A scalding wind sweeps low across the ground, and the Red String of Fate whips to the side. Above, the sky begins to writhe, swelling and pulsating as if a great heart beats within the darkness.

At first, I can't discern what I see, but then I start to make out shapes in the tumult. Snakelike creatures, as large as dragons, but without horns or limbs. They blend with the sky in colors of deep red, indigo, and black.

"Imugi," Kirin growls.

My grandmother's stories never spoke of creatures such as these, as large as rivers, and so many in number they appear to swallow the night.

I feel a pressure on my shoulder. "Stay here," Shin says, pushing me lightly toward Kirin. "Namgi, with me." As Shin turns away, Kirin frowns, though his eyes never land on the bright ribbon. Like Namgi, he can't see it.

Together Shin and Namgi move to the opening of the pavilion that faces the well-lit western bridge, the crowd stepping back to give them space.

One by one, the creatures in the sky descend into the lake outside the pavilion. As they plunge downward, gusts of wind from their bodies blow out the lanterns on the bridge, leaving only the pavilion in light. There's a resounding boom, and water from the lake splashes onto the smooth wooden floorboards. Several guests scream, hushed quickly by their neighbors. In the ensuing silence, all eyes turn to where the end of the bridge meets the pavilion. In my imagination, I conjure up the gruesome face of a snakelike dragon stretching its neck through the opening, eyes burning like fire.

The blackness undulates. Those standing nearest scatter in fear. I hold my breath.

A man steps off the bridge, followed closely by two others. They have tall, wiry bodies, dark hair, and black eyes, though something about their appearances seems familiar. They enter the pavilion, moving swiftly and silently through the crowd. Behind them, the lake is empty. No sign of the snake creatures. And yet, as I watch these men prowl nearer, I have the distinct impression that the great beasts haven't vanished. They walk among us.

The first of them reaches Shin, giving a short, succinct bow. "Lord Shin."

"Ryugi."

"We've come to bear witness for the Goddess of Moon and Memory. Where is the soul of the Sea God's bride?"

Shin hesitates for a brief moment, then speaks, his voice carrying across the pavilion. "I don't have it."

Murmurings break out in the crowd. Out of the corner of my eye, I see the tall lord of Crane House lean over to whisper something into the stout lord of Tiger's ear.

Ryugi frowns. "I don't believe you. You've never shown up

without it." His hooded gaze sweeps the assembled people. "You must have the bride. Where is she?"

Shin's eyes flit briefly to the Red String of Fate. By now it's clear the string is invisible to everyone but us. "I don't have to explain myself to you."

Ryugi steps forward with a growl. "What is this? Do you defy the goddess?"

I try to remember if I know anything about the Goddess of Moon and Memory, but though I'm familiar with most of the gods and goddesses of the realm, I have no knowledge of her.

She must be a powerful goddess, to command such a force of creatures.

When Shin doesn't immediately respond, Ryugi grows visibly frustrated, his nostrils flaring. His eyes appear to glow with a haze of red. "The goddess will have an answer, Lord Shin."

"She's no goddess of mine," Shin says coldly.

Immediately the two men standing behind Ryugi bare their teeth and reach for their swords. Namgi mirrors their actions, slipping a dagger from his belt, a wild, gleeful expression on his face.

Kirin's calm voice interjects from beside me. "No need for bloodshed. The Sea God's bride is here." He pushes me, and I stumble forward.

A brief silence follows as everyone in the courtyard stares. Then Ryugi snarls at Kirin, "You dare to mock us, Silver One? If she is a bride, then I need new eyes."

His comment draws nervous laughter from the crowd.

"If you doubt my words," Kirin says, "bring her to your goddess. She will see the girl is human and whole of soul."

A low baritone voice interrupts, Lord Tiger speaking from where he stands. "And what would keep the goddess from killing the girl and taking power for herself?"

"If she is the bride, then where is the Red String of Fate?" This question comes from Lord Crane, who watches me carefully with sharp, intelligent eyes.

"Through a series of strange occurrences, the bride's tie to the Sea God has been broken *and* her soul returned to her," Namgi says. "The strangest of those occurrences being a failed theft in this very house not but half an hour ago. Who is responsible for sending the thieves has yet to be determined, but if you have suggestions for who might have betrayed us, my lords, I am all ears."

This threat has its intended effect. Both Lord Crane and Lord Tiger step back, appearing unwilling to argue further.

"Lord Shin is a loyal servant," Kirin continues as if he hadn't been interrupted. "He would not let you take her if she truly was bound to the Sea God."

Ryugi growls. "We'll take the girl, but if we find out you've been lying to us, the wrath of the goddess will be upon you all." Ryugi nods in my direction, and one of his henchmen approaches.

I reach for my great-great-grandmother's knife. Somehow I know that going with them would be worse than having my soul stolen. A powerful goddess, yet I have no knowledge of her. My grandmother often said that the most dangerous of gods are the ones who are forgotten.

Shin steps in front of the henchman before he can reach me. "Kirin, no matter his good intent, does not speak for me."

Kirin bows his head and steps back, all deference, though I notice the clenching of his jaw.

Ryugi has clearly grown impatient with these proceedings, narrowing his eyes. "If her soul truly has returned to her, then you will not protest our taking the Sea God's bride."

"She is not the Sea God's bride," Shin says.

Ryugi growls. "Playing games, Lord Shin? I'm running out of patience. If you won't give me the bride, then I'll—"

"She is *my* bride."

A stunned silence follows this statement. Kirin looks up, shocked. Behind Shin, Namgi grins from ear to ear.

Ryugi blinks. "Lord Shin, I don't understand."

"Tell your goddess that I have taken a bride. If she wishes to meet Lady Mina, she may visit, or wait until the wedding. As it is, my bride stays with me, where she is safest. She is human, after all."

"Wedding?" I whisper.

Shin's cautious gaze meets mine. "At the end of the month," he says. He attempts to communicate something with his eyes. At first I don't understand. Then I remember the words I spoke to him earlier, before the thieves appeared to steal my soul. *Let me help you.* Perhaps this is his way of telling me that he accepts.

Ryugi scowls. "You've lost your head."

"I believe," Namgi says, "it is his heart he might have lost."

If Namgi means to distract Ryugi, his plan is successful; Ryugi turns to Namgi with almost gleeful malice. "Ay, little brother. You were quick to draw your sword earlier. So eager to take blood from your blood."

Brother? I look between Namgi and Ryugi and his men. When they entered the pavilion, something about them seemed familiar. Now, as Ryugi stands face-to-face with Namgi, the resemblance is clear—coal-black hair and eyes glittering with menace.

Although perhaps, Namgi not so much. His eyes shine bright with mischief. "Ah," he sighs. "How I've not missed you."

"Our mother asks for you. You should visit her and pay your respects."

"Mother would rip off my head, if she were to see me."

Ryugi slides his gaze over to Kirin. "I see you still fight alongside the Silver One. Tell me, does he weep in his dreams, knowing each and every one of his kind has been murdered by ours?"

This question is met with a heavy, weighted silence. I take a peek at Kirin, but his face is expressionless, giving nothing of his thoughts away.

Namgi shrugs. "I wouldn't know. I don't sleep with him."

Ryugi growls before turning back to Shin. "We will deliver this"—he sneers, voice dripping with contempt—"news to the goddess."

He signals to his companions, and they follow him from the pavilion out onto the bridge. They disappear into the darkness. There's the powerful sound of wind buffeting against the ground, and the sky fills with the heavy thunder of great beasts. The murmurs of the crowd don't pick up until the sounds fade into the distance.

I turn to Shin. "A month, you said."

The significance of the timeframe is not lost on me. If what he said in the Sea God's hall is true, then after spending thirty days in the Spirit Realm I will become a spirit, too.

"A month for you to figure out how to save the Sea God," he replies, "and a month for me to figure out how to be rid of you."

"Lord Shin." Kirin approaches from behind us. "I offer you my congratulations, though I'll admit, I find it surprising."

"Diplomatic as always," Namgi says. "Just ask him to explain himself."

Kirin looks more affronted than when Ryugi said the Imugi had killed all of his people. "I would never presume to demand an explanation."

"Are the priestesses from Fox House still in attendance?" Shin asks, either not hearing or choosing to ignore the bickering of his companions.

"They are," Kirin says. "Though now that they've witnessed the events of the night, I'm sure they'll be departing soon."

"Inform them we'll be joining their convoy," Shin orders. "I wish to consult with their mistress."

Kirin appears to want to inquire further but restrains himself. Bowing, he leaves to carry out Shin's orders.

Namgi, who was watching Kirin with a bemused expression on his face, glances around before lowering his voice. "Is it wise for *all* of us to travel to Fox House?"

"Fox House is the oldest of the houses, their mistress the wisest," Shin replies. "She will have the knowledge I seek."

"Yes. But is it safe to bring *Mina* there?" Namgi clarifies.

Namgi's question finally seems to impress upon him, because Shin glances at me, an inscrutable look passing over his features.

"Why not?" I ask, suspicious now. Shin might have agreed to help me, but I don't yet trust him. "What's wrong with Fox House?"

"You're a human," Namgi says, rather unhelpfully.

"And?"

Namgi's grin could light a candle. "The head of Fox House is a demon."

11

Two boats depart from Lotus House, one carrying Shin, Namgi, and myself, the other Kirin and three fierce-looking women, garbed in the red-and-white robes of priestesses.

Already the news of what happened at Lotus House seems to have spread throughout the city. We pass by boats traveling in the opposite direction. Upon catching sight of Shin, their occupants ask if the rumors are true, if he truly is to marry a human girl. And a Sea God's bride, no less!

Shin ignores them, closing his eyes as he leans against the prow of the boat. Instead, it's Namgi who answers by lifting one oar. "Lotus House has a lady at last!" he shouts. A cheer goes up.

No one pays me any attention, likely mistaking me for a servant.

"Are the people of the city always so interested in the affairs of the houses?" I ask, watching Namgi struggle to navigate a tight bend in the canal.

He only answers after finally managing to regain our course. "For spirits, when days often seem to blend together, any small change riles them up. That's why the arrival of the Sea God's bride is such a momentous occasion, an excuse as good as any for a celebration."

Earlier, when I walked through the city with Mask, Dai, and Miki, it seemed like the city was in a festive mood, what with all the people out on the streets, the many lanterns, food, and fireworks. Even in Lotus House it was a party.

Not like at home. Is this why the gods have abandoned us? Do they not care about the hardships of the human world because the Spirit Realm suffers no consequences?

And what of the spirits themselves, don't they remember what it was like to be human? Don't they worry for those they've left behind? Or do their memories, as Namgi implied, grow distant and hazy with time spent here in the Spirit Realm?

Outside a grand teahouse built over the canal, a crowd gathers, jostling one another to get a glimpse of our boat. I can't be sure, but I think I see a boy with thick hair slip through the crowd, an infant strapped to his back.

"It's true that the affairs of certain houses interest the spirits more than others," Namgi continues blithely. "In the Sea God's city, there are eight great houses, all of which serve the Sea God. Shin is the head of the most powerful house, the one that all the others look to for guidance and order. While houses like Spirit House protect the interests of spirits, and Tiger and Crane, soldiers and scholars, respectively, Lotus House protects the interests of the gods."

"And the gods protect humans," I say.

I know I've caught Shin's attention when he slowly sits up, watching me closely. The boat dips in the water, and I grip the seat, bracing my feet on the wooden boards.

Perhaps I shouldn't anger him. Our alliance—if I can even call it that—is tentative at best. But the sounds of merrymaking now grate upon my ears, raucous laughter and out-of-tune singing, and cutting through it all a loud and clear sound—the peal of a chime.

The boat rocks, bringing our bodies closer.

"Do you deny it, then," I ask, "that gods are meant to protect humans?"

"I do deny it." Shin's voice is low, his words as merciless and cruel as they were in the Sea God's hall. "Humans are fickle, violent creatures. Because they fear their own deaths, they are driven to war, scouring from the earth in seconds that which takes years to grow."

"Only because death shadows them closely," I retort. "Can you blame them, when death has no patience, slipping into their homes and stealing the breath from their children?"

"I can blame them," he says, "just as you blame the gods for the follies of humans."

"But it's supposed to be a circle, isn't it? The gods protect the humans, and the humans pray to and honor the gods."

"That's just like a human to think the world revolves around you, to think the rivers are for you, the sky, the *sea* is for you. You are just one of many parts of the world, and in my opinion, the one that blights them all."

Namgi's eyes dart between us. A few yards away, Kirin watches from his boat, drawn by our raised voices.

Slowly I look up, holding Shin's gaze. "So you do protect the gods," I say. "From humans."

The rest of the boat ride is spent in silence, both of us leaning away from the other on the small bench. The canal flows into a larger body of water, and we leave the luminous buildings of the city behind us, traveling into darkness. Ahead, a bright light flares up in Kirin's boat. Namgi follows suit, firing a torch that he hands to Shin.

Soon, I can't see anything beyond the light of the torches. The darkness thickens. When I grip the edge of the boat, I find the wood dewed with mist. Then suddenly, I feel a great presence all around me, as if the air is weighted. Out of the darkness looms something huge, monstrous, as large as the dragon. Hundreds, thousands of them. I grip my knife and glance at Shin and Namgi, yet neither of them appears concerned. Then I look closer. The great objects are . . .

. . . trees.

They loom out of the water, seeming to rise up endlessly into the sky. The boat drifts too close to one, and Namgi kicks off the trunk, diverting our movement.

There's a subtle vibration in the air, as if the trees are humming. We arrive at the edge of a great forest, much larger than the one within Lotus House, deeper and darker. The boat slows, skimming over pebbles. Before it comes to a stop, Shin's already up, vaulting over the side.

"The mistress of Fox House lives *here*?" I ask, staring into the dark forest. I can't make out a path through the dense thicket of trees. It's as if no one has lived here for a thousand years. No human, at least.

"Yes," Namgi says. He offers a hand to help me disembark. "A suitable habitat for a fox demon, don't you think?"

I land in the shallow water and soak the hem of my skirt. Shin has joined with Kirin and the priestesses, and together they enter the forest. "You implied that it wouldn't be wise to bring me to Fox House because their leader might . . . eat me." I shudder. "But in my grandmother's stories, fox demons are evil spirits that prey solely upon men."

"This fox demon isn't so particular. Shall we?" Namgi grabs the torch from the boat, gesturing for me to follow.

As we approach the forest, it's as if the sounds around us pick up in volume, the reedy murmur of the insects, the humming of the trees. Then we step into the forest, and the sounds stop. I pause on the threshold, unable to go farther. My stomach sinks, that familiar fear taking hold. Namgi seems to share none of my misgivings. Already the light of his torch has grown smaller with distance. I rush ahead, almost crashing into him where he's stopped to investigate some disturbance in the forest.

"What—what's wrong?" I cry. "Why did you stop?"

He glances at me with a frown. "Looks like something big came through here." He points to the trail, where a great branch has fallen onto the path and broken in two. Beside the branch is an impression in the ground, a large animal print. "I haven't been in this forest for a long time. They say the beasts, left undisturbed, can grow to enormous sizes. Tigers and snakes. Wolves and bears." Namgi raises the torch, squinting at my face. "Are you all right? You look pale."

"I'm fine," I say, perhaps too quickly.

He shrugs and moves on, walking at an even faster pace than before.

"Wait, slow down." I trip over a root, catching myself on a tree branch.

I watch the light of Namgi's torch move farther and farther away.

I try to make a run toward the light but instead end up sprawled on the ground.

Namgi returns to investigate. "Are you sure you're all right?" he asks again.

"I can't see. I need more light. Better yet, give me the torch."

"I don't know." Namgi scratches his cheek. "It seems unwise to give fire to a clumsy person in a forest."

"Please."

"It's a straight path."

"I'm afraid of forests," I blurt out, shame washing over me. How weak and human I must appear to him. When Namgi doesn't respond, I brush by him, trudging forward.

I've only walked a few paces when he slips his arm into mine.

"I'm afraid of a lot of things," he says, "but not the darkness. I can see in the dark, you know. That must be why. Really, I don't need this torch, but you do, so I'll hold it for you. Sometimes I can be thoughtless. And I like to tease. But you can depend upon me."

He prattles on, and I concentrate on the sound of his voice. The path ends in a small clearing where Shin, Kirin, and the priestesses wait for us.

"We don't have time to waste," Kirin says.

Shin's eyes glide from Namgi to me, then he hands Kirin his torch. "Go on ahead and light the path."

Kirin immediately obeys, accompanied by the Fox House priestesses. We leave the clearing, advancing even deeper into the forest. With Kirin in front and Namgi bringing up the rear, I now notice details I hadn't before—there are scuffs in the dirt, the path worn from use.

After a few minutes, Shin breaks the silence. "I thought you were fearless." He holds back a stray branch for me to duck under, the leaves brushing over my hair.

I glance at him to see if he's mocking me, but his gaze is questioning.

"Have you no fears, then?" I ask.

"If I did," he says, letting the branch fall behind me, "I would not share them with you."

I scoff. "Because fears are weaknesses?"

"I have no weaknesses."

"Just the Sea God." I watch him carefully for a reaction, but he gives nothing away. "Is he your only fear, too?"

Shin's eyes meet mine, a crease forming between his brows. Yet I don't sense any anger from him. He's trying to determine something about me, as I am about him.

"We're almost there," he says.

A light gleams at the end of the path. We must have walked a fair distance, yet I hadn't noticed. As with Namgi, our conversation distracted me from my fear of the forest. He turns from me, stepping ahead on the path.

"Was I right to believe what you said earlier," I ask, "that you were promising me the month?" He looks back. I lift up my arm, the Red String of Fate glistening brightly between us. "Even should our tie be broken, you won't stop me from completing my task?"

"I can give you that, at least."

"Even though I'm one of the humans you so despise."

For a moment, he says nothing, then hesitantly, "I don't . . . despise humans. All spirits were once humans, after all, and they comprise most of the realm . . ."

"Then why—"

He shakes his head. "You claim the gods should love and care for humans. I disagree. I don't think love can be bought or earned or even prayed for. It must be freely given."

For once, I don't jump to argue with him, mulling over his words. "I can respect a belief such as that," I say finally.

"And I can respect your determination to save your people," he says. "You won't accomplish such a feat, but I can respect that you'll try."

I scowl. "Mine was a genuine compliment."

Shin laughs, the sound so unexpected that for a moment, he looks less like the lord of a great house and more like a boy from my village.

The trees begin to thin around us, spaced farther apart. Moonlight slips through the canopy, and Kirin and Namgi extinguish their torches. A glimmer of mist coats the forest floor. Figures robed in red and white move gracefully among the trees.

Our party approaches a small temple; its walls stand open to the forest. A few short steps lead up to an elegant wooden platform where two women wait.

The younger woman glides forward to greet the priestesses who traveled with us from Lotus House. She then turns to Shin, bowing. "We've been expecting you, Lord Shin."

Kirin frowns. "Your sentries notified you of our coming?"

"Our goddess knows all." This time, it is the older woman who speaks. From her white dress and feathered hat, it's clear she must hold an honored position among the women. She turns her airy gaze out to the forest. "Look, here she comes now."

At first, all I see is the deep green of the woods, speckled with small pockets of moonlight. Then movement disturbs the peace. Through the forest comes a white fox, its long, elegant tail split in two. Nimbly, it leaps over a small stream and up the steps of the temple, approaching on padded feet.

The fox's glittering gaze is riveted on me. She's so lovely—her eyes amber flecked with pure gold. Her fur is mostly white, with silver around her pointed ears and the tufts of her split tail.

Suddenly the fox lunges forward, her sharp teeth bared.

"No!" the younger priestess screams. At first I think she's warning of the demon, but then I realize she's reaching out toward Shin. He's drawn his sword, the sharp blade angled against the fox's neck.

The fox's eyes slide toward him, fiercely intelligent, then it ducks beneath the blade, dodging between us to bite down on the Red String of Fate. The fox gnashes down, wringing and shaking it to the point that if it were a regular ribbon, it would have shredded to pieces. Abruptly the fox pulls back, sitting on its haunches and licking its paw. The Red String of Fate shimmers brightly, undamaged.

"How dare you raise steel against our goddess!" the young priestess hisses.

Before Shin can respond, a voice answers, deep and sonorous. "And why shouldn't he, to protect what matters most?"

The powerful voice comes from the elder priestess, though her demeanor has changed. When before her eyes were cloudy and dazed, now they shine with an uncanny light—amber with specks of gold.

"You see it, then," Shin says, his eyes not on the priestess, but on the white fox. "The Red String of Fate."

"It shines bright." It's the priestess again who answers. The fox is speaking *through* her.

"What do you mean by the Red String of Fate?" Kirin studies

the air between Shin and me, which to him must appear empty. "It can't be . . ."

The fox moves forward to brush the top of her head beneath the ribbon, a low rumble humming at the back of her throat. "I've seen a fate like this before. Many years ago. It is a very dangerous type of fate, one which cannot be severed by any blade."

"There must be another way it can be broken," Kirin says.

"The only way to end a fate such as this is if one bearer should die."

There's a short pause, then Namgi asks, "So, if Mina dies, then the Red String of Fate will disappear?"

The fox shakes her head, an eerily human movement. "There is a chance that should one die, so will the other."

Namgi frowns. "But you just said that if one of them should die, the fated connection would be severed."

"If they both die, then there is no fate."

"Agh!" Namgi tugs at his hair. "This is why one should never consult a demon, or a goddess for that matter. They never give a straight answer."

"It's the same as with the Sea God," Kirin says, ignoring Namgi. "Instead, it is Shin's life that is in danger."

"Yes, but for an important difference."

When the goddess doesn't immediately continue, Kirin prompts, "And what difference is that?"

"As you can see, or *not see*, the fate is invisible, as it isn't with the Sea God. Although every Sea God's bride that arrives in this realm has a Red String of Fate, the Sea God is not fated to all of them. After all, that is not the true purpose of the Red String of Fate."

I have a suspicion that the goddess takes pleasure in withholding information until the right question is asked.

"Then what is the purpose of the Red String of Fate?" Namgi says through gritted teeth.

The fox tilts her head to the side, amber eyes glinting. "It ties soul mates to each other."

"Soul . . . mates," Kirin says slowly.

"Yes. It ties one soul to another, two halves of a whole."

For some reason I'm surprised to hear this explanation from the goddess, though this is how humans tell the myth, when the destinies of two people collide in life-altering ways. It explains the undeniable connection between lovers—like Cheong and Joon, who loved each other from the beginning.

"It's not possible," Shin says, and his words jog a memory. He said something similar when the Red String of Fate first formed between us.

My grandmother always said only the words I believe in are the ones that can hurt me. And yet, Kirin stares at me in disbelief, and even Namgi looks skeptical. As for Shin, he rubs his fingers against his wrist, as if the ribbon pains him.

I won't say the qualities he lacks that would make it impossible for me to love him, either: a caring heart, looking at me not as a burden or a weakness, but as a strength.

"I didn't ask to be fated to you," I say. "I don't want your life to be in danger because of me. I didn't know what would happen when I released my soul from the cage—I just wanted it back."

"Mina, you don't understand."

"Then tell me. What is it I don't understand?"

"We can't be soul mates . . . ," Shin says. His dark eyes lift, holding mine. "Because I don't have a soul."

12

How can Shin not have a soul?

The question plagues me all the way to Lotus House. Upon our arrival, I'm whisked away by a group of maidservants to a large bathing chamber where I'm unceremoniously stripped down, doused with hot water, and scrubbed until my skin is raw and red. Too exhausted to protest, I relax as the women trim and buff my nails and smooth rich oils along my arms and legs. The only time I speak is when I catch sight of one of the maidservants leaving the chamber with my battered dress. "My knife!" I exclaim. The maidservant returns and places it on a low shelf within reach.

They call me "Lady Mina" and "Shin's bride," guiding me from the salt baths across the warm, heady chamber to dip my toes into the cool stream that runs through the north side. Their chatter is filled with excitement and wonder, their words pattering around me like summer rain.

"She's so young to be a bride, barely sixteen!"

"How romantic, don't you think? That Lord Shin should fall for her in one night."

"What do you think captivated him so?"

"Her bright face!"

"Her nimble body."

"Her thick hair. It really is lovely." A warm set of hands massages my scalp, while another slips perfumed fingers through my hair, the scents of lavender and hibiscus washing over me. Finally I'm left alone to soak in the central bath of the chamber, steam curling up around me in pleasant, lazy swirls.

My thoughts drift to just an hour earlier. What did Shin mean when he said he didn't have a soul? He spoke as if stating an undeniable truth. And neither Kirin nor Namgi contradicted him. But I was taught that everything has a soul, from the emperor to the lowliest of humans, from the birds to the rocks in the stream.

I lift my arm, and water spills from my hand, as does the Red String of Fate, slipping across the chamber to disappear through the far wall. I wonder where Shin is now. He received a missive and left on another boat with Kirin, while Namgi took me back to the house. Slowly, the Red String of Fate begins to shift across the room in a diagonal motion. He must be on the move.

"Lady Mina?" The maidservants have returned. They help me out of the water, placing a warm cup of barley tea into my hands to sip while one sweeps a turtle shell comb through my hair. I'm then garbed in a light summer dress with a pale blue skirt and white jacket, the sleeves embroidered with pink flowers. It even has a pocket for my knife. Afterward, we leave the main building of Lotus House and walk across the same open field I traveled with Shin and Namgi earlier.

Dawn streaks pink across the horizon. I've been awake for the whole night. I'm half asleep by the time the maidservants lead me to a room with a soft pallet of silk blankets. I lay my head down on the beaded pillow. Within seconds, I'm asleep.

My grandmother once told me the story of when the storms first began.

A long time ago, our people were ruled by a benevolent emperor blessed by the gods. Loved by them. By the Sea God, most of all. The world was prosperous then.

It was said that the emperor and the Sea God had a brotherly bond that was unbreakable, that one could not exist without the other.

Then one day, a conqueror came to our kingdom, and although our brave emperor fought him, he was defeated, his murdered body tossed from the cliffs into the sea.

It was the loss of the emperor that threw the Sea God into his vengeful wrath. And the usurper, triumphant after having slain the emperor and his family, learned what it was to rule a land cursed by gods.

Ironically, it was the conqueror who first sacrificed a bride to the Sea God, and in so doing, saved our people.

For five years, a terrible drought had ravaged the lands; the rivers and streams dried up. The bones of fish lay shattered in the barren riverbanks. The usurper consulted a priestess, who told him that only "a love equal to or greater than the love the Sea God bore for the emperor" could appease the god's wrath. The conqueror, who had taken up residence in the slain emperor's palace, had one child, a daughter. She was said to be the most beautiful girl in the kingdom, with pomegranate-red lips and dark-moon eyes. But more than that, it was said that she was the only person the conqueror truly loved.

She became the Sea God's first bride.

For three seasons following her sacrifice, the sea was calm, and the land was safe. Until the summer months once again arrived. This time, rain fell from the sky in sheets of icy water, flooding the rivers and fields. People drowned in their beds, children whisked away from them by fierce winds.

Another sacrifice was prepared. Another girl was thrown into the sea.

And so it continued. Year after year.

It became known. It became myth.

Nothing appeased the Sea God's wrath except the life of someone beloved.

I wake to light sweeping across my eyes and the sound of my grandmother's voice echoing from my dreams. I recognize the room I'm in as the one from the night before, where the thieves attempted to steal my soul. Though someone must have come while we were gone to tidy up. The wooden floor is polished to a gleam, and the few pieces of furniture are upright and pushed to the side. The only evidence of the fight is the hole in the window from the crossbow bolt, through which birds can now be heard singing to one another across the pond.

There's a soft knock, and the door slides open. Two maidservants enter, one carrying a tray of covered dishes, the other tools for grooming, a comb and a ribbon. The first maidservant places the tray before me and proceeds to take the lids off each mouthwatering dish. Savory soup. Grilled yellow corvina on a bed of lush greens. Chestnut rice. The last dish is a steamed egg puffing up from the stone pot like a cloud. As with the dumplings the night before, I devour the meal. The maidservants encourage me as I eat, pointing to the properties of certain dishes and asking if there are any particular foods I'd like to eat for future meals. Afterward, the second maidservant moves to sit behind me, brushing my hair and gathering it in sections for a braid.

"Could you tell me what this pavilion is used for?" I look out the window to where the pond sits serene and tranquil, but for the splash of a duck. "What is it called?"

"You are in the Lotus Pavilion, my lady," the first servant responds, a girl with rosy cheeks and a kind smile. "These are Lord Shin's personal quarters."

I blink several times. "His personal quarters? As in . . ."

"Where he sleeps, where he spends most of his time when he's not out in the city."

I look around, remembering my impression when I first entered the room last night. I thought it a storage room. It's empty but for a worn cabinet, the low shelf by the window, and the paper screen.

The second maidservant finishes with my braid and rises to her feet. Together, the maidservants fold the pallet of blankets into a neat bundle and place it against the wall.

"Thank you," I tell them.

The first maidservant lifts the tray of now empty dishes. "It's an honor to serve you, my lady." They bow and leave the room.

I wait a few minutes before moving to the cabinet and opening the doors. I know I'm prying, but Shin should have known when he put me in his room that I would look through his belongings. Inside are shelves stacked with robes of dark colors, as well as pants and belts. I rummage around but find nothing of interest. Closing the cabinet, I turn to survey the room. There's nothing here to indicate regular use, no scrolls, paintings, or board games. I move to the low shelf and reach beneath to see if there's anything hidden there.

"I can't tell if your family would be proud or horrified."

I twist around to find Nari leaning against the door.

"I'm sure they would be proud you've gotten your voice back," she says, "but somehow I can't imagine they'd be pleased about your engagement."

Last Nari saw me, I was on my way to get back my soul from Shin. Now I'm to marry him. She must be wondering what happened during the time we were apart. I could tell her the truth, but I don't want to endanger her. Even I can admit there are perilous politics astir among the gods and houses.

"Have you seen Shin? I need to speak with him. It's urgent."

Nari raises a brow but allows the change in subject. "He went with Lord Kirin to Tiger House."

Shin must suspect Lord Tiger is behind the attempted theft of my soul. "When will he return?"

"Not until tonight."

But that will be too late, a whole day wasted. Now that I have my soul back, I need to return to the Sea God. The dream reminded me—the answers I seek lie with him.

"Nari, I can't explain it, but there's somewhere I need to go. Will you help me?"

"I'm sorry, Mina," she says, her expression apologetic, "but I have orders. You're free to go anywhere you'd like, as long as it's within the grounds of Lotus House."

I stare at her in shock. Shin lied to me! He promised me that he wouldn't keep me from my task.

"Mina—" she begins.

I sweep past her out the door.

She follows me down the stairs. "You don't understand. It's for your own safety. You're human. Your body is weaker in this world."

Turning, I grab her hands. "Nari, you have to help me get to the Sea God's palace."

"The Sea God—" Her eyes widen, but then she slowly shakes her head. "I can't disobey a direct order from Lord Shin. He is the master of this house. I am sworn to him."

"Say I escaped! You helped me last night."

"Ah, Nari," a low voice drawls from the shadows beneath the stairs. "Is that why you wanted to play cards with me?" Namgi steps away from the wall he was leaning against. "And here I thought we were finally getting along."

I move in front of Nari, but though his words are for her, his eyes are on me.

"Breaking oaths, sneaking into places where you don't belong," he says. "You ask a lot of your friends."

I hesitate, then say, "I'd ask the same of my foes."

He raises a brow at the echo of yesterday's words. *Are you a friend or are you a foe?*

"There will be no escaping," Namgi says. "I'll take you myself."

13

Namgi and I leave on foot through the main gate, where the night before I'd seen party guests arriving. The guards on duty nod at him as we pass, only sparing me a cursory glance. I can tell Shin's location by the Red String of Fate. Right now it stretches behind me, indicating Shin is somewhere to the south. If I can stay north of him, he won't discover that I've left the grounds of Lotus House, at least for a little while.

Though it's early in the morning, the city is already bustling with activity, spirits purchasing fresh produce and flowers from makeshift markets set up on either side of the street. Even the canal is crowded with vendors on boats, their cargo on display as they shout out to the people on the shore. I watch as a young woman throws a tin coin into the hull of a boat with one hand, only to catch a wrapped fish with the other, pitched to her by the vendor.

"What would you like to do first?" Namgi asks, walking with his hands on the back of his head. "Shopping? Sightseeing? There's a wonderful teahouse in the market district that serves a variety of wine-spirits."

"Take me to the Sea God's palace."

I can see its winged rooftop in the distance, beneath the shadow of a great white cloud.

"The gate to the palace won't be open, you know. Not until a year from now, with the arrival of the next Sea God's bride."

I frown. That *does* present an obstacle, but I can't lose this opportunity. "I'll deal with that problem when I get there."

Namgi shrugs, gesturing for me to follow him. We set off down the street. As we walk, I study Namgi out of the corner of my eye. Like yesterday, he wears form-fitting black robes and a dagger at his waist, his hair swept back with a jade clip. People call out to him as we pass, most friendly-like, though I notice some spirits shy away at his approach. It reminds me of the party the night before, when the guests scattered in fear as the snake-men entered the pavilion.

"Like what you see?" Namgi says, having caught me staring at him.

"Last night, in the main courtyard . . ." I watch as the teasing smile slips off his face. "That man you spoke to was your brother?" Even without Ryugi *calling* him brother, the striking resemblance was too much to ignore. Both men—all of them, actually—were tall and wiry and shared the same sharp features.

"Two of them were my brothers," Namgi says after a beat of silence. "Hongi, the one in back, is more like an inbred cousin."

I shiver, remembering the events that preceded their arrival, the awful sound of long, sinuous bodies winging through the air. "Are you not a spirit, then?"

"Not a spirit, thank the gods," he says. "Not that I don't

119

appreciate spirits." He flashes a grin at a group of youths approaching us on the city street. The following eruption of giggles is admittedly impressive.

"I am not a spirit, nor am I a demon or a god." He pauses dramatically. "I am an Imugi. A beast of myth."

I look skeptically at his curly head and mischievous grin.

He laughs. "This is just my human form. This form takes a lot less energy to move, believe me. In my soul form, I am a powerful water snake. Like a dragon, but without its magic. The Imugi are a warring breed. We're born in war, and we die in war. We worship no gods, believing that we ourselves can become gods, either through living one thousand years or by fighting in one thousand battles. Only then can we be elevated from snakes to dragons.

"Of course"—Namgi grins sheepishly—"there is one shortcut to godhood, as there always is with long endeavors. The pearl of a dragon can transform an Imugi from a snake into a dragon, if he were to wish upon it. I'd heard rumors that hinted that Lord Shin had such a pearl in his possession. Being the hotheaded fool that I was, I tried to steal it. Suffice to say, I failed. It was definitely not in his room. I mean, you've seen it, there's—"

"Nothing there," I finish. Nothing but a cabinet, a paper screen, and a shelf.

"Exactly. It's as if he doesn't have any possessions. You should see *my* room. It's filled with all manner of things I've collected over the years."

"Mine as well. My grandmother is always nagging at me to

put away my things. She says, 'Mina, how are you going to handle a household of your own one day if you can't even keep your room in order?' Of course, whenever I do determine to clean it, it's only to find that she's already folded my clothes and swept the floors. She tells me to be responsible, and yet she can't help but treat me like a child. She will always see me as her youngest grandchild, the only girl in her bloodline after having only sons and grandsons. She says I'm her favorite, even though, as a grandmother, she really shouldn't have any favorites. She says I remind her of *her* grandmother, whom she misses every day."

"You are close to your grandmother."

I bite my lip, suddenly overcome with emotion.

"What of your parents?"

"They passed away when I was a child. My father at sea. My mother in childbirth."

"So it was your grandmother who raised you."

"My grandmother and grandfather, before he passed. And my eldest brother and his wife."

"I haven't seen my mother for years," Namgi says. "Not since I pledged my life to serving Shin. Most Imugi find a master to serve, to fulfill their one thousand battles, since we're not exactly a patient breed. To this end, most of my kind serve gods of death or goddesses of war. I had planned to serve the Goddess of Moon and Memory, alongside my brothers. But something had always felt wrong to me, to serve a master just to fight in meaningless battles. Stealing the pearl was my form of rebellion. When Shin caught me, he should have killed me, but instead he offered me a role in his guard. He saved me, and for that, I owe him a life debt. And my mortal life is, more or less, one thousand years."

I look at him, slightly awed. "So how old *are* you?"

Namgi flashes me his now familiar grin. "Nineteen."

Though we've been walking steadily, the Sea God's palace remains in the distance, at times appearing even farther away. Namgi leads me down one street, then another, until we reach a road that runs alongside a canal, the main feature a teahouse with low decks that stretch over the water. It's a lovely sight.

I've seen it before. We passed this building on the journey to Fox House last night, which means we've gone too far—we're now west of the Sea God's palace, when before we were to the east.

Namgi turns slowly to meet my gaze, raising his hands in a placating gesture. "Please don't be upset, Mina. As I said, the doors to the palace are barred. No one has ever gotten inside. It's enchanted. Maybe if you wait, Shin will take you himself. If anyone can breach the palace walls, it'll be him."

"I'll wait."

Namgi sighs in relief. "You won't regret your decision. There's so much for you to see in the city other than the Sea God's palace." He ducks beneath an archway into an alley lined with cramped market stalls, spirits scrambling over one another to haggle prices on a variety of items—slippers, celadon bottles of ginseng, and ink and scrolls. He stops to ogle a horse pin with silver eyes, saying with a chuckle, "Looks like Kirin."

I smile pleasantly.

I need to lose him, but how? I'm not fool enough to believe I can escape through the crowd. He'd find me within moments. He knows the area better, and the city's inhabitants are more likely to help him than a stranger. One stall sells umbrellas in silk, paper, and cloth. Another shop consists entirely of a wall of masks. There are masks painted like foxes and birds of prey. Some have slits for eyes, others holes for mouths. There are white bridal masks with red dots painted on their cheeks, grandfathers with feather eyebrows and grooves for wrinkles, and a grandmother with smiling eyes.

I'm staring at the last, when it winks at me.

Mask holds a finger to her lips, then moves her finger away, pointing. Dai darts through the throng toward us.

"Mina." Namgi appears beside me. "What are you doing?"

I quickly pick up the nearest mask—depicting a magpie, ironically—and place it over my face. "What do you think?"

Through the eyeholes, I watch Namgi grimace. "It's hideous."

I glance sideways. Dai's almost upon us. "I want it. Will you buy it for me?"

He sighs. "If you insist." He pulls from his pocket a long string of coins, turning to the shopkeeper. "How much?"

Dai arrives, sweeping in between us. In the blink of an eye, he grabs Namgi's money rope and the mask from my hand, placing it over his own face. Then he's gone, disappearing into the crowded market.

"The little thief!" Namgi runs off in pursuit.

Mask appears beside me. She grabs my hand and hauls me through a gap between stalls.

I stumble to face her, looking around to see she's brought me into a narrow alley.

"You came right on time," I say, breathless. "I was wondering how I'd lose Namgi."

She nods, her grandmother mask smiling its rosy-cheeked smile. "I know the way to the Sea God's palace. Let me show you."

"What about Dai?" I look back to the busy street. "Namgi will be furious when he realizes he's been tricked."

"Who says he'll be caught?" Mask says. "Put your faith in Dai, Mina. He might not be very bright, but he's fast!"

Mask turns, leading me down the alley. On her back, Miki is fast asleep, her little fists tucked against her cheek. Mask hunches down and places her hands more firmly beneath Miki's bottom, adjusting her hold so that the little girl is secure. She then hurries from street to alley, across bridges and gardens. Pedestrians jump out of her path to make way for a "grandmother" with a baby.

Not for the first time I wonder what she must look like beneath her grandmother mask. Walking with her back to me, I can see the hemp strings of the mask woven through the dark strands of her hair. If someone were to look out of their window down into the alley, they might mistake us for sisters.

Soon we reach the large boulevard that leads to the Sea God's palace. We hurry forward, climbing up the steps.

"The gate is open!" I shout. Namgi had said it would be closed, but there's a crack between the great doors, just big enough for a person to slip through.

I'm almost at the door when I realize Mask and Miki are no

longer with me. I look back to see Mask at the top of the stairs. Miki, now awake, peers owlishly from over the older girl's shoulder.

"Go on," Mask says. "You're almost there."

I step back from the doorway.

"Mina?" She tilts her head.

I rush toward her and grab her in a fierce embrace. "I don't know why you're helping me," I say, "but I'm thankful for it." Miki coos, and I widen my arms, snuggling into her downy hair.

Perhaps I should be wary of someone who hides her face behind a mask, but I feel her kindness and concern for me in every word she speaks, in her gentle hands that reach up to pat my back.

"I have my reasons," she says, rather mysteriously. "Now go."

She pushes me through the gate and into the Sea God's palace.

14

The Sea God's hall is empty. The throne, where he was sleeping the night before, is vacant. Somehow I'm not surprised, though I wish it were a simple matter of finding the Sea God and forcing him awake to break the curse. The noon sun has reached its apex in the sky, pounding heat against my neck. I have a sinking premonition that he isn't here—in this hall, or in the many courtyards.

The Red String of Fate tugs at my hand. I look down, noticing a subtle shift in its direction. Before, it had angled to the left as I moved across the city and Shin remained in place, but now it's a straight line, and . . . it's rippling. The color of the ribbon shifts from pale pink to deep red, like a wave cresting toward me.

Shin is coming.

Namgi must have sent a missive, alerting him to my escape. Or he sensed the change in my direction. He'll be here soon, to take me back to Lotus House, where I'll have no hope of discovering the truth about the Sea God.

I search the hall. There must be some hint as to where an errant god might have disappeared to. Yet there are no doors in the walls, and when I reach for the windows, my fingers barely brush the closed shutters. There's only the dais and the throne, and behind both—the great mural of the dragon chasing a pearl across the sky.

The dragon in the mural is not true to life, perhaps a fourth the size of the real one. And yet the depiction is mesmerizing, each scale painted a different shade of the sea, from deep indigo to jade green to viridian blue. I draw closer to the mural, reach out a hand, and press it to one of those smooth, glittering scales.

The wall gives beneath my hand, revealing a hidden door.

I step through it into a garden.

Birdsong lilts through sun-dappled trees. A stream nearby gurgles merrily. I look for signs of the Sea God, but the garden appears abandoned.

I follow a worn path overgrown with weeds and grass, passing crumbled rock walls and moss-covered statues.

Speckled sunlight winks through the trees. At one point, I glimpse a meadow in the distance, with a broad swath of flattened grass, as if a large creature had recently been taking a sunny nap.

I've walked a fair distance when I come upon a pavilion, built beside a small pond. Its design is similar to the temple of the fox goddess, with a winged rooftop and four pillars at each corner. The wooden steps creak as I make my way up them; inside, the floorboards are rough with sand and dirt. I place my hand on a pillar, warm from the sun, and look back the way I came. The Red String of Fate is now pale pink. I wonder if Shin has arrived at the palace, only to find the doors barred.

I close my eyes. It's quiet. Peaceful. The silence in the Sea God's hall felt empty, but here the silence feels expectant, like a held breath.

Out of the stillness comes the peal of a chime.

I feel the blood drain from my body. I turn toward the sound. Behind the pavilion is a pond filled with small white objects. It takes me a moment to realize what they are.

Paper boats. Hundreds of them, overlapping one another in the water.

I step off the platform and walk to the pond's edge. My toes sink into the warm, silk-smooth mud. There's a boat caught in the reeds. I lean down and pick it up. The paper is rough against my fingertips, the bottom soggy and dripping.

Slowly, I unfold the boat. My fingers brush against the first character scrawled across the surface, written in black ink. Darkness rises up, consuming me.

When I open my eyes, the world is covered in white. At first I think it's snow. The fine residue coats the leaves on the trees, even the bark of their branches. But it's not cold. And there's smoke in the air, dulling the brightness of the sun.

It was noon when I entered the garden, but now it appears to be dusk. Did I faint beside the pond?

A flake of white drifts downward, and I lift my palm to catch it. From this close, I can see that it isn't white at all, but gray with flecks of black.

Ash.

Ash everywhere, falling from the sky.

There's a muffled cough behind me. I turn to see a young woman kneeling by a stream, though this stream doesn't appear like any that I saw in the garden, its waters muddy and brackish.

"Please," the girl says, "I beg of you. Save my child." Her trembling hands spread across a bump beneath her rough dress. Tears stream down the girl's face, which, even from this distance, is frighteningly gaunt.

A small fire crackles beside her. I watch as she takes a short stick from the pile, blowing out the flame at its tip. She then pulls a paper scroll from beneath her short jacket, spreading the paper on her lap. With the blackened coal from the fire, she writes shaking words onto its mottled surface. When she's finished, she folds the sides of the paper, creasing each line carefully until it takes the shape of a boat. Raising it to her lips, she kisses the boat gently with parched lips and places it upon the water.

The paper boat gathers a layer of ash as it drifts downstream, disappearing around a bend. The girl lets out another heartbreaking cough. She stands, her movements shaky and weak.

Quickly, I rush over, reaching out my hands to steady her. "Wait! Let me help you."

She passes right through me, as if I were made of air. I turn around. As she walks away, her body slowly begins to fade.

It's as if the memory she and I exist in can only hold this one moment as she knelt beside the water's edge. For that's where I must be—inside her memory. That moment in time when she poured all her soul and hope into a paper boat. A wish for the gods.

The air grows thick with ashes. They fall from the sky, choking me. I can't breathe. I'm drowning in ashes. They bury me, weighing me down, until I'm blind and cold and aching.

"Mina!" a voice calls to me from out of the darkness.

In my mind, I see them all. I see my grandmother performing ancestral rites to honor first her son and daughter-in-law, then her husband. I see my sister-in-law, weeping beside the grave of her child. And lastly, I see this girl, a stranger to me, but just as familiar as the rest, for in her grief I recognize my own.

Why must everything we love be taken from us? Why can't we hold what we love forever in our hands, safe and warm and whole?

"Mina!" the voice persists. "It's not real. You need to wake up."

A pressure on my forehead, a burning warmth, and then—light.

I open my eyes, gasping in the fresh, lotus-scented air. I look up, not to clouds of gray and darkness, but to Shin, sweat plastered to his brow as if he'd run a great distance.

"Breathe, Mina. You'll be all right."

We're in the garden. The bright colors of the trees and the sky are almost blinding after the white and gray of the memory.

"What is this place?"

"The Sea God's garden. This pond is called the Pond of Paper Boats."

"All of those boats," I whisper. "They're prayers that were never answered."

Shin nods slowly.

"Why? Why have they have been abandoned?"

"They're just prayers, Mina."

I sit up. "*Just* prayers? They're the precious wishes of humans!"

Shin hesitates, then says coldly, "I don't care about the wishes of humans."

I stare at him, a tight feeling in my chest. His eyes are blank of expression, as if they hold no light at all. I'm the first to turn away.

"You left the house though I forbade it," he says. "Didn't you hear what the fox goddess said? My life is tied to yours. If you die, so shall I. You may not care for my life, but you should at least have a care for your own. There are many things in this realm that could kill a weak human like yourself."

"That might be true, but there are many things in *my* realm that could kill me, too. Drought. Famine." My eyes travel to the paper boat, where I dropped it on the grass. "A broken heart."

"There is nothing you can do."

Shin is right. Like he said, I'm but a weak human. How could I hope to help that girl? Even if I could find her, I have nothing to give her, nothing to offer but my own tears, and she's had enough of those to last a hundred lifetimes. She'd been at the end of her hope; all she had left was this one last prayer . . .

One last wish to the gods.

I scramble to my feet. "There *is* something I can do. That we can do. If you'll help me." Hurriedly, I grab the paper boat off the grass, turning to Shin. "I'll go back with you willingly, and I won't leave the grounds of Lotus House for the whole month, not without your permission, but first we must grant her wish."

"Mina . . ." Shin looks skeptical.

"This boat was meant for the gods, yet it never reached them. We just have to deliver the boat to whomever it was intended for."

Shin nods slowly, seeming to come to a decision. "What sort of wish was it? It should have been written on the paper." His eyes drop to the boat. It's half-unfolded. The inked characters are smudged from the water, rendering them illegible. I curse in frustration.

"It doesn't matter," Shin says, his calm, level voice surprisingly reassuring. "When you picked up the boat, you visited the moment the wish was made. Can you describe what you saw?"

"I saw a young woman." *Her bare knees in the muddy bank. Tears slipping down her face as she kissed the paper boat.* "She was with child."

Shin's lips thin, a darkness shadowing his face.

"What is it? What's wrong?"

He shakes his head. "We go to Moon House. To the Goddess of Women and Children."

15

We leave the palace through the front gate, which has remained open despite Namgi's claim that it's closed for most of the year. If Shin finds this odd, he doesn't comment on it. I look for Mask and Miki among the market stalls outside the palace but catch no sign of them, though a few spirits glance in our direction, clearly surprised to find two individuals coming out of the palace.

"This way, Mina," Shin says, and I follow him down a side street, away from the crowds. As we walk, I refold the paper boat. The characters of the wish might be smudged, but that shouldn't prevent the goddess from knowing the true heart of the wish, which often can't be expressed in words. That's why, though we celebrate the paper boat festival once a year, any human can pray to the gods at any time, whether at a shrine or where they feel closest to the gods—standing in a field while the wind blows, by the fire as it crackles brightly, on the cliffs by the sea.

This wish should have reached the goddess, regardless of the paper boat, given as it was from the heart. But perhaps the gods and goddesses of the world aren't able to hear our prayers, the connection between the human world and the spirit world broken because of the Sea God's curse.

Traveling with Shin is a different experience from traveling with Namgi or the spirits. Perhaps because he doesn't want to be stopped or recognized, he takes mostly back alleys, cutting through private courtyards and bustling kitchens and even once climbing the stairs of a teahouse to jump from the balcony onto a lower roof. As he turns back to help me, I quickly jump down, landing a little inelegantly, but on my feet. He lifts one brow, and I shrug.

As we head down a narrow street, a thought occurs to me. "Does Moon House have anything to do with the Goddess of Moon and Memory?"

"No," Shin says. "One has nothing to do with the other. Moon House is dedicated to women and children, just as Sun House is to men and the emperor."

"Emperor? But there is no emperor. He was killed years ago."

"Which is why Sun House remains empty."

Shin moves on ahead, but I follow at a slower pace now. A hundred years ago, the emperor was murdered, and the storms began. But even a god, no matter his love for the emperor, wouldn't punish an entire people for the crime of one person. In the hall, when I touched the Sea God and looked into his memories, perhaps it was from that moment when the emperor was killed. What happened on that cliff so long ago that left an emperor murdered, two worlds torn apart, and a kingdom cursed for a hundred years?

"There it is," Shin says grimly, pointing across the way. "Moon House."

I've been so caught up in my thoughts, I didn't realize we'd traveled to the outskirts of the city. Ahead of us stretches a long, shallow canal, debris floating across its muddied surface. Crumbled buildings with broken doors and shuttered windows border the dirt pathways on either side of the canal. After the babble and crush of the inner-city streets, the empty silence is unnerving, as is the lack of color. The Red String of Fate is the only brightness against the dull gray buildings. Desolation hangs thickly in the air.

Even in a city of gods, there are places like this.

At the end of the canal—beyond a shattered gate, its arch cracked in two—is a large building, like a crescent moon on its side. At the center of the house is a door ripped from its hinges, leaving only a gaping, black hole.

A shiver runs down my neck. Reaching into the pocket of my dress, I grip the paper boat.

This would be easier if Moon House didn't appear so foreboding. Hundreds of windows look down on me like black, depthless eyes. I can't see beyond the threshold of the door. The air grows colder as we draw near. A bitter breeze swirls out from the doorway and scrapes against my skin. I take a deep breath, stepping into darkness.

Warmth envelops me, and I blink, surprised. Considering the

size of Moon House, I thought it would be cavernous, drafty, and damp. But the room I've entered is small, with a low ceiling and closed walls. I don't see any doors leading deeper into the building. It's as if the entirety of Moon House—which, from the outside looked as if it were several stories high, with many floors and hallways—consists of this one small room. Its only inhabitant is a woman.

She sits on a cushion behind a low table at the very back of the room. Beside her is a fire, crackling in its grate. It casts the woman in shadow. All I can see are the whites of her eyes and the curve of her red lips.

A loud clicking sound draws my gaze downward. The woman has one hand lifted to the table. The sound comes from her long, curved nails tapping against the surface.

I lower my head in a bow and wait for her to speak, staring at the uneven floors. They're scattered with dirt and splinters of wood. The incessant clicking of her nails continues as they *tap, tap, tap* upon the table.

The paper boat feels heavy in my hands.

Finally the tapping ceases.

I look up. The goddess's eyes are focused beyond my shoulder, a bitter smile creeping over her wide mouth.

"What do we have here?" she says, her voice oily smooth, as if she eats the hearts of clams day in and out. "Why, if it isn't Lord Shin. What have I done to deserve such an honor?"

"The honor is ours," Shin says evenly. "We've come to ask you for a favor."

"We . . . ?" Her eyes slide to me. "And who are *we*?"

"My name is Mina," I say, stepping forward. "I have a wish."

The goddess blinks. "A wish?"

"It's not for me." I lift up the paper boat. "I've come on behalf of another."

She holds out one hand, heavy with jeweled rings. I begin to hand over the boat, but she clicks her tongue. "First, I require payment."

I stare at her smooth white hand, palm up and steady in the air. I'm reminded of the girl's hands as she put the boat in the water. The way they trembled.

The goddess, impatient, snaps her fingers, and I blink away the image. "I won't grant the wish unless I'm paid."

My throat feels dry, and I have to swallow saliva to speak. "I have a knife. It belonged to my great-great-grandmother. It's all I have."

The goddess scowls, and her fingers curl back into the shadows. "Worthless. I won't grant the wish unless I'm paid in gold." She turns away from me, from the paper boat I still hold outstretched before her.

"I don't understand," I whisper. "You're a goddess of mothers. Of *children*. With or without gold, you should want to answer her prayer."

"Don't be foolish, girl. Nothing in this world is ever freely given."

Tears spring unbidden to my eyes. "She was by the bank of a stream. She was crying. And all the hope that she had she poured into a wish to *you*. She believed in you. What more could you want?"

The goddess doesn't even blink. She stares at me, as if *I'm* the one who should be pitied. As if I'm the one who doesn't understand.

Shin throws a string of gold coins onto the table. She snatches the coins up, and they disappear into the sleeve of her dress.

Reaching out, the goddess plucks the paper boat from my feeble grasp. I watch as her hands run along the paper, her nails scratching the charcoal ink.

She starts laughing, a terrible high-pitched sound. "Where did you get this boat, girl? Do you know how old this prayer is? Months old. Years old. This girl is dead. Her child is dead. Her prayer was never answered. This is just a memory, one forgotten a long time ago." Lifting her hand in the air, she flings the paper boat into the fire.

"No!" I scream, lunging forward. My hand rips through the flames. A terrible sound comes from my throat, an agonized cry that has less to do with my burning hand and more to do with my breaking heart.

Shin grabs me from behind, pulling me back. He drags me from the room, the sound of the goddess's laughter ringing loudly in my ears.

Outside on the street he releases me, ripping a piece of cloth from his sleeve and forming a makeshift bandage. "We have to get you back to Lotus House," he says.

"How could she? How could she not *care*? She's the goddess of—of children!"

He reaches for my hand, but I back away. "Mina," he says carefully, "we need to treat the wound or it will fester."

"What is *wrong* with this world? What is wrong with the gods?" I can't stop shouting. Tears stream down my cheeks, and my heart beats wildly in my chest. Shin manages to catch my injured hand. With the torn cloth, he wraps the wound. I feel nothing, a strange numbness having overtaken my body.

"They love them," I whisper. It sounds like an accusation.

Shin ties the knot, looking up. "They . . . ?"

"My people. Everyone. My grandmother. Every day she goes to the shrine to pray, kneeling on the floor for hours, though her joints ache and her back hurts. My sister-in-law. Even when she lost her child, she never blamed the gods, though she walks in silence and cries when she thinks no one is watching. The people of my village. The storms may blow away their crops, but still they leave offerings to the gods of harvest. Because the world may be corrupt and broken, but as long as there are gods, there is hope."

If I'd found pity in Shin's eyes, I might have turned away from him. Indifference would have been even worse. But there's something in his gaze that strikes through the numbness until I feel it—the pain, the ache. There's compassion there. "Mina . . ."

"I love them." It sounds like a confession, and I realize— haltingly—that it is. Whenever I ran through the rice fields, the long-necked cranes billowing their great wings as if in greeting; whenever I climbed the cliffs, the breeze urging me onward; when- ever I looked out to sea, the sunlight on the water like laughter, I felt love. I felt loved.

How could the gods abandon those who love them?

I don't realize I've spoken aloud until Shin releases my hand, looking out over the desolate canal. "There's nothing you can do."

He's said these words before. In the garden, he said there was nothing I could do to help the girl. He said a similar sentiment when we first met, that I would fail like all the brides before.

He was right, in the end, but while it gained him nothing to be right, it costs me everything to be wrong.

"You're as much at fault as the rest of them."

Shin laughs harshly. "You would compare me to a goddess who takes bribes for prayers, who laughs at the pain of others?"

"No. You're worse than her." His shoulders tense, and I feel a pang of regret, but my pain makes me want to lash out. "You make false promises. You give me hope with one word and despair with the next."

"I've given you a place in my home to keep you safe, servants to provide for your every need, my people to guard you—"

"With orders to keep me from leaving."

"Because there's already been a threat against your life! Thieves have never attempted to steal the soul of the Sea God's bride before. When I went to confront Lord Bom of Tiger House this morning, he'd fled the city. Until I discover who's behind the threats, you have to be patient. Give me time. It hasn't even been a day."

"One day in the last month of my life." I know I'm being dramatic, but I feel the rage and pain burning me up inside.

"What do you want from me, Mina?"

"I want nothing from you." I curl my burned hand, wincing at the pain. "Only the Sea God can help me now."

Shin narrows his eyes. "What does he have to do with this?"

"Because once the curse is lifted—"

Shin scoffs, a cruel sound. "You don't get it, do you, Mina?"

"What don't I get?" I point back toward the gaping door of Moon House. "You didn't see her, the girl in the memory. She was suffering. She was crying. All she had left was her hope, and in the end, it wasn't enough. When will it be enough?"

Shin turns abruptly, his eyes a mixture of fury and despair. "It will never be enough! Don't you see, Mina? There is no curse upon the Sea God. He *chose* to seclude himself because he couldn't face his own grief. He's the one who abandoned your people. Who abandoned all of us!"

Shin breaks his gaze away, trembling. There's a tic in his jaw, and a slight redness at the corners of his eyes.

"You hate the Sea God," I whisper.

He closes his eyes. Unconsciously, he moves his hand to his chest. "The Sea God. The Goddess of Women and Children. All of us are unworthy. All of us deserve to be forgotten."

Us.

Realization hits me. "You're a god."

His answer is in the way his breathing turns ragged. His fingers, already pressed to his chest, dig into the cloth of his robes.

"Shin, what are you the god of?"

At first I think he won't answer, but then he shakes his head.

"Nothing anymore." He speaks so softly I have to strain to hear him. "You have to believe in something to be the god of it."

Night has fallen by the time we arrive back at Lotus House. Shin dismisses the servants who rush out to greet us, instead calling for Kirin. Together we head to the pavilion on the pond. In the upper room, someone has already spread out the blankets on the floor. I sink to my knees on the silk sheets, using my good hand to steady myself. I attempt to curl the fingers of my left hand and grimace at the sharp pain.

I look up to find Shin watching me.

"Can I . . . ?" he asks.

I nod.

Crouching beside me, he takes my hand and slowly unwraps the bandage. I wince as he peels it away. The skin beneath is raw and bleeding in patches.

He stares at my hand, a crease forming between his brows. "Why did you put your hand in the fire? You already knew it was too late to answer the wish. It was just paper."

"I know, but . . ." I hesitate, trying to explain to him something that even I don't quite understand. "In that moment, doing nothing hurt more than putting my hand in the fire."

There's a sharp rap on the door.

Kirin strides in, bowing low. His keen eyes glance at Shin's hand, still holding my own. "You called for me?"

"Mina's been hurt."

"Ah, I see."

I frown at the two of them, the unspoken words thick in the air. Why had Shin asked for Kirin and not a physician?

As Shin releases my hand, Kirin reaches inside his robes and pulls out a small silver dagger. With a quick motion, he makes a deep cut across his palm. Blood the color of starlight oozes from the wound.

I only have a moment to gape before he grabs my wrist, placing his now bloodied hand over my burned one.

His silver blood seeps into my wounds, and soon the blistering pain of the burns subsides and is replaced with a cooling sensation. A minute or two passes before he lifts his hand from mine, revealing the skin underneath—unblemished and smooth. "It will be sore for several days," Kirin says, "but then it should pass."

I turn my hand in the candlelight. The only evidence of the wound is in the redness at the edges of the palm. "Kirin." I look up. "Thank—"

I blink at the empty space where he was standing. He's already through the door, sliding it closed behind him.

"You should rest," Shin says, nodding to indicate the blankets. "You must be exhausted."

He moves through the room to extinguish the many candles. At the far wall, he lifts the paper screen, carrying it over and placing it carefully atop the blankets.

I realize we're meant to sleep beside one another, with the screen between us. I'm too exhausted to protest. My hand still aches, and to my great horror, hot tears begin to slip down my cheeks. I hurry to the edge of the pallet, pulling the blankets over my shoulder.

On his side of the screen, Shin blows out the candle, and the solid shadow of him disappears from view.

I roll to my back, listening to Shin's movements—the soft rustle of clothing as he undresses, the breath of a sigh as he settles onto the blankets. Earlier, he went to Tiger House to question their lord on the attempted theft of my soul. Even resenting the Sea God, he tries his hardest to protect him. The Red String of Fate glistens in the air, leaping from my hand across the blankets and through the paper screen.

In the dark and quiet, the events of the day rush back to me. Not just the terrible encounter with the goddess, but the moment in the garden, when I witnessed the last wish of a girl at the end of her hope. All those unanswered prayers, floating stagnant and forgotten. My thoughts wander to my own prayers, the ones I made every year at the paper boat festival, but also the ones I whispered into the darkness, when I thought no one was listening.

No, that's not true. I thought *someone* was listening. Because even in moments of despair, I believed the gods were watching over us. We were never alone because we were beloved by them.

Or so I thought. Or so I believed. The image of the girl, trembling on the bank of the stream, is imprinted in my mind. To think, in the moment of her greatest sorrow, she was truly alone.

I almost wish my soul were a bird again, then it could fly away from here, and no one—no gods, not even me—would be able to feel what I feel now. Stranded in another world, by my own choice, with no hope of saving the ones I love.

Hours pass before I finally fall into a restless sleep filled with dreams of the dragon and a voice calling me from a distance, begging me to save him.

16

In the morning, Shin is gone. The paper screen is folded and pushed up against the wall. I rub my eyes, sore from crying myself to sleep. I sit up gingerly, careful not to put pressure on my hand. Something in the corner catches my eye. On the low shelf below the window is a small object. I blink, leaning forward.

It's the paper boat.

I stumble to the shelf. The boat's edges are charred from the fire, but otherwise it's whole.

How . . . ?

Leaning against the side of the boat is a pink-and-white flower, plucked from the lake. A lotus in bloom, the petals open to reveal its star-colored center. Shin must have gone back to retrieve the boat in the night, after I'd fallen asleep.

I bring the boat and the flower to my chest. A strange feeling burns inside me. My eyes follow the ribbon as it winds its way out the window, pale red against the morning sunlight.

Although Kirin dispelled most of the pain, my hand takes a couple of days to fully recover. After that first night, Shin doesn't return to the room. I learn from Nari that a courier arrived the morning after our visit to Moon House, and Shin left with Namgi and Kirin in pursuit of the thieves. Two men that fit the thieves' description—one bearlike, the other weasel-like—were seen leaving the city.

Though the days are long, I keep busy. Betrothal gifts arrive from all the prominent houses—tea sets, celadon vases, mother-of-pearl jewelry boxes, wall scrolls with paintings of landscapes and poems, and a huge chest of embroidered silk blankets. It makes me wonder what will happen to these items once the truth of our betrothal is revealed. The same servants from my first morning at Lotus House attend me, sisters who have served Shin for many years, though you wouldn't be able to tell from their youthful appearances. I help them with chores around the house. We scrub blankets in water pulled from the lake, then hang them out to dry in the south fields, like great clouds billowing in the wind.

Though no one forbids me from leaving the grounds, I remain behind the walls of Lotus House. I spend the days collecting acorns and drying flowers to hang them upside down in Shin's room, livening up the empty space. The younger maidservant and I even attempt to draw a landscape on the paper screen.

After I get underfoot one too many times, the older sister finally orders me outside. I wander to the main pavilion, meandering down to the water's edge. I find a small rowboat, push it into the lake, and climb over the side. Lying on my back, I gaze up into the sky. It's a clear day, with only a few fish, and what looks like a humpback whale in the distance.

I close my eyes, drifting off.

Suddenly there's a sharp yelp, and the boat jerks to a stop. "Hey, watch it!"

I scramble to my knees and peer over the side.

Dai floats on his back in the water with Miki balanced on his stomach, looking very much like an otter that's caught a Miki-shaped fish.

"Dai!" I shout. "What are you doing? Get out of the water—it's dangerous."

"I'm swimming," Dai says matter-of-factly, as if he isn't floating in the middle of a lake with an infant balanced on his stomach.

A voice comes from behind me. "Don't worry, Mina. Dai won't let Miki come to harm."

I turn to find Mask sitting across from me in the boat, her grandmother mask rosy-cheeked and smiling. She's completely dry.

I gape at her. "Are you a goddess?"

"I'm a spirit. I told you that the first time we met."

I look around at the clear, open sky. "Spirits can fly?"

"Some spirits. Not me, though. I'm a lesser spirit, remember?"

"Then how—"

"It's a nice day out." Mask tips her face up. Her painted red cheeks seem to grow larger beneath the sun. I can see the long, slender line of her neck.

There's an old fishing rod at the bottom of the boat. She leans over, picks it up, and drops a line into the water.

"There's no hook," I say, "or bait."

"Oh, I don't want to catch anything," she says confusingly.

The boat has been drifting, but now, as if caught by a small breeze, it begins to glide across the lake.

"I've been watching for you in the marketplace," Mask says, "but you haven't left the house."

"Kirin said I wasn't to use my hand. The burns . . ."

"Mm." A noncommittal noise. Her face remains showing its pleasant expression, but there's a hint of reproach in that "mm."

"I've been helping the maidservants with the cleaning," I say, somewhat defensively. "They're spirits, like yourself. We're brightening up Shin's—the room I've been staying in. It's very bare, you see. I've been bringing in flowers from the gardens. The younger maidservant found some pots of ink, and we painted a landscape on the paper screen. Mountains and some trees."

Mask tilts her head to the side, musing, "For a girl whose hand was burned, you've been using it quite a lot."

I blush deeply. "Yes, well, it doesn't hurt so much today."

Mask nods lightly.

I look away, my eyes catching movement in the water. Where are Miki and Dai? We're not moving very fast, but it would be difficult for Dai to keep up with the boat, balancing an infant on his stomach.

I peer over the side to see Dai has grabbed hold of the fishing line. He and Miki are being tugged along.

"When you first arrived, you were determined to save the Sea God."

I grimace, hunching my shoulders. "I was. I am. I just—I wonder if it's even possible."

She gives another vague "mm," which, for some inexplicable reason, makes me want to pour my soul out to her.

"We visited the Goddess of Women and Children," I blurt out. "I brought her the wish of a young woman who was with child. The goddess saw the girl, saw how she suffered, and didn't *care*. She laughed. The girl was crying, her child was dying, and the goddess was *laughing*. She has no love, no sympathy for humans." I shake my head. "It's hopeless. My task is hopeless. And it made me realize . . . maybe I'm not the Sea God's true bride. Maybe I'm not the one who can save him."

When Mask doesn't say anything, I add quietly, "Why is it all up to me?"

"Is it?"

"The myth says only a bride of the Sea God can save him. If that's not my fate, then what is?"

I wait for Mask to say something wise, but then she shrugs. "Tell me this, Mina. If there was no myth of the Sea God's bride, what would you do? Would you give up? What if someone told you your fate was to sit around all day and eat dumplings?"

"That sounds like a wonderful fate!" Dai says from somewhere over the side of the boat.

Mask leans forward. "What if someone told you your fate was to climb up the highest waterfall and jump off? Or to hurt the person you love most in the world? Or worse, to hurt the person who loves *you* most in the world? Fate is a tricky thing. It's not for you, or me, or even the gods, to question what it is . . . or is not." She takes my hand, and though she can't see the Red String of Fate, her thumb brushes along the ribbon. Slowly, she lifts her face and looks across the lake. I follow the direction of her gaze.

Shin waits for me on the shore.

"Don't chase fate, Mina. Let fate chase you."

I turn back to see Mask has disappeared. I peer over the edge of the boat. Dai and Miki are nowhere to be seen.

The boat slowly changes direction and heads toward the shore.

Shin wades between the shallow reeds, grabbing the boat by the nose and dragging it from the water. I hop out as it reaches the shore, patting down the skirt of my dress.

Turning, I meet Shin's gaze. The Red String of Fate flutters in the air between us.

I study him to see if I notice any godlike qualities. I think of the gods I've met so far. He's taller than the Sea God. He's less frightening than the fox goddess. And he's honorable, unlike the Goddess of Women and Children. Every action he's taken has been to protect either his house or the city, even the stealing of my soul.

A tall, not very frightening, honorable god without a soul. How did my fate get entangled with his?

"Did you find what you were looking for?" I ask.

"Not quite. We lost the thieves' trail in the mountains east of the city." He studies me just as carefully. "You didn't attempt to leave the house."

"I promised I wouldn't." I promised I wouldn't leave the grounds of Lotus House if we granted the girl her wish. Even though her wish was never fulfilled, he still kept his end of the bargain.

"I didn't find the thieves, but I found this." He pulls a strip of cloth from his jacket.

Taking it from him, I smooth my fingers over a red, gold, and black stitching of a tiger depicted in a powerful leap with its claws extended.

I hand it back, lifting my gaze to his. "Tiger House."

Shin nods grimly. "When I visited Lord Bom last week, he denied having sent the thieves. Lord Bom was a great military tactician in his lifetime, and leaving behind such an obvious token seems either careless or . . . deliberate. Regardless, I can't ignore it."

"You said no one has ever attempted to steal the soul of a bride before. Why do you think they are now?"

"The only reason I can think of is they mean to harm the Sea God through you, not knowing you're no longer tied to him. I couldn't risk the chance they might succeed. It's why I gave the order for you to remain at the house—should there be an attack, my guards would be better suited to defend you."

I know that he only takes precautions for the Sea God's sake first, and now himself. But still, I have a fleeting, reckless thought: *What if he should wish to protect me for no one's sake but my own?*

"Of course," he says slowly, his brow furrowing, "it's possible the night they came to steal your soul, their intention was to restore the Red String of Fate . . ."

"And by doing so, kill me and the Sea God in turn?" I crinkle my nose. "I'd rather go without such help. My soul is safely where it belongs, inside of me."

When Shin turns away, I wince at my careless words. After all, he has claimed that he has no soul.

But when he glances back, his expression isn't pained but thoughtful. "Walk with me?"

We head around the bridge toward the far side of the lake, where most of the house activity is located. Servants unload baskets of rice and vegetables from boats tied to the docks. I look for Mask and Dai on the lake, but they're nowhere in sight.

Though Shin and I walk in silence, it's a companionable sort. I feel more myself than I have all week—because of my talk with Mask, but also because Shin is here. The Red String of Fate, though a friendly glimmer at the corner of my eye, was also a constant reminder of his absence. Something about him makes me feel braver, like I can be the person he believes me to be.

I don't realize I'm staring at the Red String of Fate until I look up to find Shin's eyes upon it as well, then he lifts his gaze.

"Kirin was frustrated with me while we were in the mountains. We were supposed to be tracking the thieves, but I was distracted. Every now and then the Red String of Fate would ripple or glimmer, and I thought to myself, *What is she doing? Probably up to all kinds of mischief.*"

He shakes his head with a half-smile. "I was surprised when I returned only to discover you hadn't left the house at all."

153

My first instinct is to deny his words, the feeling of embarrassment acute, but I surprise myself by speaking truthfully. "After the encounter with the Goddess of Women and Children, I felt discouraged. My faith was badly wounded. It was hard for me to accept that a goddess wouldn't care about a prayer that was given with so much love."

An echo of that awful feeling returns, and I bring my hand to my neck. When I look up, I find Shin watching me, and I feel suddenly vulnerable.

I drop my hand. "Well, I *am* glad you're back," I say, throwing a bit of levity into my voice. "At least with you around, there's more for my heart to do than mope." Shin goes still. I realize, belatedly, how this might sound. "That is, I don't have time to stew on melancholy thoughts. I'm too busy trying to get the best of you. It's easier to be brave when you're boiling mad."

He raises a brow. "Only you could change your mind from a compliment to an insult halfway through."

We step onto the docks and walk across the thick boards until we reach the very end, where a boat is moored to a post. I recognize it as the one we took to Fox House. As Shin leans down to untie the rope, I feel a strange pain in my chest. "Where are you going? You just returned."

And maybe it's the raw feelings from earlier, but I don't want him to leave. And the realization of this makes me feel confused and upset. My cheeks grow hot, and I'm glad that he's occupied with the boat.

"Outside Moon House," Shin says, the boat rocking gently beneath him, "you claimed that I hated the Sea God. The truth

154

is, I don't. Resent him, yes. Pity and doubt him, every day. But never hate him. I don't know if I believe he's . . . cursed, or that the curse isn't one he inflicted upon himself. But maybe my own feelings have gotten in the way of seeing things clearly."

He turns back, holding his hand out to me. "For years, Lotus House has protected the Sea God by severing the tie that makes him mortal through his connection with a human bride, and for a time, blocking a wound from bleeding out. But a wound, not tended properly, *will* reopen; it must be healed."

I take his hand and step into the boat, settling on one of the seats. He sits opposite me, reaching for the oars.

"But the Sea God wasn't in the throne room or the garden," I say.

"He has to be somewhere. We'll go every day if we must."

Hope is a heady feeling. I sense it billowing up inside me, as if the magpie were unfurling its wings. In this moment with Shin, the Red String of Fate bright like a flame between us, anything feels possible.

17

We leave the boat in the canal outside the palace and enter the Sea God's garden through the door in the painting.

Even abandoned as it is, the garden is beautiful. Flower petals flitter across the pebbled pathway, catching in the billowy pleats of my skirt. A slight drizzle permeates the air, and I wonder if a storm might be brewing somewhere to the east.

At the pond a small wind has blown all the paper boats to the far shore, leaving the waters closest noticeably bare. While Shin inspects the pavilion, I wander down to the bank and bend to pick up a stone.

My grandfather used to skip pebbles across the surface of the pond in our garden. When we were younger, Joon and I would count the times the pebbles would hit the water before they disappeared.

Turning my hand just so, I fling the stone across the water. There's a loud plopping sound as it sinks. I glance over my shoulder to see Shin come around the side of the pavilion. He looks unimpressed.

As I reach down to pick up another pebble, my fingers brush against something rough. This one is different from the rest, etched with a drawing of a lotus flower. The lines are too neat for the carving to have been a natural occurrence. Someone must have painstakingly taken a knife and chiseled the eight oval-shaped petals and the star-colored heart. It reminds me of the lotus Shin left beside the paper boat, still floating in its shallow bowl. I pocket the pebble.

Out of the corner of my eye, I see Shin take up position beneath a tree at the far side of the pavilion, keeping a watchful lookout. We agreed that no amount of searching would result in us finding the god, that our best course of action was to wait.

For the next half hour, I sink rocks up and down the shoreline, giving up when the clouds fill the sky. I plop down beside the pond. My grandfather always said the times he felt most at peace were while sitting by the pond in our garden, watching the ducks as they swam leisurely by. Except there are no ducks in this pond. Just paper boats. Like a school of unruly minnows, they crowd the northern shore.

One boat has escaped the cluster, drifting toward the center of the pond.

As it comes closer, I see that it's not like the other boats. It's lopsided with clumsy, uneven folds, half submerged in the water. A rough red thread runs down the center of the boat, as if it was ripped in half and then stitched back together again.

A chill sweeps through me. I know this boat.

I was the one who found the paper for it, pressing it against my lips as I whispered my prayer into the cool sheet. I was the one who folded it with trembling hands.

It's *my* boat, the one with my wish. Not any of the childish wishes I made at the paper boat festival, but another one. One I never set upon the river.

I rush forward, wading into the pond.

"Mina!" Shin shouts from behind me.

I don't listen, too intent on reaching the boat. I make a grab for it. My foot snags on an upturned tree root. Flailing, I go under.

I come out a half second later, spewing water, looking around, only to find an empty pond.

The boat is gone. Did I imagine it? My guilt dredging up the memory of a prayer?

Soaked, I slog my way back to shore. I'm prepared to get an earful from Shin, who in all likelihood is furious with me for doing something even I can admit was reckless. But when I look up, I almost fall back into the water.

Lying on the grass before me is the dragon, and beside the dragon is the Sea God.

The dragon curls its body protectively around the sleeping god, resting its enormous horned head beside the boy's. Its large whiskers tangle with the Sea God's soft hair, and when the dragon lets out a huff of breath, the boy's hair rises, caught in the warm breeze.

The dragon's eyes are open, watching me, sea dark and bright with intelligence. I take a tentative step out of the water, warily anticipating any sudden movements made by the dragon, but like a giant cat, it seems content to just lie there. I approach slowly, waiting for the moment when the dragon decides to devour me whole.

I must be hesitating too long, because the dragon begins to growl low in its throat. The pebbles tremble beneath my feet. The dragon's eyes flit between me and the Sea God, impatient. Demanding. If anything, the dragon seems to be urging me *toward* the Sea God. I take the last few steps, and with one quick glance at the dragon, I lay my hand on the boy-god's. As before, I'm drawn into a blinding light.

The first thing I notice is that I'm still in the garden, though now it's shrouded in mist, as when I first woke in the Spirit Realm.

The second—

"Shin!" He's lying, facedown and unmoving, at the edge of the pond. I scramble forward, falling to my knees beside him. I turn him over and trail my fingers over his lips. Relief washes over me when I feel the warmth of his breath. Though, had I taken a moment, I'd have seen the Red String of Fate, bright in the mist, and known he was unharmed. As long as the string remains intact, both of us are safe, our lives tethered to each other.

Easing his body off the ground, I cradle him in my lap.

"He's all right, you know. He's only sleeping."

I look up. Before me stands the Sea God. The luxurious folds of his robes soak up the water in the muddied bank. He doesn't seem to notice. Behind him the mist has thinned, and I can make out the shadow of the dragon within.

The Sea God's gaze shifts from Shin to me. "My soul tells me you are my bride."

I blink in surprise.

"You are suitable." He tilts his head to the side, dark hair falling across deep-lashed eyes. "I like the way you look. Your hair is like the warm bark of trees, and your eyes are like the sea at night. I can see the moon in them. Two moons. Two seas at night."

I swallow thickly, unsure what to say. This is the first time we've spoken. "You are very romantic, Sea God."

"Not really," he says. Turning from me, he walks to the edge of the pond. He places one slender finger into the pond, and ripples splinter across the water. "Just lonely."

I don't know where to begin. Just as in the throne room, I'm struck with an overwhelming feeling of protectiveness for this boy, caught in nightmares and shrouded in sorrow. It doesn't seem right to start making demands of him. Save my people. End the storms. Wake up and be as you once were, whole and happy.

In my lap, Shin groans, though his eyes remain closed. Gently I sweep his hair to the side from where it's plastered to his brow.

"He's fighting it," the Sea God says. "He wants to wake."

I look to the boy-god, torn between staying in this moment

with him and helping Shin. Somehow I know even now time is running out, and soon the boy and the dragon will disappear, and I'll be forced out of the dream.

"You could tell him a story," the boy-god says.

My heart stills. A story? Convincing a god to wake after a hundred years seems impossible, but a story I can tell. I've told hundreds of stories to my brothers and the village children. A story for the Sea God, and for Shin. But which one should I choose?

Shin shifts in my lap. My eyes drift from him to the Sea God and back, lingering on Shin.

Shin, who protects the Sea God from those who would harm him, even as he resents the god for abandoning him, and the story comes to me, as if it were waiting all along.

Taking a deep breath, I begin. "Once upon a time, there were two brothers. The younger brother was poor and lived in a shack, but he was kindhearted and good, while the older brother lived in a large house and was rich, but he was cruel and filled with greed.

"One morning, the younger brother heard a pitiful sound echoing through the wood. He followed the sound, finding a baby swallow that had fallen from its nest, crying out in pain from its wounded wing. Taking the swallow back to his home, the younger brother rubbed medicine into the swallow's joints and made a little cast from sticks and string to keep the wing from bending. He then placed the swallow back into its nest, and when winter came, it flew away to the south.

"The following spring, the swallow returned and dropped a seed into the younger brother's garden, where it grew into five large gourds. When the younger brother cracked open the first gourd, mountains of rice spilled out, more rice than he could eat in his entire lifetime. The second gourd held gold and jewels. The third held a water goddess, who then cracked open the last two, one which held small carpenters and the other timber. In a day, they built the younger brother a magnificent mansion.

"The older brother, having heard of his younger brother's fortune, came to his brother's mansion and asked him how he could become so wealthy in such a short amount of time. To which the younger brother explained about the swallow.

"The older brother, thinking himself very clever, built a nest and waited until a swallow came to lay her eggs. He then proceeded to push one baby swallow out of the nest, where it broke its wing. Like his younger brother, the older brother put ointment on the wing and stitched a cast. In the winter, when the swallow flew to the south, he waited eagerly for its return. Just as he'd predicted, the swallow flew back in the spring and dropped a seed into the older brother's garden. As before, five gourds grew from the seed.

"The older brother, joyous, cracked open the first gourd, only for an army of demons to issue forth. They beat him with sticks, berating him for his greed and cruelty. Still, the older brother thought there might be treasures in store for him, so he cracked open the second gourd, only for it to be filled with debt collectors who took all his money. The third gourd opened to a rush of filthy water that flooded and destroyed his house and swept the other two gourds away. He was left with nothing.

"Realizing his terrible mistake, the older brother ran to his younger brother, begging for help. Now, never has the older brother been good or kind to the younger brother. In fact, he had gone out of his way to be openly cruel and vindictive. But when he arrived at his younger brother's home—expecting to be turned away, as he himself would have turned away his brother had their circumstances been switched—the younger invited the older into his home, saying, 'You are my brother, and what is mine is yours.' He split half of his wealth with his brother, and the older brother, realizing the depth of his brother's love, knew for the first time true remorse and shame. He became a humble and good man, and together, the brothers grew old and happy, surrounded by their families and loved ones."

As I was speaking, the Sea God remained by the pond.

His voice is quiet. "What is the meaning of this story?"

I gaze at his back, the tremble of his slight shoulders. "There is no meaning, just a . . . feeling, maybe."

"And what is that?"

"That there is no place you can go so far away from forgiveness. Not from someone who loves you."

At least, that's what I always thought when I heard this particular story. I wanted to believe that even if one of us should make a mistake, my brother would forgive me, and that I would forgive him.

"Forgiveness," the Sea God says. "I will never be forgiven for what I have done."

He lifts his hand from the water, placing his fingers on his forehead. Droplets trickle down his face, moving over and under his closed eyes like tears. "I have a headache. Leave me."

"Wait," I say. "There's something you need to know. My people—"

The dragon raises its head from within the mist and blows a cool breath across my face.

I collapse unconscious, only to wake to an empty garden with Shin beside me.

"Mina." Shin struggles to sit up, fighting off the last vestiges of sleep. His voice is laced with concern. "Are you all right?"

"I—I'm fine," I say, startled by his presence. When he was asleep, he was vulnerable, and I felt protective of him. But now I'm the one who feels oddly exposed.

Like that morning I discovered he'd gone back for the paper boat, an odd feeling lodges in my chest, as if my heart were full. Something changed between us that day, or maybe it was the night before, when we brought the wish to the goddess. Though I'm not ready to put a name to the feeling just yet.

I turn away. "The Sea God was just here, Shin. I was in his dream."

Shin says nothing, though his brow is furrowed.

"What does it mean?" I ask.

"I don't know," he says. Then, hesitating, he adds, "The Sea God has never shown himself to a bride before."

All around us the fog has dissipated.

"Let's go back, Mina. We've lingered here long enough."

He reaches for my hand, and it feels natural to slide my palm against his, taking comfort in his steady strength. When we hold hands like this, the Red String of Fate disappears altogether. It's how it would seem if we were in the mortal realm, where fate is hidden from the eye.

18

Kirin and Namgi are waiting for us on the dock when we arrive back at Lotus House. "A missive came for you when you were away," Kirin says, handing over a scroll. "From Crane House."

Shin unwinds the string, opening the scroll to reveal a short message written in elegant, sweeping calligraphy. "Lord Yu claims he has news of Lord Bom's treachery," he informs us. "He says to come at once."

I turn to Namgi. "On my first night in the Spirit Realm, you said Crane House was home to scholars."

"That's right." Namgi nods. "Crane House is home to the greatest scholars who've ever lived."

"Then . . ." This time I address Shin. "Can I come with you? I would speak to a scholar, or Lord Yu himself, about the Sea God. Perhaps someone has knowledge of his past."

Shin looks hesitant, so Namgi says, "With Kirin, you, and myself, Mina will be safe."

Shin nods reluctantly, and I hurry off to the pavilion to change my dress—still smelling faintly of pondweed—into a more decorative one, with a light blue jacket and pink skirt. I keep my great-great-grandmother's knife around my neck and my lotus-carved pebble tucked inside a silk bag tied to my waist.

Together, Shin, Namgi, Kirin, and I make our way toward Crane House, which lies northeast of the palace. The setting sun gilds the buildings in a hazy golden glow. Spirits with long poles flit in and out of buildings, lighting candles in their lanterns.

Immediately Shin and Kirin fall into deep discussion, presumably over the plans to expose Lord Tiger.

The air reverberates with a low humming sound, as if there's a great waterfall nearby.

"What was the Sea God like?" Namgi asks from where he walks beside me.

I think of the expression on the Sea God's face as he looked at the pond. "He wasn't at all what I expected. He was . . . melancholy, as if he'd lost something and forgotten what it was."

Namgi kicks a loose stone. "And the dragon was with him? I'd give anything to see the dragon again."

The longing in his voice is palpable. His profile is stark in the shadows cast by the lanterns. I remember what he told me before—that his kind, the Imugi, fight in endless battles so that one day they might become dragons.

"What are the differences between an Imugi and a dragon?" I ask.

"There are only a few differences, but they are great. While

Imugi are creatures of salt and fire, a dragon is a being of wind and water. While an Imugi's magic burns bright and fast like a shooting star, a dragon's power is like a river—slow and steady, but limitless. It's rumored a dragon's pearl can grant any wish. Dragons are also three times the size of an Imugi, and universally benevolent and good. Not like Imugi. Imugi are evil."

"But, Namgi," I say slowly, *"you're* an Imugi."

Namgi cackles. "Yes, I am!" A school of approaching carp darts away in panic.

Ahead of us, Kirin looks over his shoulder, his silvery eyes landing on Namgi, caught by his laughter.

"Perhaps the biggest difference," Namgi says, "is that dragons are solitary creatures while Imugi only exist in groups. Like wolves, we live and die alongside our brothers, and we're rarely alone. I'm the only rogue that I know of. Most Imugi can't survive without a pack."

Namgi must catch my expression, because he reaches out to pat me lightly on the shoulder. "Don't worry, Mina. I have Shin and Kirin. They're all the brothers I need."

I glance at Kirin to see if he's heard these last words, but he's turned away again.

We arrive at Crane House, a great black-and-white fortress several stories high, with a curved rooftop shaped like the wings of a crane. A servant dressed in similar colors shows us to an elegant room with beautifully sanded floors of deep oak. On either side of a long table are shelves lined with scrolls stacked in neat piles and stitched books bound with thread.

A library. There must be hundreds, thousands of stories here—histories, myths, poetry, and songs. The memories of spirits and gods might be hazy, but not the memories of books. Stories are eternal. Perhaps in one of these scrolls is the story of the Sea God, of what happened a hundred years ago to make him succumb to an endless sleep.

In the garden, the Sea God said he'll never be forgiven. But what must he be forgiven for? If he feels guilt over abandoning his people, then why doesn't he just return to us?

The excitement of seeing all these books diminishes at the overwhelming prospect of searching through each one for a clue to the Sea God's past. Even if I had a year, it would be impossible.

The servant, who left to inform Lord Crane of our arrival, returns. "My lord will receive you now."

Kirin steps forward, but Shin shakes his head.

"Stay with Mina," he orders. "Namgi will join me in meeting with Lord Crane."

Kirin's lips thin slightly, but he only bows.

Shin turns to me, his eyes softening. "After Lord Crane and I finish our discussion, I'll call for you, and we'll speak with him. Together."

"Thank you, my lord," I say, then bow, as it seems appropriate.

Shin and Namgi follow the servant out of the room. I stand and make my way toward the closest shelf, trailing my fingers across the paper scrolls, alternatively smooth and rough in places.

Kirin is clearly annoyed about being left to watch over me,

speaking not a word. I'm not so thrilled myself. Unlike Namgi, who's all warmth and bluster, Kirin is as cold as the silver in his eyes.

But his blood was warm. I remember the way it oozed from his hand, pooling over my wound until the pain was gone entirely.

"I never thanked you properly for healing my hand," I say, shifting my body so that I face him. "Thank you. It was truly appreciated."

"I didn't do it for you."

I sigh, glad the women in my family have a thicker skin than most. In any case, Kirin's words are far less painful than the burn from the goddess's fire.

"Are you a god?" I ask, thinking of the magic in his blood. "Or a beast of myth?"

"I am not a god."

Which means he's a beast of myth. But not a sea snake. The night I first arrived, when the goddess's servants appeared, Namgi's brothers had called Kirin the Silver One, saying the Imugi had butchered the last of his kind.

I have enough sense of self-preservation not to bring *that* up.

"It's strange to think Namgi is of a kind with those other sea snakes, who all seemed very cruel and awful. Namgi has only ever been friendly to me." I pause, adding with a grin, "And perhaps a bit mischievous."

Kirin shakes his head. "Never trust an Imugi."

I stare at him. "I trust Namgi."

"Then you're a fool."

I scowl, hurt for Namgi, who not a half hour earlier had spoken so affectionately about Kirin. "I trust Namgi far more than I trust you," I retort. "He's forthright and sincere. He told me how he met Shin, and why he serves him. While you've told me nothing of yourself."

I hesitate, wondering if I've gone too far with my impulsive words. Kirin truly does appear upset—the first sign of real emotion I've seen from him.

"Because I'm unlikable, you think I'm disloyal," he says, his voice icy. "Yet I've served Shin far longer than Namgi has. I've never known a time when I haven't stood by his side. He's my leader, but more than that, he's my friend. I trust him with my life."

Kirin pauses, then his gaze turns to me with a look of middling horror. "I can't believe you exasperated me into actually defending myself against your ridiculous claims."

I sidle forward, turning to flash him a wide grin. "It makes it easier to talk to you, knowing you're a little human."

I know I've said something wrong when the reluctant smile on his lips disappears.

"I am *not* human," he says coldly.

For the next half hour, neither of us says a word. I move farther into the rows of shelves, which extend deeper than I first thought. It truly would be impossible to go through each scroll and book, even if the method of categorization were clear. As I walk, I realize the room is much larger than the outside view of Crane House suggested, which was taller rather than wider. It's both similar and opposite to Moon House, where the room the goddess resided in was tiny compared to how her home appeared from the outside.

I continue to explore the library, turning corners when I meet them, until, at the end of a particularly long row of bookshelves, I reach a door. I'm surprised only because I thought the library was confined to a single room. The door is slightly ajar. I peek through to find a short set of stairs leading downward.

I know I should go back. If Shin returns and finds me missing, he will not be pleased. And yet, this is Crane House, home of scholars—what harm could there be in such a place?

I slip past the door, tread lightly down the stairs, and enter a narrow corridor dimly lit by lanterns with low-burning candles. On either side are rooms purposed for reading and writing and other scholarly pursuits, scattered with paper scrolls, ink, and brushes.

At the end of the hall is a private study, larger than the rest. Scrolls of poetry hang on the walls alongside paintings of nature. A single writing table is positioned at the back of the room before a paper screen.

It's a beautiful screen, four times the length of the one in Shin's room and twice its height. Each of its panels shows the life stages of a crane, from newborn hatchling to the last panel, which shows the crane in flight, the only splash of color the bright red of its crowned head.

"Forgive me. I wasn't prepared for visitors, or I might have tidied up a bit."

I turn to face a tall, elderly scholar standing in the doorway.

"Lord Yu," I say, recognizing him from that first night at Lotus House. I bow low. "Excuse my intrusion. I was waiting in the room above and came upon the stairs—"

"Did I appear offended?" Lord Yu says. "Come, please sit." He nods, indicating the small table before the paper screen. Moving to a side cabinet, he produces a tray with a bottle and two porcelain cups. "Do you enjoy the taste of wine-spirits?"

"I've never had the opportunity to find out," I say, taking the seat opposite him.

He lifts the bottle and pours some of the golden liquid into a cup. Accepting the cup with two hands, I turn my face away to drink it entirely, as I've seen my brothers do. The liquor tastes bitter in my mouth.

"Now," Lord Crane says. "Tell me the questions you have."

I must look surprised, because he adds, "You must have questions you seek answers to, a young girl with a homeland in peril, a Sea God's bride with a mystery to unravel."

"Then you must guess my question before I ask it."

"Nevertheless, you must ask for me to answer."

"How do I lift the curse upon the Sea God?"

"You didn't have to come to me for the answer to that question. The answer is in the myth: *Only a true bride of the Sea God can bring an end to his insatiable wrath.* The bride who shares a Red String of Fate with the Sea God has the power to break the curse."

"I don't understand," I say, frustrated. "Every bride arrives with a Red String of Fate."

Lord Yu refills both cups, then pushes mine toward me. He doesn't speak until I've emptied it of the golden liquid. "All brides share a Red String of Fate with the Sea God, but that is only a spell to protect them. Otherwise Lord Shin would not be able to cut the fate, as he does every year. After all, a true fate cannot be broken with the edge of a blade."

I nod slowly; the fox goddess said as much.

Lord Yu continues. "The bride who loves him, the one he loves in return—only she has the power to turn myth into truth. Should this fate form, it will be invisible to all but the Sea God and his bride."

Instinctively, my eyes dart to the Red String of Fate tying me to Shin. *An invisible fate.* Lord Crane doesn't seem to notice the direction of my gaze, pouring a third cup.

"Then it's hopeless," I say. "Until the fated bride is thrown into the sea, the Sea God will not wake."

More girls will be sacrificed. More lives will be lost to the storms.

"Not so hopeless as it seems," he replies. "It is possible to *form* such a fate. After all, attachment, or what the poet-scholars call love, is also a choice. Two people can choose each other out of necessity. Or duty. In this way, even a Red String of Fate can be unmade, if one party should form a stronger connection with another."

A month for you to figure out how to save the Sea God and a month for me to figure out how to be rid of you. This is the answer Shin has been searching for.

Lord Crane pushes the cup toward me. Is this my third or fourth cup? When I move to pick it up, I'm struck by a brief spell of light-headedness.

"You have your answer on how to break the curse. Form a Red String of Fate with the Sea God. That is, if you haven't already with someone else."

I look up, alerted to a change in Lord Crane's voice. He was speaking in a rhythmic cadence, almost hypnotizing in its quality, like that of a storyteller's. But now there's something false about his voice, a spark of avarice.

His eyes linger on my hand. "I heard a curious rumor that Shin, like the death god Shiki before him, found himself bound by an unexpected fate."

Suddenly he lashes out, grabbing my wrist. I try to pull away, but his grip is viselike, powerful for an elderly scholar. But that was my mistake for thinking he was anything other than a spirit with inhuman strength.

At the same time, the Red String of Fate starts thrashing. Something must be happening on the other end. *Shin!* Is he being attacked?

I try to tug my hand away, my heart racing, my head clouded from the wine-spirits. Why was Lord Crane here, when he should have been meeting with Shin?

"I sent a missive to Lotus House with every intention of parting Shin from your side," Lord Crane seethes. "How furious I was when I discovered you accompanied him here. Luckily, you separated yourself from the Silver One. It's been a long time since I was human. Was I ever such a fool?"

"You are still a fool," I grit out, "if you think to kill Shin through me. Afterward, when I'm left bleeding on the floor, Shin will be very much alive, and he will have his revenge."

My words must pierce through his triumph, because Lord Yu looks doubtful. He loosens his grip.

Seizing this opportunity, I reach for my knife, slicing it through the air between us. Lord Yu howls, stumbling back, his hand to his cheek, where my blade has left its mark.

I fall, hitting the floor just as a shout rises in the hall and the door bursts open.

19

Shin barrels into the room. He takes one look at me on my side, the table turned over, and the tea set now in pieces on the floor, and an incredible fury seems to overtake him. He grabs Lord Yu by the collar and throws him up against the wall. "I should kill you for this!"

Lord Yu appears almost gleeful as he gasps, "You found her quicker than I thought. It's as if you were guided by an invisible fate. I wasn't certain before, but I am now."

"Mina!" Namgi's by my side, helping me to stand. "Are you hurt?"

Outside in the hall there are the sounds of battle, shouts and steel against steel. Kirin must be holding off the guards.

"I'm fine," I say. "I nicked him with my knife." Lord Yu's cheek bleeds freely now.

"Let's go," Shin says, dropping Lord Yu to the floor. He turns, reaching for me. I wince as his hand closes over my wrist.

He pushes up the sleeve of my dress. A great bruise has already formed beneath the skin where Lord Crane grabbed me.

He takes in the bruise; he says not a word, though his eyes seem to somehow grow even darker. Twisting away from me, he seizes his sword.

Namgi grabs him from behind. "Shin, stop! Lord Yu is the head of Crane House. Even you can't kill him without angering the other houses. We have to go before we're overwhelmed." As if to emphasize Namgi's words, there's a great thundering of feet on the floorboards above us, guards of Crane House gathering to defend their lord and home.

Shin reaches for me again, this time taking my hand.

Out in the hall, Kirin stands above the unconscious bodies of five guards, his white robes pristine, as if he hadn't just been in a scuffle.

"Lord Shin . . . ," he begins, but Shin brushes by him. Guilt sweeps through me—had I not left Kirin's side, this wouldn't have happened. And yet, I can't regret the actions that led me to Lord Yu; although he was treacherous, he did share knowledge.

Neither Shin nor I speak as we traverse the long hallway back to the library, leaving unchallenged through the great doors we entered not an hour ago.

Shin's face is set, his expression grim. He doesn't let go of my hand until we've walked a far distance.

"What happened after you left me?" I ask. Over my shoulder, I see Namgi and Kirin spread out, watching our backs.

"Lord Bom was there when I arrived." Shin shakes his head. "But he had soldiers with him. It was a trap. Crane and Tiger were working together. They meant to keep me occupied until they could get to you." He growls, clearly frustrated with himself. "I should have anticipated this. You're in danger because of me."

I should tell him what I discovered from Lord Crane: The curse upon the Sea God can be lifted if he forms a Red String of Fate with a bride. And in turn, Shin's and my fate can be unmade, if either of us were to make a stronger connection with another.

The answer seems clear. For both of us to have what we want, I should form a bond with the Sea God. Then Shin will be free, and my people will be saved. The path I'm supposed to take is right in front of me.

Why, then, do I feel as if I've lost my way?

As we walk, I become aware of a low, rumbling sound. I noticed it on our journey to Crane House, though it was in the distance. It's louder now; I can feel my bones humming in answer. The air grows cooler, and a heavy mist rises to the height of my ankles. A chill wind catches the strands of my loosened braid, unraveled in the tumult.

"Is that a waterfall?" I ask.

Shin stops to remove his outer robe, placing the long jacket over my shoulders. Immediately I stop shivering, the jacket warm with the heat from his body. "It's the river."

The way he says "river" suggests it's not an ordinary body of water. The rising mist thickens. I pull Shin's robe tighter around me, breathing in crystals of ice that catch sharply in my throat. Ahead is a river shrouded in mist. It's not overly wide—I can see the far shore—but it's loud, the strong current buffeting large objects on the surface.

"Is that . . . ?" I edge closer to the shore. It takes me a moment to grasp what I'm seeing. A pale hand, a bloodless face. The objects aren't debris, but *people*. They float on the river, their bodies half-submerged. I count four, five, six individuals, and those are just the ones closest to the shore. More float ever closer to this point in the river, and even more have already passed. They're all so still. Too still . . .

I catch sight of a thrashing movement. In the middle of the river, a child struggles against the current. Her cries are faint, almost noiseless against the onslaught of rushing water. Her desperate arms reach up, breaching the surface, only to get sucked down again, too exhausted to keep afloat.

I rush forward, but Shin stretches out his arm to block my path. "You can't go into the river," he says. "The current is too swift. It'll sweep you away."

"I have to help her."

"I'm afraid it's impossible. Only the dead can enter the River of Souls."

I've heard of this river before; Mask mentioned it the night we first met. But she also mentioned that spirits can pull themselves from the river, should their will be strong enough.

I watch as the little girl struggles to keep her head above the water. The other bodies have their eyes closed, as if in sleep, but the girl refuses to accept the course of the river. She wants to live.

Shin curses beneath his breath.

I follow his gaze farther up the shore. A man approaches the water. From this distance, I can't see his face, but he's tall, with black, shoulder-length hair. The waters nearest the shore calm with his approach, and he wades into the depths. While the rest of the river rushes powerfully along, a circle of smooth water surrounds him.

"Who is he?" I ask.

"The death god, Shiki," Shin says. "One of the more powerful gods, and no friend of mine."

Shiki. *The one who Shin fought for the soul of last year's bride, Hyeri.*

Moving slowly, the god approaches the little girl, halting a short distance from her. The girl—out of breath, out of strength—catches sight of him. She resumes her struggle, but this time, in his direction. It's slow progress, but her will is strong. She refuses to give in to the relentless current. Finally, reaching the god, she grasps on to his robes. He takes her up in his arms, cradling her close. Weary from her ordeal, she falls limp.

The death god begins to walk with the girl toward the opposite shore. Halfway across the river, he stops, turning to stare directly at us. Balancing the child with one arm, he uses the other to point to a bridge spanning the length of the river, his meaning clear. When Shin nods back that he's understood, the death god continues his slow advance through the water.

Kirin and Namgi wait for us at the edge of the bridge.

"Is it wise to meet the death god alone?" Kirin says, once we've drawn close. If he's still upset from earlier, he doesn't show it.

"Shin will be fine, as long he's with Mina," Namgi answers. "Shiki has a soft spot for Sea God's brides."

Whether Shin agrees or not, he doesn't argue further, stepping onto the wooden slats of the bridge. Neither Kirin nor Namgi moves to stop me as I follow him into the mist.

It's thicker here than it was by the shore. The atmosphere feels familiar, and I wonder if this is the same bridge I found myself on when I first woke in the Sea God's realm.

I follow the Red String of Fate to the middle of the bridge, where Shin waits, peering into the mist.

"What lies on the other side of the river?" I ask.

"Star House," Shin answers, "where the death god resides. Other than that, mountains and mist. The fog thickens the farther from the city you venture. You can wander in the mist for weeks and come out where you started, or on the other side of the city. It's why I lost the thieves' trail. In the mist, it's difficult to keep track of anything. Spirits often get lost in it, trying to find a way to return to the world of the living, but it's not possible. Once you come down the river, you can't go back."

I shiver at the thought. "What do you think Shiki wishes to speak with you about?"

"In truth, I can't say. Last we met, we clashed. With words and weapons. I had taken the soul of the bride, as I have every year, yet Shiki, having grown protective of the girl, demanded its return. When I refused, we fought."

"And yet her soul was returned to her," I say, the implication being that the outcome had been in Shiki's favor. In my mind, I envision the memory of Hyeri, peering out from the palanquin's window, her eyes alight with curiosity and laughter.

"She had interrupted the fight. She was . . . dying, apart from her soul for too long. And Shiki, the God of Death, could do nothing. I returned her soul then, if only to stop him from complaining."

"Ah," I say. "So Shiki won in the end"—Shin scowls—"because he had a friend like you."

Shin shakes his head but doesn't deny my words. "Proper thanks he gave me. After saving her life, he called me a 'bastard without a soul,' and left. I haven't spoken to or seen him since."

Shin's story has revealed more than he might have intended. For Shiki's sake, he saved Hyeri, giving rise to rumor and scorn against himself.

"How can you be certain that you don't have a soul?" I ask.

"Every being has a soul, whether it's hidden inside you, as it is for humans, or in a different form, as it is for beasts of myth. Gods also have souls. For the Goddess of Moon and Memory, her soul is the moon. For the Sea God, his soul is the dragon of the East Sea. For household gods, their souls are the hearth; for gods of the mountains, rivers, and lakes, their souls—"

"Are the mountains, rivers, and lakes," I finish.

He nods. "And so when the mountains, rivers, and lakes are destroyed, so are the gods. Because when the rivers are polluted and the forests burn, the gods fade and disappear. I am a god who has lost his soul and with it, all my memories of who I once was, of what I was meant to protect. In this way, I should have disappeared a long time ago."

The pain in his voice is unmistakable. He closes his eyes. More than anything I want to comfort him in this moment, and yet I don't have the words. Even when my soul was a magpie, I knew it still existed, just outside myself. It wasn't lost. It wasn't forgotten.

I think of all the many things Shin has done for me: saving me from Lord Crane, bringing me to the Sea God, retrieving the paper boat. He might not believe he has a soul, but I do.

I reach to my waist and unknot the silk bag, tilting it forward until the object within rolls onto my palm. Shin turns, drawn by my movements.

"Look, Shin," I say with a smile. "I found your soul."

I lift my palm. At the center sits the pebble with the carving of the lotus flower.

He says nothing for a few minutes, and I wonder if I've offended him. But then he reaches out his hand, brushing his fingers across the pebble and my open palm.

"It might not be as large as a mountain or as bright as the moon," I say as he lifts his eyes to meet mine, a heartbreaking, vulnerable look in their dark depths, "but it's just as beautiful because it's *your* soul. It's strong, resilient, and steadfast. And stubborn." He laughs softly. "And worthy, just as you are."

Shin's breath catches.

My heart begins to beat painfully in my chest. "Well?" I say, lifting my hand. "Will you accept it?"

But instead of taking the pebble, he slips his hand over mine, the pebble pressed between our palms, holding tight. "If I take it," he says, "I won't ever let go."

It's not a question, and yet I feel as if he's waiting for my answer.

Then he tenses, his eyes narrowing on something past my shoulder. He pulls me to his side. Death steps out of the mist.

20

The death god is a young man with handsome features—a long nose and wide lips. His skin is moon pale, so unlike the vibrant, fun-loving Hyeri, who before she was sacrificed to the Sea God was famed in all the seaside villages for looking as if she held the sun beneath her skin. There's something melancholy about the god, the dark circles beneath his eyes that suggest a want of sleep, his serious expression. Suddenly I'm glad this god of death has Hyeri, who was so full of life.

The death god comes to a halt a few paces away. "My guards reported seeing you at the border of my lands," he says in a voice deep and without inflection. "What were you searching for in the mist?"

"Thieves broke into my house," Shin says. "I was following their trail, but lost it in the mountains."

"What did you discover?"

"A plot concocted by Crane and Tiger. To kill me and overthrow the Sea God."

"Ah," the death god remarks. "Lord Yu and Lord Bom are

ambitious. The more spirits that arrive in this realm, the stronger their houses grow. But death should never be encouraged."

I must make a sound at that, because the god's gaze turns to me.

"But you are the God of Death," I say. "Does your power not grow with each new death that enters this world?"

"I am a death god, but my purpose lies in the balance between death and life. When the scale is tipped too far in favor of one, the imbalance disrupts the unity of both worlds, the human realm and the realm of spirits." He approaches the railing of the bridge, staring down at the rushing waters below. The death god's face shows the first sign of emotion—apprehension. "The river is rising. Eventually, it'll overflow onto the bank, bringing with it spirits who have no desire for this world. With so many lost spirits walking the Sea God's city, the Spirit Realm will become a sorrowful place indeed."

Shin frowns. "Is there no way to stop the river from rising?"

"The source of the river is in the human realm, where life ends and death begins. As we have no power over that which brings death—battles, starvation, and disease—there is little that can be done."

"What about the Sea God?" I ask. "The storms have destroyed so much. The warlords battle over what little is left, sowing chaos and leaving behind devastation in their wake." I step away from Shin to face both him and Shiki, the spray of the river on my neck. "The Sea God's curse is no longer a problem for just the human world alone, but for the world of spirits and gods as well. We need to put things right before it's too late. Before both of our realms are destroyed."

"I've seen this look before," Shiki says. "On the face of some-one beloved. Is it an expression all the brides of the Sea God share? A potent mixture. Hope. Determination. Fury."

Hyeri. He's speaking of Hyeri.

He turns his gaze to Shin. So far, neither one of them has brought up the incident that separated them as allies and friends. Instinctively, I take a step toward Shin, as if I can block him from any harsh words.

"I'm afraid I've been unfair to you," Shiki begins, to Shin's surprise and mine. "You've protected this city when no one else would. While others would wish to abandon, overthrow, or even kill the Sea God, you've protected him and the brides, and in turn, kept peace and order in this realm. I apologize for many things, but mostly I apologize for making the weight you carry a little heavier."

I stare at Shiki, stunned by this extraordinary apology.

"And I think," Shiki says softly, "perhaps, now you understand me a little more."

I glance between them, wondering what he means by these last words.

"I'll take my leave," Shiki says. As he turns, he addresses me. "You would be a welcome guest at my house . . ."

"Mina," I say.

"Lady Mina. I know my Hyeri would be glad to see you."

"And I her. It would be an honor."

He bows, then slips into the mist.

Shin and I leave the bridge. Joining Kirin and Namgi, we head into the city.

It's full dark now, the streets aglow with many lanterns, their candles dimmed by the wind. The farther we travel from the river, the warmer it gets, until I no longer have a need for Shin's over-robe. I take it off, looking ahead to where he walks with Kirin. Shin appears to be doing all the talking, while Kirin walks with his head down. It's clear Kirin is being reprimanded for what happened at Crane House.

"Don't worry too much, Mina," Namgi says, following the direction of my gaze and correctly guessing my thoughts. "Kirin would feel worse if Shin said nothing. This way, he knows exactly how he failed Shin, and will do better next time. If anything, Shin will trust Kirin even more now, since in order to prove himself, Kirin will be even more attentive and dependable. In other words," Namgi drawls, "he'll be unbearable."

The streets are deserted, probably due to a sudden sweltering heat, despite that evenings here are usually cooler.

"Though I do feel for Kirin," Namgi continues. "He never gets in trouble. Not like me."

"You have a kind heart, Namgi."

"Kirin does as well." I must look doubtful, because he hurries to explain. "He forms attachments slowly, but when he does, he's the most loyal friend, fiercely protective of those he cares about. He would do anything for Shin."

"And you?" I ask softly.

Namgi says nothing, though a shadow falls across his face. "When I look at Kirin, I see only him, a bright light in the darkness. When he looks at me, he sees only the darkness."

We reach the central marketplace of the city. At the far side is the Sea God's palace, looming beneath a sea of stars. Hundreds of night stalls border the street, and yet they're oddly quiet, without merchants to hawk their wares. There's silence all around, a stillness like death.

"Namgi . . . ," I say. "Where are all the people?"

Namgi peers at the empty market, then glances behind us to the deserted street. His brow furrows, and he reaches for his sword at his waist.

Suddenly all around us falls a heavy curtain of darkness, as if a cloak were thrown over the stars.

I look up and scream. Above us, forked tongue lashing out, is a monstrous sea snake.

21

"Mina, watch out!" Namgi pushes me to the side, then leaps out of the way as the sea snake whips its tail downward, piercing the cobblestones where we were standing. Namgi's the first to scramble to his feet. He races across the street toward me, but the snake lashes its tail to the side, catching and hurling him against a building.

"Namgi!" I scream, rushing forward.

"Stay back!" Namgi shouts. He lifts his face, and I stumble to a halt. The irises of his eyes are bleeding outward, black creeping over the white. A shadow falls over his body, obscuring his features. His shape darkens and warps, then begins to elongate. Spears of darkness shoot out from his body, and a terrible, inhuman cry roars from within the shadowy depths.

Above, the sea snake grows agitated, lashing its tail back and forth. I leap behind a crumbled wall to avoid a blow that would sever my spirit from my body.

Sounds of battle crash from across the market, where more Imugi converge upon Shin and Kirin.

Abruptly Namgi's roar cuts off. I whip my head in his direction. Slivers of shadow drift from his body like smoke from a fire. Where the curly-haired boy once was lies a great sea snake coiled upon itself. With a low rumble, its long, sinuous body begins to unwind and stretch, reaching its full, incredible length. Black and red scales flicker in the torchlight.

The words Namgi spoke to me while strolling through the market ring in my ears. *In my soul form, I am a powerful water snake. Like a dragon, but without its magic.* Yet Namgi's soul form appears different from the Imugi that hovers above us, with its serpent-like features, slitted nostrils, and red eyes. Namgi's features are that of a dragon. He has a narrower snout and smooth, glimmering scales. His eyes are his own, a deep black with that ever-present spark of mischief.

Raising his head, Namgi lets out a harrowing cry. Red light crawls up his throat and erupts from his mouth in black fire, catching the enemy Imugi in its blast. Namgi takes to the air, rising as if lifted by the wind itself. The two Imugi collide, snapping their powerful jaws. Namgi's teeth shred through the smaller snake's brittle skin. Fat droplets of viscous blood drip from great wounds, sizzling upon impact with the earth.

My attention is diverted from the battle by the sharp sound of something fast approaching, a whizzing in the air. On instinct I duck. The bolt of a crossbow flies over my head, lodging in a wooden plank. Atop a roof across the street, a figure crouches— the weasel-like thief from the first night. He meets my gaze with a sneer, looking smug even though he missed.

Then I remember his partner, the bearlike thief. Arms wrap

around my neck, hauling me off the ground and dragging me backward into the shadows of a building. I claw at the viselike grip, but my attacker's strength is too great. I struggle to breathe, my arms weakening, my vision blackening at the edges.

Suddenly the bearlike thief releases me, howling with pain. I twist around to catch a blurred glimpse of Mask leaping from his back, where she's embedded a knife to the hilt.

"Come, Mina," she shouts, grabbing my hand. We sprint through a maze of streets. Above us, Namgi and his brethren fight in a vicious battle.

Every now and then I see a face peeking from behind a window, quickly closing shut as Mask and I hurtle past. When we've run far enough, Mask darts into a building, pulling me in with her.

I bend over, hands on my knees, trying to catch my breath. We're in a pawnshop, the narrow shelves packed with an assortment of items—pottery, paper, and even firecrackers stuffed into woven baskets. Mask hurries over to a barrel and pulls out two daggers.

She hands one to me, the blade twice the length of my knife. "Do you know how to use this?"

"A little," I say, testing the weight of it in my hand. "My grandmother taught me."

Mask smiles at that, her eyes squinting through the holes of the mask. The pattering of feet on the street outside gives a short warning before Dai hurries into the room, Miki on his back.

"Are you all right, Mina?" he says. "Is she all right, Mask?"

"She's fine. And I'm fine, too, thank you for asking!"

Miki stares at me with wide, tear-filled eyes.

"It's dangerous for you two to be here," I say. Miki might be an infant, but Dai's just a child himself. "For now, go hide."

Dai doesn't argue. He moves to the corner at the back of the shop, crouching down and humming a soft lullaby when Miki starts to whimper. Together, Mask and I pile baskets in front of the children to conceal them from view.

Across the shop the Red String of Fate flutters, curving to the left. Like Namgi, Shin and Kirin must be engaging with the Imugi. My stomach twists, fear like a dagger, to think of Shin fighting against those monstrous beasts.

There's a loud crash at the front of the store. The light of a lantern sweeps over the dark interior of the shop.

"Little bird," the voice of the bearlike thief croons. "For running away, you've earned a slow death. Your friend, an even slower one."

Once the thieves meant to steal my soul. Now the bear and the weasel are assassins, meant to snuff me out entirely.

Mask taps my shoulder, gaining my attention. She points to herself and the right row of shelves, then to me and the left. I nod to indicate I understand. Moving silently, we part ways, going separately through the cluttered store. I keep close to the floor, hidden from view by wooden chests and stacked crates. At the end of the row I press my back against a shelf, peering around it to see the assassin standing in front of the door, a sword in one hand, lantern in the other.

"It seems you're wanted dead by quite a number of people in this realm. Lord Crane, for one, but also the great mistress whom the Imugi serve. What have you done, little bird, to attract the ire of a goddess?"

It's a question I'd like to know the answer to myself.

Mask lets out a loud battle cry, leaping down from a high shelf. The bear-assassin twists around, raising his sword. Their weapons clash, the sound ringing out like a bell.

Quickly Mask falls to the floor, rolling and slicing her dagger across his legs. Crying out, he drops the lantern, where it shatters upon a stack of scrolls, setting them on fire. Before Mask can slip away, he reaches and grabs her by the braid, yanking her head back. Her mask slips, and for a moment I glimpse rosy cheeks and a full mouth, bared in a grimace.

Screaming my own battle cry, I rush forward. He lets go of Mask to meet my attack. I feel the impact of our clashed weapons in a sharp pain rippling up my arm. All around us the fire now rages into an inferno.

"Mina!" I turn to see Mask has recovered and now holds a pile of firecrackers, her intent clear.

The assassin moves for another strike, and this time my borrowed dagger shatters upon contact. With a triumphant grin, he raises his sword.

Dai springs forward, grabs the arm of the bear-assassin, and bites down hard. Howling, the assassin drops his sword. Quickly I grab it, plunging it through his heavy robes and into the floorboards.

"Now!" I shout.

Mask throws the firecrackers into the fire, and they go off with a crackling boom.

We barrel out of the front, half-singed and coughing from the heavy smoke, as the store goes up in flames.

Outside, I hold Dai and Miki close. If it weren't for them and Mask, I would have surely been lost.

"Hurry." Mask pulls us to a stand. "We can't stay out here on the street. We need to find shelter."

Dai takes my hand, and together we follow Mask, who's already a distance ahead, peering around a corner.

Suddenly she turns, a look of panic etched onto her grandmother mask.

"Look out!" she screams.

A huge sea snake erupts from between the buildings to our right. Its tail whips out, knocking me to one side, Dai and Miki to the other.

My body slams into the wall of a building. Dust rises around me, and I cough, disoriented, my ears dully ringing. A cry of pain shakes me out of my stupor. Dai. *Miki.* I scramble to my feet.

A short distance away, the snake has the two of them cornered against a building, caged in on either side by its coiling body. They're trapped. I see the moment Dai realizes the same. His hand darts to his shoulder. Quickly he unties the knots of his sack, swinging Miki around and cradling her against his chest. He turns to the wall of the building, baring his back to the great snake. I watch, horrified as Dai leans over Miki, blocking her body with his own.

The snake lifts its tail, slashing it downward.

"No!" I scream.

Dai cries out. A deep slash gouges his back. He falls to his knees, Miki still held tightly in his grasp.

"No, please stop!" I lurch forward.

The snake raises its tail once more.

"Stop!" I look around desperately. "Someone, help—"

There's a sharp whistle of sound. A golden arrow shoots down from the sky, embedding deep into the back of the snake's neck. The snake writhes, howling. Another arrow finds its throat, cutting off its scream. The snake twists and falls, transforming into a man, eyes glassy and cold.

Out of the sky comes a great beast, what looks like a horse but with hooves of fire. A woman sits upon the beast, one arm pulling back the string of a large horn bow. Her hair falls down to her waist. Her eyes are like flaming candles. A bolt of lightning flashes and silhouettes her against the darkness. She's the most awe-inspiring being I've ever seen, terrible and terrifying at once. Slowly she turns her mount, her bright gaze upon me.

"Goddess!"

Shin stands on the roof of the closest building, and with him is Kirin. Both show signs of the battle in their ripped clothing and their swords that drip with blood. "Call away your servants," he commands, "and leave this city."

Servants? Then *she* must be the Goddess of Moon and Memory. More Imugi have gathered in the sky above her. Yet if she is their mistress—I shift my gaze to the man on the ground, his body slowly fading—why did she kill one of them?

"Give me the girl," the goddess says, "and I will leave in peace."

"I already told your servant, Ryugi. Lady Mina is no longer the Sea God's bride, but my own."

This answer seems to displease her more than placate her, her grip tightening on the bow. "Then why does she walk in the Sea God's gardens? Why does she tell him stories to tempt his heart? Your bride. The Sea God's bride. It does not matter. To me, she is an enemy."

Slowly she begins to lead her mount toward me. Behind her, Shin leaps from roof to roof, but he won't make it in time. The goddess lifts her bow, the arrow pointed directly at my heart.

Then a body lurches into view, knocking me over. "Dai!" He wraps his arms around my neck, surprisingly strong for a young boy, let alone a badly wounded one. I try to push him away, but he holds tight. Across the street Miki wails in Mask's arms. "Dai," I beg, "you have to let go." But he refuses. Even battered and bleeding, he thinks only of protecting me.

I lift my gaze to the goddess, only to see her watching us, very still upon her mount. For a second, I could swear I see a deep longing in her expression, but then her eyes harden, even as she lowers her bow. "How cowardly, to hide behind a child. But you won't be with him always, and when you're alone, when you least expect it, I will appear before you. And I will take what belongs to me."

I bite my lip to keep from retorting, *My soul belongs to me.*

The horse rises in the air. Golden cinders leap from its hooves to sizzle in the wind. It gallops upward into the sky, the sea snakes swarming around the goddess.

One sea snake breaks off from the rest and falls to the ground. The snake's body shrinks to a human shape, revealing a sweaty, scratched, but altogether uninjured Namgi.

Dai's body goes limp, and I catch him, cradling him in my lap.

Shin arrives, crouching down beside me. "We need to get him back to Lotus House."

I nod, and gently he lifts Dai in his arms.

Together our battle-worn party moves off, Mask holding an inconsolable Miki, whose cries echo the worry in my heart. As we hurry down the street, I look over my shoulder one last time. The lanterns in the street have all blown out during the battle. The only light comes from the moon, full and glowing, eclipsed by the lone figure of the goddess.

22

Dai is placed in Namgi's room, one of the two rooms on the bottom floor of the Lotus Pavilion, the other belonging to Kirin. I wait outside in the hall with Miki in my arms, her little body trembling every few minutes. The tremors began when she was first separated from Dai, after he'd saved her from the Imugi. On the walk back to Lotus House, she exhausted herself from crying, yet the trembling hasn't stopped. She releases another shiver, and I hold her close.

The door to Namgi's room slides open, and Shin steps out, followed by Kirin.

"How is he?" I ask quietly.

Kirin tightens the bandages around his hand. "He's strong, for such a small person. He'll pull through."

Reaching out, Shin lightly brushes back the wisps of hair that have escaped the tangle of my braid, clinging to my forehead and cheeks. The gentleness of his touch almost undoes the fragile walls I've built around my heart.

"I thought you were asleep," he says. By now, dawn must be breaking over the horizon.

"I want to see him."

Shin nods, stepping away from the door. As I pass, he says gently, "He'll be all right, Mina."

Fighting back tears, I hold his gaze, then Kirin's. "Thank you."

Kirin hesitates, then nods.

I enter the room, and Shin closes the door behind me.

Pink and yellow light filters through a closed window, lending a hazy glow to the room. Mask sits on the floor beside Dai, leaning over to pat down the blankets around him. Speaking in hushed voices, neither has noticed my entrance.

"I did good, didn't I, Mask?" Dai is whispering. "I protected them. Both of them. Like we said we would."

"Yes," Mask says softly, "you were very brave."

In my arms, Miki lets out a gurgle, drawing the attention of Dai. "Miki!" he croaks, opening his arms, only to wince in pain. He draws back into the blankets.

I hurry over, kneeling on the opposite side of the pallet, across from Mask.

I cover my mouth with my hand. "Oh, Dai . . ."

His black hair is pushed back from his face, revealing mottled bruises along his forehead and jaw. His face is pale, and there's a cut at the edge of his lips. The blankets obscure the rest of his body, but I can tell he's in pain by the way he holds himself, lying stiffly on his side, and by the way he keeps himself from reaching for Miki.

"Mask was just saying how brave I am," Dai says. "Remember

this moment, Mina. I will need you to recall it later, when I'm better and she's being mean to me again."

Mask chuckles, the expression on her mask that of a smiling grandmother.

"I agree with Mask, Dai," I say. "You were so very brave. It was terrible, seeing you and Miki beneath the shadow of the Imugi. But you protected her. And you, not so much bigger than her yourself."

"I sometimes forget," Dai says, "how small I am. I wasn't always so small, you see."

I frown. "I'm not sure what you mean."

"When spirits first enter this realm, we are given a choice to take any form we want," he explains. "If we happened to die a young man, we could take the form of an old man. If we died an old man, we could take the form of a little boy. But Miki died when she was only a baby. She hadn't had a chance to dream of being older than she already was. When deciding what type of body I should take, I thought of Miki. I thought, *I must be little like she is to understand what she's feeling*. I'm a boy, after all—what do I know about what it's like to be a little girl?"

He chuckles to himself. Beside him, Mask laughs her muffled laugh, and Miki trembles in my arms.

"Do you know how much I love Miki?" he continues. "When she gurgles, like she does when she's happy, I feel like my heart grows to ten times its normal size. When she is sad, I feel like my heart is breaking. I would give my life a hundred times for Miki."

The tears that I was holding back slip down my cheeks. I know he would; he almost did today.

"Do you know how much I love Miki? I came down from heaven so I could be with her."

"H-heaven?" I ask.

He smiles, a faraway look in his eyes. "Beyond this world, there are others. One of those other worlds is heaven. That's where I was, you see. I was waiting for my wife to join me, but then Miki . . . she's my great-granddaughter. My wife would never forgive me if I left Miki to float alone down the River of Souls. I came down from heaven, and I picked her up out of the water, and I've never put her down since. I spoil her, I think. She is my Miki. I love her."

Miki reaches for him, and I can't deny her. Carefully, I place her in his arms. "She is not very heavy," he whispers. "She is light. And if my wife passes through and straight up into heaven, she'll just have to wait. But she won't mind, because she knows I will be with our Miki."

Across Dai, Mask takes my hand, and together we watch as Miki lays her head on his shoulder, her trembling having stopped, safe in his arms again. The small furrow wrinkling her brow disappears, and she falls into a peaceful slumber.

"Do you know how much I love you, Miki?" Dai whispers softly. "Even I don't know. My love for you is endless. Deep and endless, like the sea."

In the morning, I wake to sunlight on my face and Dai drooling on my sleeve. Mask and Miki are nowhere to be found, though all four of us fell asleep together on the small pallet. Dai's face has regained most of its color. I adjust his blankets, careful not to wake him.

Outside, Miki sits on Mask's lap as they watch Namgi and Nari play a board game with white and black stones for markers. Namgi picks up one of the black stones from the bowl, hovering it over the board. Mask makes a *tsk* sound. He moves his hand to hover over another position. When she nods, he places it on the board.

"This is unfair," Nari says, picking up a white stone from her bowl. "I thought I was to play a young Imugi, not a grandmother of interminable age."

I glance between Namgi and Mask. Last night, I witnessed Namgi's transformation into a monstrous sea snake, and Dai revealed that he and Mask were not as their appearances might have implied. And yet, in the morning sunlight, Mask and Namgi look as they always have, familiar and good.

I take a seat beside Mask, tickling Miki's toes. "Where are Shin and Kirin?"

"Crane House," Nari replies. "Where, by now, Lord Crane must have come to regret all his wrongdoings."

Namgi chuckles at that, but as the day grows longer and Shin and Kirin don't return, I wonder what could be keeping them, and if Lord Crane has revealed to Shin what he had divulged to me.

Even a Red String of Fate can be unmade, if one party should form a stronger connection with another. How will Shin react to this information? Since the moment our fate was first formed, he wanted to destroy it because of the risk to his own life. With that reasoning, he won't desire to form a bond with another soul. Which means only I can break our tie by choosing the Sea God, and having him choose me in return.

Soon, day becomes night, and everyone separates to their own sleeping chambers—Miki and Mask to join Dai in Namgi's room; Namgi to Kirin's room, where he'll be bedding for the next few days as Dai recovers; and me, alone, to the floor above.

Moving to the far wall, I pick up the large bedroll and spread it down the middle of the floor, patting the blankets until they're smooth and flat. I hesitate before going to the paper screen, dragging it over the blankets so that the bedroll is divided. Finished, I take off my short silk jacket and untie the strings of my skirt. I let both fall to the floor before kicking them to the side. In my thin white shift, I crawl beneath the blankets. I stay awake awhile longer, sensitive to every sound outside the door, but when an hour passes and no one appears, I fall asleep.

I'm dreaming of the dragon as it rose from the sea—its eyes upon me, dark and fathomless—when I'm startled awake by a sound. I blink, disoriented. Moonlight seeps through the window. The shadows of clouds drift slowly across the paper screen. It can't be too far past midnight.

Again, the sound. An unmistakable cry of pain. *Shin!*

Scrambling out of the blankets, I push aside the screen. Shin tosses and turns on the bedding, his robes askew. He must have returned to Lotus House and gone to bed without changing. I quickly check him for visible wounds but find none. A nightmare, then? Sweat beads his brow, and his body trembles, as if taken by a chill.

I crouch beside him and grab his shoulders, giving a rough shake. "Shin, wake up!"

His eyes fly open. "Mina?"

I press the back of my hand to his forehead. "You don't have a fever. How do you feel?"

He starts to sit up, and I quickly move to help him. Once he's upright, I hurry to the low shelf and grab the bowl there, plucking the paper boat from the water and placing it gently aside. I test the water with my fingertips, relieved to find it cool. Returning to Shin's side, I soak a cloth in the water and bring it to his forehead.

"You were having a nightmare," I say as I dab the sweat from his brow. "Do you remember what it was about?"

He shakes his head slowly, his dark eyes intent upon my face. "I spoke to Lord Crane. He knows about the Red String of Fate between us. He admitted to sending the thieves to steal your soul, and failing that, contracted the same to kill you."

A shiver runs through me. Mask, Dai, and I might have defeated the bear-assassin, but the weasel is still out there.

I dip the cloth again and bring it to his neck. "Did he say anything else?"

He must have told Shin about how the Red String of Fate can be broken.

"No."

I look up. Shin meets my gaze, his expression inscrutable. Is he . . . lying? But why would he lie about knowing the truth?

"He told me some things as well," I say. "He said that the way to break the curse upon the Sea God is to form a fated connection with him, the same as between lovers. As for the Red String of Fate we share, he said—"

"You're wrong," Shin interrupts. "I think I have a fever."

I was disoriented before, upon waking, but reason has now returned. According to Nari, spirits and gods cannot become ill.

Shin lifts his hand to brush his fingers against his face. The movement draws my attention to his bare forearm and his robes that are askew, having fallen wide at his neck in his sleep. Suddenly, my shoulders feel very exposed without my jacket. Neither of us is dressed to be having this conversation.

"I'll fetch Kirin." I get up, almost tripping when the skirt of my dress snags on something. I look down to see Shin holding on to the back of it, his hand a fist. He notices it, too, and releases me abruptly, turning his face away.

I hesitate, then kneel on the blankets. "Do you want me to stay?"

He looks at me, and I have my answer in the open longing in his eyes.

I move to smooth down his pillow. And then he's reaching for me, and I go to him, his arms circling around me. His breath whispers against my neck as he pulls me close.

It seems impossible that I'll fall asleep, the tension humming painfully beneath my skin, but eventually I'm lulled into a peaceful slumber, every one of my heartbeats an echo of his.

23

I wake to thunder rumbling in the distance and a *knowing* in my heart of what I must do.

"Shin," I say, turning to face him. I hesitate. He's asleep. Unlike the restlessness of last night, he looks at peace, his brow smooth, his lips slightly parted. I'd give anything to make his slumber last a little longer. But I can't do this alone.

"Shin," I say again.

"Mina?" He blinks sleepily. "What's wrong?"

"I need to go somewhere."

He frowns, watching me closely. "Where?"

"To the Sea God's palace."

His eyes darken, but he nods. "All right."

He stands, grabs a fresh set of robes from the cabinet, and leaves the room. Hurriedly I dress in a coral skirt and white jacket, rushing down the stairs. Shin waits with Namgi and Kirin outside, the air coated in a heavy mist. In the east, dark clouds gather over the mountains.

"Something's not right," Kirin says. "That storm appears unnatural."

"If it's traveling over the eastern mountains," Namgi says, "it's from the world of humans." They exchange an inscrutable glance.

"Let's go," Shin says.

The heavy mist extends across the whole city, seeming to roll along the ground like swirls of clouds. The doors to the Sea God's palace are closed, so Namgi scales the wall and throws down a rope for Shin and Kirin to climb, with me clinging to Shin's back. Over the wall, the Sea God's garden is eerily quiet, the blanketing fog like ghostly tendrils reaching out as if to beckon us into the mist.

Shin leads the way with Namgi, as always, beside me. It's Kirin I'm surprised to find walking to my left.

"You've decided, then," Kirin says, a chill in his voice. "What you want."

His animosity is palpable. "What are you trying to say?" I ask.

"Last night, Lord Crane was eager to divulge to us the knowledge he shared with you, that the Red String of Fate between yourself and Shin can be unmade, should you form a connection with the Sea God."

So Shin *does* know. I look to him where he walks a few paces ahead. The fog is so thick it's unlikely he can hear our words.

"It's not just my decision to make," I say. "Shin can also form a connection with someone else."

"Modesty doesn't suit you. The one who will make the choice will be you."

"My feelings are not so simple," I whisper.

"Neither does indecisiveness."

I flinch, though I don't blame Kirin. I see now how loyal he is to Shin.

"That's unfair to Mina," Namgi protests. "It's not so easy for her to follow her heart. She has a duty to her family, her people."

Kirin growls. "Then I should praise Mina for her sense of loyalty, and condemn you for your lack of it."

Namgi tenses. "I have loyalty."

"Is that why you abandoned your brothers, your family, your *blood*? Leaving them doesn't make you less of a monster, Namgi." Kirin's voice is cold, ruthless. "It just makes you a traitor."

Namgi holds himself very still; then his shoulders sag, the fight seeming to leave him. He says, in a defeated voice so unlike his own, "Sometimes you don't find family in your own blood, but elsewhere."

And though Kirin was the one with the harsh words, it's he who turns away, as if pained.

Namgi separates from us, and the fog swallows him whole. When he doesn't return after a few minutes, I ask worriedly, "Should we go after him? He might get lost in this fog."

From the murky depths comes a muffled shout.

"Namgi!" Kirin cries out, his hand reaching to his sword belt.

"Go to him," I say. "I'll follow the Red String of Fate to Shin."

He meets my gaze, then nods, disappearing into the mist.

Rain begins to fall, and soon my dress is soaked through. Perhaps it was a mistake to go in search of the Sea God instead of waiting out the storm, but deep down inside I knew when I woke this morning that if I didn't look for him now, I might not look for him ever. I might step off the path I chose for myself when I jumped into the sea and instead follow my heart.

The rain lightens to a low drizzle. I follow the Red String of Fate as it parts the mist, flitting along the dewy air to the pavilion by the Pond of Paper Boats. This is where I find Shin, standing at the center of the elegant wooden structure. With him is the Sea God.

If Shin is surprised to find the Sea God awake, he's careful not to show it, perhaps wary like I am that the god might flee, taking with him the chance to solve the mystery of his enchantment.

"Have you come to tell me another story?" the boy-god asks. He's dressed in the same grand robes he wore when I first laid eyes on him, an emblem of the dragon embroidered in silver on his chest. Once more, I'm struck by how like a child he is, wanting to hear a story rather than face the truth.

I immediately chide myself. My grandmother would scold me for such a thought. Sometimes, only through a story can a truth be heard.

"If that is what would please you most," I say. Though I'm unsure of what story to tell.

I meet Shin's gaze over the boy-god's shoulder. I settle on Joon's favorite, a love story.

"A long time ago, there lived a woodcutter at the edge of a great forest. He was young, strong, and kind. He was also very lonely. One night, as he was traveling back home, he heard laughter through the woods. Curious, he followed the lovely sounds.

Beneath a magnificent golden tree, he found two heavenly maidens swimming in a small rock pond, their beautiful white dresses streaming out behind them. The heavenly maidens had taken off their wings and had hung them over a low branch of the golden tree."

Heavy raindrops begin to hit the rooftop of the pavilion. I raise my voice to be heard.

"Though the woodcutter counted three sets of wings upon the branch, there were only two heavenly maidens in the pond. Then a hint of white in the verdant green caught the woodcutter's eye. A third maiden was approaching through the woods. She came to the rock pond, but didn't slip into the water. Instead, she looked up through the trees, to the stars, closing one eye as if to see them clearer. The woodcutter fell in love, then and there. And so, he stole her wings."

Both Shin and the Sea God frown at this, though neither speaks a word, listening carefully.

"When her sisters returned to the heavens, their strong wings carrying them up into the sky, the youngest heavenly maiden was left alone and wingless. It was then the young woodcutter came to her, offering the jacket from his back. She accepted it, charmed by his humility and love for her. They built a life together. They could not have children, for she was not of his world, but for a long time, they were happy."

The Sea God turns his face toward the garden, as if distracted.

"But as it is with life, the woodcutter grew older and wiser. He realized that his love of a moment was nothing to the love built over a lifetime. Although it weighed on his soul, he knew what he had to do. For he knew that if he truly loved the heavenly maiden, he would have to let her go."

As I say these last words, my eyes meet Shin's. His face holds a heartrending expression. Taking a deep breath, I finish the story.

"In the night, he went into the forest and dug up her wings from where he'd buried them beneath the golden tree. He laid them beside his wife as she slept and went back to the forest to weep.

"The next night, he returned to his house, only to find that the heavenly maiden was no longer there, and the wings were gone. With tears in his eyes, he went outside to peer up at the sky to see that one more star had appeared in the heavens. And although he cried for what he had lost, he was filled with joy. For he knew, then, that the heavenly maiden had returned to where she belonged."

As I speak the last word, the Sea God lifts his face to look out into the storm. His hand goes to his chest, fingers digging into the fabric. "There's a tugging at my soul." Suddenly he leaps from the pavilion, rushing into the rain.

"Wait!" I follow. I hear Shin shout from behind me, but the rain muffles all sound. The fog rises up around me, and soon I lose my way. I try to turn back toward the pavilion, but I can't tell if I'm going in the right direction. Even the Red String of Fate is barely visible in the heavy mist.

My foot catches on the ground, and I stumble forward, landing on a grand sweep of stairs. I recognize them as those that I climbed when I first arrived in this city. Above are the gates of the Sea God's palace, the doors now open. How am I here, when I'd been in the garden?

Behind me is the unmistakable clop of hooves on stone. I turn to face the figure approaching from within the mist. The Goddess of Moon and Memory. Like before, her mount is a great horse with flames for hooves. "I warned you what would happen," she says, "if I were to meet you alone."

"That I would die because you would kill me."

She watches me through cool, impassive eyes. "Are you not afraid?"

"I am. But tell me, would it be the same if I wasn't the Sea God's bride? If I was a child, like Dai? If I was someone who believed you could help me?"

"You are none of those things."

"I am the last."

Her eyes flicker for a brief moment, then look away. "You are mistaken." From her wide sleeve, she pulls out two paper boats.

I immediately recognize the boat in her left hand, with its red, uneven stiches. It's my wish. "How do you have that?"

"I am the Goddess of Moon and Memory. In this boat is the memory of a wish you once made."

"Did you see what the wish was?"

She watches me carefully. "No. I cannot see this memory, because it is one that is tied closely with your soul." I reach for it, but she holds back. "What would you trade me for this piece of your soul?"

I look up at her and say nothing. If this is a contest of wills, she has won, for I would give anything to have that memory returned to me, to throw it into the fire where it belongs. She tucks the first boat into the sleeve of her dress, instead handing over the second boat, the one I'd momentarily forgotten in the need for my own.

"This belongs to someone you know. Perhaps you can return it to her."

The goddess looks over my shoulder, and I follow her gaze. The rain is so thick that for a moment I don't recognize the young woman walking through the downpour.

Shim Cheong.

24

Shim Cheong is dressed in an elaborate bridal gown. Her long sleeves drag on the ground, and red circles are painted onto her pale cheeks. Her black hair is swept back and knotted beneath a headpiece of jade and gold. *Why is she here?* A bride is only sent down once a year. Until the storms begin again next summer, there should be no need for another bride, let alone *Shim Cheong*, who I hoped to spare with my own sacrifice.

I turn, but the goddess is no longer beside me to answer my questions. There's a sharp cry of pain as Cheong stumbles on her long gown.

"Cheong!" I rush over to where she's fallen.

She gasps. "Mina?"

I help her stand, tucking the paper boat into the jacket of my dress and hauling her up by the arms. "Are you all right? Are you hurt?"

She stares at me through dark, luminous eyes that shimmer with tears. "Oh, Mina, I'm so glad to see you. Joon was devastated when you jumped into the sea."

"Cheong, why are you here?"

A ghostly pallor steals over her face. "I was sacrificed."

For a moment, I just stare at her, unable to form words. "But . . . but why?"

"We had thought they had ended . . ." Her beautiful eyes glaze over, terror-stricken. "But then the storms began anew, more terrible than before. Whole villages have been swept away into the sea. Husbands separated from their wives, children from their mothers. The council of village elders met and determined that we angered the Sea God when you went in place of me. They ordered soldiers to storm our home. Your family fought bravely to protect me. Brother-in-law. Sister-in-law. Your grandmother, who was the fiercest of them all. And Joon."

Cheong chokes on his name, and I don't think she'll be able to go on, but then she takes a steadying breath and continues. "But I was taken away, dressed as you see, and thrown into the water. Though even as I was caught and pulled beneath the waves, I knew it was a mistake. A wrath such as this cannot be appeased with just one life. The Sea God's anger is too great, too powerful. I fear, this time, the storm will destroy us all."

I stare at her, wanting only to deny her words, but know she wouldn't speak such terrible forebodings if she didn't believe them. I think of Namgi and Kirin, who, earlier this morning, said the storm appeared otherworldly, arriving over the eastern mountains where the human world ends and the river begins.

I'm struck with a terrible thought.

"Mina?" Cheong says.

"Wait here," I say. I don't want to leave her, but I have to know for sure. Picking up my skirts, I sprint toward the river.

Soon, I hear the roar of raging rapids. Out of the mist, the river looms loud and furious. Shiki stands at the water's edge, his eyes hollow with grief. I see whole families caught in the rapids—mothers, fathers, and children. Unlike the girl from the night before, none of the dead struggle against the current. They lie still, as if they've given up all hope. Why is this happening? Why have the storms returned?

The Sea God. Fury sweeps through my body.

I head back in the direction of the palace, sprinting up the steps to the open gate. Cheong cries out my name, but I don't stop. I run past one courtyard after another. The rain is less here, but still it falls. I feel it sliding down my face in droplets that burn across my lips. It tastes of the sea. I reach the last courtyard and enter the hall.

Rain falls through cracks in the ceiling, battering against the cold stone. The Sea God is on the floor beside the throne, his hand gripping his chest. It's the same motion he made when he left the pavilion in a hurry. *There's a tugging at my soul.* Was it the pull of the Red String of Fate? But his wrist is bare, as was Shim Cheong's. Had they shared a true fate, it would have been visible to her and strange enough that she would have remarked upon it.

The Sea God lets out an agonized cry. I rush over to him, hesitating as I reach out. Last I touched him, I was pulled into his memories. I take a deep breath and grab his shoulder. A blinding light rises up to swallow me whole.

There's a wall of sound, like a forest of trees in the wind, and then I'm released abruptly.

I stand on the edge of a cliff facing the sea at dusk. The setting sun casts a golden pathway of light across the darkening water.

I turn slowly, taking in my surroundings. The air smells of fresh honeysuckle. A warm breeze brushes against my skin, blowing the hair from my cheek.

Back home we have our own sea cliffs. They lie a mile outside our small village. Joon and I would often race each other up to the top, breathless and laughing.

On our way down, we'd sometimes catch sight of Shim Cheong making her way up, her hand grasped tightly in her father's. It would take them hours to reach the small meadow at the top of the cliff, but still they would make the climb. Patient, beautiful Shim Cheong and her father, whose murky eyes could never see the sunset, but who loved those daily walks beside his daughter, smiling as she described the world to him, tinged by the light of her love.

I blink, dissolving the memory.

And then I see him crumpled at the edge of the cliff. The Sea God. I rush forward, falling to my knees. His robes are shredded and muddied with dirt. I move my hand across the silk, and my fingers slide against something warm and wet.

Blood. The whole back of his robes is covered with it.

I cry out. "What happened? Who has done this to you?"

The Sea God, who's been staring out at the sea, turns his face to look up at me. His eyes are glassy, his lovely face contorted with pain.

"The pain is nothing," he whispers, his voice less that of a god's and more that of a boy's, small and breaking. "The pain is nothing compared with what I've done. I've failed them all."

"No," I say, smoothing wet strands of hair from his eyes. "You can make it right again. I'll help you. There must be a way—"

Abruptly the Sea God reaches up, grabbing hold of my wrist. His eyes meet mine, and I gasp. I can see flames, a whole city burning inside his eyes. He releases me, and I'm flung backward, knocking my head against the ground. When I come to, I'm back in the Sea God's hall.

I stare upward at the painting of the dragon on the wall. Then I remember. The rain. *The storm.*

Getting off the floor, I stumble to the Sea God. Quickly I examine his robes for blood, but they're smooth, only damp from the rain.

The Sea God groans, sitting up. I move forward to help him, but he raises a hand to stop me. "What are you doing here?"

"I came to speak with you. Where were we just then? The cliff by the sea . . . Was it the human world? Why were you bleeding?"

"Stop! I'm the one who asks the questions. Why do you tell such sorrowful stories?" he cries. "Do you mean to break my heart? You should know, it was broken a long time ago."

"Whatever happened on that cliff, is that the reason why the storms began? Was it a human who did that to you? Is that why you stopped protecting us? Is that why you abandoned us?"

He curls inward, as if to shield himself from my words. His voice is small, tired. "You say you are the Sea God's bride, but how can you be when yours words fill me with such shame? The one who hurts me . . . is you."

Outside, thunder rumbles over the palace. The rain continues to pour through cracks in the ceiling, rattling against the wooden floorboards. A part of me wants to leave, abandon the Sea God to his sorrow and fate. But another part of me wishes to stay, because even in my anger and frustration, my heart aches for him. In many ways, he reminds me of Joon when he was younger—a warrior now, but bullied by the other village children as a boy. He was bighearted and too kind. I used to scream at the older girls and boys who would tease and call him names. How dare they hurt my brother, who I loved most in the world.

Gently, I reach out and wrap my arms around the Sea God.

"What are you—" he protests.

I hold tight, lending him my warmth and my strength. "When I was little, I used to pray to you. When the storms raged and the waves broke against the shores, I was afraid, yet I believed in you. When the seas were calm and my brother and I played safely in the tide, I was happy, and I believed in you."

"But no longer," the boy-god mumbles.

"I believe in you still. Sometimes it's hard, and I doubt myself, but I never doubt you. How can I doubt the sea, the wind, the waves? I wish I could bear some of your burden for you. Holding you now, I can feel how heavy it is."

He starts to sob, and I wrap my arms around his neck, as if I could hold him together with just my strength. "I wish you could know, even after everything, even after the storms and the sorrow, how much your people miss you, and how we love you," I say. "We will always love you, because you are ours. You are our sea, and our storms, and our sunlight breaking out over a new day. You are our hope. We've been waiting for you for such a long time. Come back to us. Please come back."

My dress was already soaked from the rain, but now the Sea God's warm tears seep into my shoulder. Through the ceiling, the rain falls around us, an endless symphony cradling us in our grief.

25

Shin, Namgi, and Kirin wait for me on the steps of the palace. I'm reminded of the first night when they stood before me in the Sea God's hall. Enemies. Strangers. Shin appeared so distant from me then, just as he appears now.

"Where is Shim Cheong?" I shout to be heard over the lashing rain.

"Shiki offered her shelter at Star House," Namgi answers. "She'll be safe there."

"We have to get out of this storm," Kirin says.

Shin turns and moves down the stairs. I meet Namgi's gaze, but he just shakes his head. Is Shin angry with me for rushing out into the fog?

The streets are flooded. The four of us make our way around overturned carts and lantern boats snuffed of their candles. Shin and Kirin lead the way, clearing the path of debris, while Namgi and I follow behind. The water is up to our knees; any higher and we might be in danger of being swept away. Luckily, the current isn't as strong as it is in the river. I gasp as a body floats by, a woman with her eyes closed, her hands on her stomach as if in slumber. Namgi grasps my shoulders, urging me onward.

Back at Lotus House, Shin leads us to the main pavilion. The first floor is already flooded, so we climb the stairs to the second floor. Everyone is here, all the people who call Lotus House their home. I see my handmaidens, as well as the washerwomen, cooks, and guards. Mask sits on a cushion beside Dai, who holds Miki. Nari is escorting a few older spirits to a corner, plying them with hot tea to warm their bodies. I head over to the balcony. The waters from the lake have risen to lap over the bridges. The only light for miles is from the torches that blaze all around the perimeter. To someone standing in the distance, the pavilion must appear like a candle in a vast sea.

As I press my hand to the railing, something crinkles in my sleeve. I reach inside and remove a paper boat—the one the Goddess of Moon and Memory gave me. The one with Shim Cheong's wish.

The paper boat feels light in my hands. The folds are neat, the paper smooth. Slowly, I unfold the creases, waiting for the familiar fogginess, the feeling of being pulled into a memory. Nothing happens.

The boat is open. There is only one short sentence written on the paper.

I expect the words to say *Let me not marry the Sea God* or *Let me stay with Joon* or *End the storms forever*, but all that's written on the paper—in Shim Cheong's elegant writing—is:

Please let my father live a long and happy life.

I carefully fold the paper boat and place it back into the sleeve of my jacket.

"This storm is unnatural," Kirin says, addressing everyone in the pavilion. "The river has flooded, and the dead are floating in the streets. Something must be done, and soon."

"We must send out boats to collect the dead," Nari insists, "and set them back on their course down the river."

"Meanwhile," Namgi adds, "the river must be stopped from flowing into our world. If we can dam the source, we can block the dead from entering."

"That will mean ghosts in the human world," Mask says vehemently. "Without vessels to contain them, the restless spirits will haunt the living, spreading dread and panic. More deaths will follow."

Kirin shakes his head. "It can't be helped."

"No," I say, and everyone turns their attention to me. "All of these solutions are only temporary. The real source of the dead are the storms that steal their lives. They are the cause of everything. They are what we need to stop."

Namgi looks around the room, then back at me. "I don't deny the truth of your words, Mina," he says gently. "But if the Sea God hasn't ended the storms in a hundred years, what makes you think he'll end them now?"

A painful throb begins at the base of my skull, making it difficult to shape the thoughts in my head. "At Crane House the other night, Lord Yu shared some knowledge with me." I'm careful not to look at Shin. "In order to lift the curse upon the Sea God, the bride must form a true fate with him."

"A true fate?" Namgi frowns. "What do you mean?" I forgot he hadn't been with Shin and Kirin when they questioned Lord Crane.

"One between soul mates," I say.

"And you believe you are that bride," Kirin says. The room is quiet, expectant. I wait for the whispers and looks of derision. Who am I to believe I am the Sea God's true bride? I am not a great beauty, nor am I particularly skilled in anything.

"It's possible you are," Kirin continues, and I startle in surprise. Of all people, I would think him the most doubtful. "Before you, no bride has ever spoken to the Sea God. And though this storm is terrible, it's a change in a routine that has remained unchanged for a hundred years."

"The bride who just arrived," Namgi adds, "Shim Cheong. She didn't have a Red String of Fate."

Now the whispers begin, but not like I expected. Spirits turn to one another in excitement, awed by the possibility that the myth of the Sea God's bride might be fulfilled at last.

"It doesn't matter," Shin says, his first words since entering the pavilion, "because you don't love him."

The throbbing at the back of my skull intensifies.

"And you'd be a fool to think he could ever love you."

The room goes silent. I know he's speaking out of his own hurt, but a painful warmth gathers behind my eyes. And maybe it's childish of me to flee, but I can't help it. I rush from the room, spirits moving out of the way to let me pass. I sprint down the flight of stairs to the first floor. The rain lashes my face as I step from the shelter of the pavilion. The water from the lake has climbed halfway up the rise of the hill. I don't cross the bridge but slip down the grassy bank until my feet touch the water.

I think I understand finally what it means to be the Sea God's bride. It's not a burden or an honor. To be the Sea God's bride is not to be the most beautiful girl in the village, nor is it to be the one to break the curse. To be the Sea God's bride, she must do one thing: She must love him.

I am not the Sea God's bride.

I've failed my people. I've failed my family. My grandmother. My brothers. My sister-in-law. Cheong. I've failed them all.

And there is no hope, because love can't be bought or earned or even prayed for. It must be freely given. And I have given my heart to someone, but he is not the Sea God.

The rain continues to lash the earth. The water from the lake rises, soaking my slippers. I step back just as a whoosh of sound sweeps by me. The bolt of a crossbow lodges at my feet. A branch snaps beneath the bridge. My hand instinctively reaches for my knife.

From out of the darkness steps a familiar figure. The weasel-like assassin. I pull out my knife, but it's too late. He loads another bolt, aims, and releases.

I twist to the side, but I'm not fast enough. The bolt pierces my shoulder. I scream in pain.

I hear a shout from the pavilion. *Nari*. The assassin must hear it, too, because he flees, scuttling back into the dark.

I collapse onto the ground, my cheek pressed against the

damp earth. My limp arm stretches out beside me. Blood pools beneath me, spreading like a warm blanket. The ribbon shimmers, then slowly begins to fade.

"No," I whisper. The Red String of Fate ties my soul to Shin's. If I should die, so will he . . .

The rain blends with the tears on my face. My breaths turn ragged, and I can feel my vision blackening at the edges.

My last thoughts are a jumble of images—my brother, moving away from me across the bridge; the Sea God weeping on a cliff by the sea; and Shin, as he was only this morning, sunlight like water streaming over his face.

26

All my life, I've believed in the myth of the Sea God's bride, passed down from grandmother to grandmother since the storms first appeared, when the kingdom was destroyed by conquerors from the West and the emperor thrown from the cliffs into the sea. The Sea God, who loved the emperor like a brother, sent the storms to punish the usurpers—the lashing rains were said to be his tears, the thunder his cries. The droughts were those years he'd felt the emptiness in his heart.

But how much of myth is truth? And what do you do when your belief in it is breaking?

"There's nothing more I can do for her." Kirin's voice is muffled, seeming to come from far away. "I've closed her wound, but she's lost much blood and her pulse is weak."

"What of the assassin?" Namgi asks. His voice is hoarse, as if he's been shouting.

"He fled when she screamed. Lord Yu must have sent him as a last attempt in killing Shin."

I'm in Shin's room, looking down at my body from above. I

wonder if this is how the magpie views the world. I wonder if I *am* the magpie, fluttering about. I don't think so, though. No one seems to notice me hovering above their heads.

Namgi and Kirin stand beside me where I lie on a pallet of silk blankets. But Shin isn't with them. Is he all right? Namgi and Kirin would be more upset if he were hurt, wouldn't they?

I look to my body to see the Red String of Fate is no longer tied to my hand. I remember the way the string flickered into nothing. The fox goddess said that it could only be severed if either Shin or I should die.

Did I . . . die, as I lay bleeding by the lake? But if I'm dead, my spirit should be in the river, not here floating beside my body . . .

I drift out the window. A beautiful rainbow arcs through the sky. Distracted, my soul flies upward. I wonder, if I soared high enough, could I breach the heavens?

There's a tickle in my ear, and then Dai's voice. "Don't go so far away, Mina. If you go too far, you won't be able to come back."

I turn and float back to the small room.

Namgi and Kirin are no longer with me. Dai now sits beside my body, Miki in his lap.

"The storms have stopped," he says. "There's a feeling in the air, as if they've stopped forever."

I float to Dai's side, gazing down at his face. His wounds from the Imugi attack are mostly healed; the bruises are not as dark as they were before, and his face has regained its color. Miki whimpers as she watches my sleeping form, her little fist against her mouth.

"Don't worry, Miki," Dai says. "Mina will be all right. She'll wake up when she's ready."

I glance out the window to see it's now dusk. Time seems to work strangely in this in-between state. When I look back, Dai and Miki are gone.

The door slides open. Namgi steps into the room. He pauses by the door and I float to stand beside him, peering at the room. Besides the cabinet and the paper screen, there are several more pieces of furniture in the room: a chest for my clothes, a small table and mirror for my hair ornaments. The low shelf beneath the window is cluttered with items I've scavenged from the gardens—dried flowers, pebbles, and acorns. On the shelf beneath the window the paper boat floats in a shallow bowl of water.

"This room was empty before," Namgi says. "And then you filled it with all these things. Is that a good metaphor for how you've filled all our lives?"

Slowly, he moves across the room. "If you were awake, you would tease me. *Namgi*, you would say, *how clever you are.*" He pauses at my bedside, peering at my still face. "I really thought you'd wake for that one."

Taking the blankets, he raises them to my chin, then leans down to kiss me on the brow. "Sleep well, my friend, though not for too long. Some of us are not as strong as you are."

I frown. What does he mean? But then my mind fogs, and time seems to slip away from me. Morning sunlight pierces the room the next time I become aware of my surroundings.

I'm surprised to find Kirin at my bedside. He holds a cool

cloth to my forehead, a furrow between his brows. Even when I'm asleep, he's displeased with me. I sigh, wishing to fly away from his disappointment. But then he puts aside the cloth and stands, moving to the other side of the pallet. He hesitates, then steps into the direct path of sunlight that is shining brightly onto my face.

I float over to the side of my body to see what he was frowning at. There's sweat on my brow.

I don't know how long Kirin stands there, watching over me without a word, his body blocking the sunlight.

He doesn't move until there's a knock on the door; his head turns toward the sound.

The fog from before rises up again, darker, more menacing, and I drift into a void. It's an inescapable nothingness. A place without time or meaning, just an aching in my heart that I'm dying, and there's nothing I can do to save myself.

The next time I come back, it's full night, and Shin is beside me. The room is dark, the moon hidden beneath clouds.

"I killed the assassin," he says, his eyes in shadow. I frown at the way his voice sounds, flat, empty. "I dragged him through the streets. He was begging for me to spare his life. He was in terrible agony. Yet he hurt you, and for that, I knew no pain would be too great."

He stops speaking. I move closer, needing to see his eyes through the shadows.

"But when I arrived at the river, I realized none of it mattered. It was raining, and you were dying . . ." Slowly, he reaches out and takes my limp wrist in his hand, lowering his head until his forehead rests against it. "The fox goddess said the Red String of Fate would break if one of us should die. Like a fool, I took her words plainly." He sucks in a harsh breath. "I should rejoice that it's gone and I'm still alive. But strange, Mina, why do I feel like this? I don't need a Red String of Fate to tell me that if you should die, so will I."

No! I want to tell him that the goddess must have been mistaken, but the dark fog comes for me again, a place of unconsciousness so deep it feels like the end of despair. A part of me knows this isn't a place I should be—that if I drift too deep within it, I will be lost forever. But I don't know how to find my way back. There is no Red String of Fate to guide me.

I drift deeper into the nothingness, my legs drawn to my chest and my head bowed over my knees. I've never felt so alone. Is this how the Sea God has felt for a hundred years?

Out of the darkness, I hear a voice. Strange, but it sounds like *my* voice, singing.

> *Beneath the sea, the dragon sleeps*
> *What is he dreaming of?*
>
> *Beneath the sea, the dragon sleeps*
> *When will he wake?*
>
> *On a dragon's pearl,*
> *your wish will leap.*
>
> *On a dragon's pearl,*
> *your wish will leap.*

Only my grandmother knew that song. Her grandmother taught it to her when she was a girl, a long time ago.

My grandmother.

A soft hand takes my own, squeezing. "Mina. You need to wake up. How can you save the Sea God, yet not save yourself?" Her voice is clear. It's as if she's right beside me, whispering into my ear.

It's different, I want to say. *I was badly wounded. I lost a lot of blood.*

She clicks her tongue. "No excuses, Mina. Wake up. Wake up, now!"

I open my eyes.

"Mina!" A half dozen voices cry out my name. I look up to see that I'm surrounded. On one side of my pallet are Mask, Dai, and Miki. On the other side are Namgi, Nari, and Kirin.

Dai moves first, toppling over to grab me around the waist. "You scared us!" he says.

"Be careful," Kirin scolds, pulling Dai up by the sleeve. "I closed the wound, but it'll take time to fully heal."

"Are you hungry?" Nari asks. "Do you want me to get you anything to eat?"

"What about a drink?" Namgi suggests. "Liquor helps with the pain." Now it's Namgi's turn to get pulled away from the bed as Nari grabs him by the ear.

"I'm glad you've returned to us," Mask says from where she sits beside me, Miki in her lap. Reaching out a hand, she gently brushes a few strands from my face.

I look around the room, then find my voice. "Where is Shin?"

The room goes silent as each person looks at the other.

"He was here up until a few minutes ago," Namgi says finally. "He's hardly left your side."

I don't understand. Then where is he now?

"Don't concern yourself with him," Mask says. "He'll be back soon. Meanwhile, get some rest." She turns and begins to give orders for food to be brought up and a bath prepared. Everyone scrambles to obey, each careful not to meet my eyes.

I curl my hands in my lap. Where once the Red String of Fate sparkled, my palm is now bare, as if the tie between Shin and myself never existed at all.

27

On Kirin's orders, I'm confined to the room for the rest of the day, though I'm allowed visitors. Mask and Dai visit with Miki in the morning, and in the afternoon, Namgi and Nari, separately. But not Shin. The possibilities as to why are endless, plaguing me all day and distracting me from my well-wishers. Does he feel guilt for his harsh words the night of the storm? Is he angry with me for fleeing when I knew the assassin was still out there? I not only put myself in danger, but him as well . . .

There's a light tap on the door. I sit up as it slides open, and Cheong steps into the room. I blink in surprise.

She's changed out of her ceremonial wedding gown from last I saw her, now wearing a simple dress of blue and white. Her black hair is braided and coiled behind her head, like that of a married woman.

"Mina!" She glides across the room, settling gracefully beside my pallet. "I wanted to come sooner, but I wasn't allowed inside. How are you? Are you all right?"

"I'm fine," I say, suddenly overcome with shyness. Even

though we grew up in the same village, I never truly spoke to Cheong. She was older and intimidating in her beauty. Really, *no one* spoke to her except for Joon.

People told stories about her and praised her devotion to her father, whom the villagers called Shim the Blind. Some even envied her; I know I've been guilty of that. But not one of us paused to ask her how she felt. Until now, it never occurred to me how lonely her life must have been.

Cheong puts to the side a cloth-wrapped package she's brought with her, gazing around the room at the paintings on the walls, the stitched notebooks and the scrolls stacked in neat piles on the desk. She moves her hands to her lap, smoothing down each pleat of her dress, a gesture my sister-in-law, Soojin, often made when she was nervous. Through the window, the sky outside is bright and clear.

"Forgive me, Mina," Cheong says. "Will you let me talk a little bit? There are some things I'd like to say to you."

"Yes, of course," I quickly reassure her.

She nods, hesitating a moment more before finally speaking. "In my life, there are two women I respect the most. One is your grandmother. She is the strongest person I've ever met. She defended Joon and me when others berated us for choosing love over duty. I was chosen to be the Sea God's bride, but she taught me that my life was my own, and no one else's. She made me believe that I could have a life beyond the one that was expected of me, a life . . . that I *wanted*."

Cheong stops fiddling with her skirt to take my hand. "The other woman I respect most in the world is you. When you took my place, I was filled with so many emotions. Relief. Gratitude. Guilt. And yet, that moment when you jumped onto the prow of the boat, I was filled with an emotion I'd never felt before: hope. You make me believe in wonders."

I don't know what to say, feeling both overwhelmed and incredibly honored.

"I've never had a sister," she says softly. "I'm so glad that I have you now."

"And I, you," I whisper, swallowing thickly.

She reaches for the package she set aside and gracefully unties the silk knot of the ribbon. The cloth folds back to reveal a dress with a skirt the color of peach blossoms and a yellow jacket embroidered with small pink flowers.

I gasp. "It's beautiful."

"Do you like it? It's a gift. From Lady Hyeri. She was going to bring it over herself, but I asked if I could be the bearer, and have a moment alone with you. May I?"

I nod, and she takes my arm to help me stand. Careful of my shoulder, she wraps the peach blossom skirt around my body, tying the string secure at my chest. She then holds the yellow jacket up for me, and I slide my arms into the sleeves. She moves behind me, and I feel the gentle tug of a comb as she sections out my hair and braids it in a long plait, securing it with a pink ribbon. Finally she turns me to face her. Taking the two ribbons at the front of my dress, she makes a knot, looping one ribbon and slipping the other through the hole. She adjusts the length until it falls elegantly across the front of my dress. Finished, she steps back to admire her work.

"It's a lovely dress, Cheong," I say. "But what is the occasion?"

"There's to be a festival in the city tonight, to celebrate the ending of the storms."

I remember Dai at my bedside. *The storms have stopped. There's a feeling in the air, as if they've stopped forever.*

Could it be true? But what has changed? The last I saw the Sea God, he was in despair.

Cheong lifts her gaze, her eyes bright. "You must go. After all, there are rumors in the city. They say the Sea God's storms stopped because of you."

28

Walking with Namgi and Nari in the city later, I'm struck by the change in the atmosphere. The city is always brimming with warmth and light, but tonight, it's as if the people have released their joy onto the streets. Acrobats jump and leap to the beat of barrel drums. Food cart sellers hand out sweet rice cakes and silk candy. The aftermath of the storm is visible in the broken rafters and missing beams, though cleaned and patched up in the last few days. I jump back as two young girls run by carrying a large barrel. One opens the lid to release hundreds of golden carp with bells tied to their fins. As the fish dart away, a chorus of chimes peals throughout the city.

Even delighted as I am by the sights and sounds, I can't help feeling a little wistful. After Cheong left, I eagerly awaited Shin's arrival, but as the sun sank behind the mountains, I lost hope that he would come. Not to let Cheong's gift go to waste, I asked Nari and Namgi to take me into the city.

"Mina," Nari says, arching a brow, "I believe you have an admirer."

I look—perhaps too eagerly—over my shoulder. A small group of boys, around Dai's age, gathers beneath the awning of a teashop. They throw furtive glances in our direction. One boy is pushed forward from the others. In his hands he holds a paper boat. "Lady," he says, shyly approaching, "will you grant me a wish?"

"I'm not a goddess," I tell him, though I gentle my words with a smile.

He brushes the hair back from his face, revealing mischievous eyes. "Please, lady. Only you can make my wish come true."

I lift a brow, curious now. I take the boat and open it as Namgi leans over my shoulder to read the words the boy has scrawled across the paper. Namgi's guffaw of laughter startles a passing school of fish that breaks around us like shooting stars.

In the tumult, I motion the boy closer, leaning down to give him a kiss on the cheek.

He cups his hands reverently to his face; then, turning, he shouts to his friends, "Look! I got a kiss from the Sea God's bride!" The boys whoop and holler. One by one, they press their lips to the boy's cheek, as if to share my kiss between them.

Looking around, I notice that many people are staring at us, at *me*. One small girl even lifts her hand to point.

"Does this have anything to do with what Cheong said?" I ask Nari. "That there are rumors in the city that say the storms have stopped because of me?"

Nari nods. "The night of the storm, many of the city's people saw you rush up the steps and through the gate of the Sea God's palace. Less than an hour after you emerged, the winds and rain

241

died down and a rainbow appeared." Even Nari, who's always calm and collected, has a hint of wonder in her voice. "Never has a rainbow appeared after a storm. There are rumors that it was also seen in the world above, a bridge between worlds. The people are taking it as a sign that the storms have ended for good and that the myth has finally come true."

I try to make sense of her words. "And what of the Sea God?"

Namgi shakes his head. "The gate to the palace is closed. No one has seen him."

Was it a coincidence that the storm stopped after I left the palace? An hour later was around the time I was attacked by the assassin and the Red String of Fate was cut. Lord Crane said I would know if I were the Sea God's bride, as a Red String of Fate would form between the Sea God and myself. But just as it was when I woke, my hand is empty.

Cheers up ahead distract me from my thoughts. A crowd is gathered beneath a great tree. It grows out from the middle of the street, bright lanterns winking between the leaves of its massive canopy. From the largest branch of the tree dangles a swing. It's built of two ropes with a plank of wood for a seat. A girl around my age stands on the seat, bending her knees to bring the swing up into the air. The crowd gasps, clapping and whistling as the girl swings higher and higher.

Namgi, Nari, and I join the others, lending our voices to the shouts and cheers.

Back and forth, the girl rises as her momentum grows. Soon, she's reached a height where she's almost horizontal with the ground.

As she swings back down, she takes one hand off the rope and waves to the crowd. I cheer the loudest as the girl slows the swing, jumping off with a flourish and bow.

Afterward, the girl approaches. "Would you like to give it a try?"

"I don't know . . ."

"Don't worry. If you fall, one of your guards will catch you."

I look over my shoulder to see Namgi flirting with a boy in the crowd. But Nari, standing close by, nods in encouragement.

The girl drags me to the swing and helps me stand on the wooden plank. I curl my fists on each rope.

"Ready?" the girl asks.

"Should my knees be shaking?"

"Probably not. Here we go!" She runs, lifting me up, and I tighten my grip on the ropes.

"Bend your legs!" she shouts, letting go. "Move your body with the swing!"

I take several quick breaths, inhaling and exhaling. I've never been on a swing before, but I *have* played games at festivals, and this one is like all the rest—if you only trust yourself, it can be fun.

As the girl instructs, I bend my knees and move my body to the rhythm of the swing. Back and forth. The higher I rise, the more of the city I can see over the crowd. Children run down the many streets, trailing fish-shaped kites with golden streamers. Groups of individuals gather to play street games; others sit around storyteller stalls, listening raptly to the tales being unraveled. Strands of my braid come loose and flutter about my face. I close my eyes and feel the wind.

When I've finally exhausted the strength in my arms and legs, I slow the swing, bracing my body until it comes to a stop. The crowd cheers as I hop off the plank and help the next girl up.

As I move away, I'm caught by a sudden awareness. My heart catches in my chest. I turn toward the tree. Beneath its sweeping branches Shin waits. He's dressed simply in dark blue robes, his hair falling across his brow. He looks like a young man out to enjoy himself at a festival rather than the lord of a great house.

At my approach, he steps forward to meet me.

I take in the dark circles beneath his eyes, his lips red against the pallor of his skin. "You look awful—when was the last time you slept?" At the same time, he says, "You look beautiful."

He scowls. "Is that all you have to say to me?"

"I can say more. Where have you been all day? Why didn't you come to see me when I woke? Are you angry with me?"

Shin looks as if he'll respond, then seems to change his mind, glancing around us. We've attracted an audience. He looks meaningfully toward the canal, and I follow him to the edge, where he pays a boatman to lend us his small rowboat. Careful not to catch my dress, I take Shin's hand. His grip is steady, only letting go when I've settled onto the bench.

Shin drags the oars through the water in an easy, fluid motion until we've reached the middle of the canal. Pulling in the oars, he lets the boat drift. There are only a few other vessels out on the water, but they're closer to the shore. It's as if we're alone on the river. I listen to the croon of the water and the creak of the wood. A dozen floating lanterns surround us, glowing brightly.

"You asked where I've been all day," Shin says. "I was at the

Sea God's palace. I wanted to determine the truth for myself. The doors of the gate were barred. When I tried to climb over the wall, a force prevented me from entering. Whether the storms have ended"—his eyes move to the shore, where spirits gather to place paper lanterns on the water—"you can see for yourself that many believe so. We'll have to wait until next year to be certain."

I dip my hand in the water, letting droplets slip through my fingers like pearls. "What happens now?" I'm careful to keep my voice steady. "The Red String of Fate is broken. In a week's time, I'll have spent a month in the Spirit Realm." The implication of my words is clear; in one week, I'll become a spirit. I straighten, pressing my hands into my lap. "My main concern is Shim Cheong. Is there a way for her to return to the human realm?"

Shin watches me, though it's difficult to make out his expression. "What about you? Do you wish to return?"

My breath catches. "Can I?"

"The second question you asked was why I didn't come to you after you woke. The reason is because I had gone to Spirit House, to consult your ancestors."

"My ancestors?" I ask, not understanding. "What do you mean?"

"You can speak to your family members who've passed before you, at least those who've climbed from the river to remain in the Spirit Realm. Many spirits still receive ancestral rites from their children and grandchildren. If you were a spirit yourself, you would instinctively know this."

I've always wondered if the gifts of food and other offerings we leave beside the graves of our loved ones ever reach the Spirit Realm. I smile in wonder at the thought.

"Ancestors are invested in their descendants, and are often wise after many years of living in the Spirit Realm. I thought I could ask them for help. But as they're not my ancestors, I wasn't allowed to speak with them. On another day, I'll take you to them."

I'm struck with a rush of emotions, relief that my ancestors might know a way to return Shim Cheong to the world above, that I might even return. And uncertainty, because I have so little time left.

"And what of my last question?" I ask softly. "Are you angry with me? Because of what happened with the assassin?"

"No," he answers. "That wasn't your fault."

He lifts his hand to his chest, an unconscious movement. He did the same outside Moon House, when he first told me he was a god that had lost everything he was once sworn to protect.

"The truth is, I *was* angry. Earlier, not then. The story you told the Sea God, about the woodcutter and the heavenly maiden. In the end she returned home, to the place where she longed to be."

He takes a deep breath. "I know that all you ever wanted was to save your family. That's why you jumped into the sea. That's been the reason behind every decision you've made, however reckless, however brave."

His eyes find mine. "I *was* angry, but not at you. I was angry at the fate I'd been given. Because I realized that in order for you to have what you want, I'd have to lose the only thing I've ever wanted."

I can hardly breathe; my heart is in my throat.

Shin slips his hand into his robes at his chest and pulls out a silk purse. He unknots the drawstring, and the pebble carved with the lotus flower tumbles out.

"I'll return you home, Mina. I promise. But it might take longer than a week." He curls his hand around the pebble. "In order to remain a human, you'd have to tie your life to an immortal. I may not be the god of a river, a mountain, or a lake, but I am a god, and I would tie my life to yours, if you'll have me."

I'm overwhelmed with emotion. We no longer share a Red String of Fate, but he's willing to do this, for me.

"I—"

There's a sizzling burst of a sound, followed by a scream.

A dark cloud spreads over the city, and I look up to find a hundred shadows creeping over the moon.

The Imugi are here.

29

Shin and I run through the streets, spirits rushing to duck into buildings or leaping into the canal as Imugi rain fire down upon the city.

Up ahead, a bolt strikes a teashop, burning a hole through the tiered roof. Patrons barrel out of the smoking doorway, tripping over themselves in their panic and fear. I rush over and help a woman to her feet, while Shin carries a boy to the canal, dropping him in the shallow water to douse the flames on his jacket. More screams pierce the night, not too far from us. I watch as Shin tenses, his head instinctively canting toward the sound.

"Go," I tell him. I motion toward the remaining teashop patrons, huddling and coughing on the ground. "I'll help the rest of them, and then hurry to Lotus House. I know the way."

Down the street an Imugi roars, followed by more screams. "Lotus House," Shin repeats. "No more than an hour." I nod, and he holds my gaze for a searing second before running off in the direction of the screams.

I help the rest of the teahouse patrons to the canal, crowded now with spirits eager to escape the fires.

After the last is safe in the water, I sprint down the streets, retracing the steps I walked earlier with Namgi and Nari. Though this time, instead of joy, I feel only heartache as I pass over broken lanterns and crushed kites.

I'm almost at the bridge that leads to Lotus House when I hear an awful slithering sound. I dash into an alley and back against the wall just as an Imugi prowls by, failing to notice me in the shadows.

The alley I've stepped into is deserted, with only a small alcove down the way that appears to house a shrine. I recognize the familiar stone tablet and the bowl for offerings. Incense sticks trickle smoke into the air. Most likely it's dedicated to a local god, a place for spirits to gather and ask favors from the deity.

As I draw nearer, the strong scent of incense washes over me, smoky and bitter. Then I notice an object floating in the bowl of offerings. It's a paper boat, ripped in half and stitched back together again.

A chill runs down my spine. Slowly, I lift my eyes to read the characters scratched onto the stone.

This shrine is dedicated to the Goddess of Moon and Memory.

Soft laughter floats down the alley.

I turn to face the goddess.

She wears a simple white gown with a red sash around her waist. Even without her great mount, she's terrifying, twice my height with candles in her eyes. She lifts her chin slightly, eyes flickering. "Why don't you pick up your wish? Let us discover your deepest desire."

I swallow my fear. "The Imugi are your servants, aren't they? Why have you allowed them to wreak such devastation? Don't you think this city and its people have suffered enough?"

She continues as if I hadn't spoken. "Once I see your memory, it will belong to me. I will have that part of you that wishes to be the Sea God's bride."

The puzzle of her words falls into place, and I think I finally understand what she wants. I turn toward the bowl and pick up the boat. When I look back, I bite my tongue to keep from crying out. The goddess stands beside me, having moved silently from a distance. She's now close enough that I can see the candles in her eyes, the flames burning brightly. I unfold the paper boat and hold it out to her.

"Do you relinquish it willingly?"

During the storms, she told me that she couldn't see the memory because it was too closely tied to my soul. Only by relinquishing it will she have power over me.

"Will you call away the Imugi if I give you this memory?"

The goddess watches me carefully; the flames in her eyes hold steady. "Yes."

"Then I give it to you willingly."

She smiles, triumphant. "Then you are a fool. Because though you might have saved the city tonight, you have thrown away your chance to save it forever. The memory contained in this boat belongs to me now, and I will destroy it, along with your desire to be the Sea God's bride."

She grabs the paper, and the memory rises up, taking hold.

I'm in the garden behind my house, and with me is the goddess. Like the wish I'd found in the Pond of Paper Boats, the memory is clouded, as if seen through a veil of mist. The goddess appears out of place, standing regally beside my grandfather's pond.

As she stares at the scene before her, the goddess's look of anticipation turns slowly into one of confusion. I brace myself and follow her gaze.

A girl kneels beside a broken shrine. An old woman stands above her, her work-roughened hands trembling over the girl's lowered head.

I close my eyes. After all, I don't have to see this memory to remember it.

"Mina," my grandmother cries, "what have you done?"

All around me are the shattered remains of the shrine. The food, the little I'd sacrificed from my own meals and dedicated to the Goddess of Women and Children, smashed upon the floor. The worn rush mat, the one I knelt upon every day for hours, my forehead pressed against the earth, torn to pieces.

I look at my grandmother, wincing at the sharp pain of tears in my eyes. "Were my offerings too little for the goddess? My prayers too weak?

Perhaps I should forsake her altogether. A goddess who is forsaken will die the same as those she's forgotten."

My grandmother gasps in horror. "Be angry at the goddess, Mina. But never"—she grabs my trembling shoulders—"never lose your faith in her."

Behind us, there's a keening sound, followed by a crash. My grandmother picks up her skirt and flees, pulled by the agonized cries of my sister-in-law, driven mad with grief. Guilt overwhelms me. What is my pain compared to hers?

I reach out and slowly trail my fingers over the offerings laid out upon the shrine—the star-and-moon chime to bring luck and happiness, the bowls of rice and broth to bring health and a long life, and the paper boat to guide my niece safely home. Though every year at the paper boat festival I make the same wishes—a good harvest, health for my family and loved ones—this year I brought the boat home to place on the shrine because I wanted nothing between the goddess and my prayer.

Snatching the paper boat from the shrine, I tear it in half.

Like the boat, the goddess and I are ripped from the memory. Back in the alley, we stumble away from the shrine.

"You tricked me!" the goddess shouts. "That was not your wish to be the Sea God's bride!"

I should feel triumphant. She assumed wrong. She thought by stealing the memory of when I wished to be the Sea God's bride, she could steal that desire from me. But I never made a wish to be his bride, or even that I should be the one to save him.

The goddess and I can agree on one thing. It is true that a wish is a piece of your soul. Because a true wish is something that if it never came true, it might break your heart.

Even though it's quiet in the alley, I can hear the goddess's servants slithering above us.

"Your sister," the goddess says quietly. "She lost her child."

There's something odd about her voice. And then I realize what it is—she sounds mournful. Tears slip down her cheeks. The candles in her eyes have gone out.

"My sister by marriage, my eldest brother's wife. She lost a daughter."

The goddess backs away, a hand pressed to her chest. "I must go," she says. The wind picks up in the alley. The goddess's dress billows out. White and red feathers peel off from the fabric to swirl in a storm around her. The wind whips out, and I raise my hand against the rush of feathers and dust.

When the wind dies down, I'm alone once more.

Even with the retreat of the goddess, the Imugi still rage throughout the city. From my position in the alley, I can hear their screams, the tremor of large bodies moving through the streets. My heart aches every time a quieter cry haunts the night. There were so many children at the festival. I think of the boy asking shyly for a kiss, the girl joyous on the swing, the people of this city celebrating the ending of the storms. That must have been why the goddess attacked in the first place. But why did she leave? An image flashes through my mind of her face after she saw the memory, the dimmed flames of her candlelit eyes.

Was it pity I saw in her eyes?

No matter the reason, she left without calling away the Imugi, therefore breaking our bargain. This city that but a few days ago was flooded from the storm now burns with fire.

I think of the Sea God's nightmare, the burning city in his eyes. This city now mirrors that of his memory, smoke billowing up to choke the clouds. When does it end?

Above, a figure leaps across the rooftops, his shadow falling over me.

Kirin.

I sprint down the alley to where it opens up onto a wide street. A large sea snake thrashes down the length of it, knocking against buildings that crumble upon impact.

Kirin gathers speed and jumps off the edge of a roof. In one quick motion, he unsheathes his sword and plunges the blade into the snake's neck. The beast lets out a terrible scream. Kirin leaps out of the way as the snake's body begins to writhe in its death throes, spewing blood and venom. I duck behind a stand of barrels as blood splatters across the wall, burning quickly through the wood.

Kirin drops to the ground beside me. "Mina! What are you doing here? Are you all right?"

"I'm fine. I was on my way to meet Shin at Lotus House."

"We'll go together." He turns north, only to stop, his eyes narrowing. "Is that—"

I follow his gaze. Namgi in his Imugi form dips erratically through the sky. Following on his tail is a whole swarm of snakes.

"That fool!" Kirin shouts. "He's luring them out of the city. But he won't make it that way." Kirin races off in Namgi's direction, and I hurry to follow. We're almost by the river when Namgi goes under, disappearing beneath the swarm. There's a terrible crack, and the swarm breaks apart. Namgi, transformed back into his human body, drops from the sky.

"Namgi!" Kirin cries out. We race down the street, turning the corner to see Namgi battered and broken on the ground. Kirin rushes forward, dropping beside Namgi's limp form. He takes a knife from his waist, raising the blade to his palm. But before he can make the cut, Namgi's hand jerks upward, grabbing his wrist.

"Don't, Kirin," he says, blood thick in his throat. "My wounds can't be healed so easily. Not this time."

He's not wrong, but that doesn't stop Kirin from growling in frustration. "Why do you have to be so reckless?" he shouts. "I thought you desired more than anything to become a dragon. Did you forget? An Imugi can only become a dragon after *living* one thousand years."

Namgi coughs. Even with blood slipping from between his teeth, he smiles. "That's right. One thousand years. I couldn't believe those fools who thought they could become dragons by fighting in endless battles. Don't they understand what a dragon truly *is*? The Imugi live for death and destruction, but a dragon is the manifestation of peace." Namgi coughs again, and this time it takes longer for the tremors to subside. Kirin grabs his hand and Namgi looks up at him with young, fearful eyes. "I wanted—I wanted to be a dragon, Kirin. More than anything. I wanted to be wise and good. I wanted to be whole."

Kirin's grip tightens. "You are, Namgi."

Before our eyes, Namgi's body begins to fade.

I look desperately from Namgi to Kirin. "What's happening?"

"He's losing his soul," Kirin chokes. "Hurry, we need to get him to the river. Help me, Mina."

Together we manage to get Namgi onto Kirin's back. I take the lead, checking around corners to see if there are any snakes in our path.

Around and above us, the battle rages on. I catch sight of the death god Shiki jumping from rooftop to rooftop, leading a band of warriors with bows slung low across their backs. I look for Shin in the group, disappointed not to find him among their number.

We reach the river. Unlike the night of the storm, it's calm. Few bodies float on the surface. Kirin and I gently lift Namgi from Kirin's back and lay him by the shore.

"Look for Namgi," Kirin says, unbuttoning his jacket. "He should be coming down the river."

The thought terrifies me. Only the recently deceased float down the River of Souls. Is Namgi . . . dead? He's lying so still. A curl of hair falls over his pale face. Without his vibrant soul to light him up, he looks empty . . .

"Mina!" Kirin shouts.

I snap my head from Namgi's body to the river. I need to concentrate. He isn't gone. Not yet.

At first all I see are strangers, older men and women, ghostly shadows in the water. But then . . .

"There!" I point to a familiar lanky body. Namgi floats face-down on the surface. I look over to Kirin to find him approaching the river.

"Kirin," I say, suddenly realizing what he plans to do, "Shin said only the dead can enter the river. The current will sweep your soul away."

"I'm not going into the river."

Kirin steps to the very edge, the water lapping at his feet. His body begins to tremble, and his skin emits a beautiful silver light. The human shape of him morphs, changing. There's a burst of illumination, like a star exploding. A beast of myth emerges from the light, its hooves clopping on the stone. Where once Kirin stood, there now stands a magnificent four-legged beast with two horns and a mane of white fire. It has the shape, body, and legs of a deer, but the height and strength of a horse.

"Kirin?" I whisper, and the beast gazes at me with silver eyes. It tosses its head back, jabbing its hooves in the air. It then leaps from the bank onto the water. The beast doesn't sink but walks on the surface. With every step of its hooves, radiant light pulses outward, trailing incandescence.

Kirin reaches Namgi's body in the river, nudging his shoulder with his nose. When Namgi opens his eyes, I sigh with relief. With Kirin's prodding, Namgi grabs on to Kirin's neck and pulls himself onto the beast's broad back. Slowly, so as not to let Namgi fall, Kirin begins heading back to shore.

A loud screech draws my gaze to the sky. A sea snake circles in the air above the river, eyeing Kirin and Namgi. If it attacks, it will be disastrous. Even if Kirin can fight in his beast form, he can't risk dropping Namgi.

With one hand, I grab my great-great-grandmother's knife, and my skirt with the other. Turning, I sprint from the river, back toward the city. When I hear the scream in the air, I know the sea snake has spotted me. I pump my legs, moving as fast as I can.

I know what I'm doing is reckless. Namgi and Kirin would never ask me to risk my life for theirs. But I can't help it. It's true that people do the most desperate things for those they love. Some might even call it a sacrifice—maybe that's what people believed when I jumped into the sea in place of Shim Cheong. But I think it might be the other way around. I think it would be a terrible sacrifice to do nothing.

And never was it for anyone's sake but my own. I couldn't endure in a world where I did nothing, where I let those I love suffer and be hurt. If I had stayed home, if I had never run after Joon, if I had never jumped into the sea, there would have been such a hole in my heart—the emptiness of having done nothing at all.

Still, as I look at the snakes chasing me, the snakes in front of me, blocking my way, I wish the circumstances weren't always so dire.

I've reached the main boulevard outside the Sea God's palace. The wide-open space is overrun with sea snakes slithering down every alley and climbing over the many rooftops. I'm surrounded. My chest pounds with the pressure from my lungs. My shoulder aches from the wound left by the assassin.

The sea snakes converge upon me, large and terrifying. I brandish my knife with two hands. I can see the faces of people watching me from the buildings. Earlier, a boy had called me the Sea God's bride and asked me for a kiss. I won't disappoint him now. After all, I am a Sea God's bride. Maybe not *the* Sea God's bride, but a girl who wished, in a world far distant from this one, for a different fate from the one I'd been given, one I could grasp on to and never let go.

A tremendous roar shakes the city.

I look up.

The dragon crashes down from the sky.

The dragon is massive, three times the size of the largest snake. It sweeps its long tail through the street, hurtling Imugi against buildings. As a pack, the Imugi attempt to close in on the dragon, but it lashes out, thrashing and flailing. A freezing wind picks up. Shards of ice like glass whip out from the air, piercing the thick hides of the snakes. One by one, the snakes fall to the ground, transforming into men. The rest take to the air, screaming their defeat.

The dragon, terrible and bloody, lets out another roar. It twists its head wildly in search of a new enemy.

I take a step back, only to trip on the steps of the Sea God's palace. The dragon catches the movement. Unlike on the boat, when my anger gave me courage, my fear overwhelms me. The dragon prowls across the distance between us, all four of its curved claws digging great holes in the broken ground.

"Mina!"

Shin stands on the roof of the nearest building. He leaps off, rolls on the ground, then sprints toward me. Reaching me, he pulls me into his arms. He smells of sweat, blood, and salt. I hold him close and draw strength from his heartbeats.

He releases me, placing his body between the dragon and me. "I won't let you hurt her."

I catch my breath, reminded of Joon and Cheong on the boat.

The dragon lowers its head, baring row upon row of deadly fangs. Shin unsheathes his sword, his hand opening to reposition itself, grasping the hilt strongly. His shoulders tense, ready to strike.

A new voice interrupts. "My soul would never hurt my bride."

The Sea God stands on the steps of the palace.

He's dressed in full ceremonial robes. The gilded seal upon his chest depicts the dragon as it appears now, powerful and ferocious. The god himself looks pale, but undeniably awake.

Then the rumors are true. The Sea God woke because of that night, when I held him in my arms as his sorrow rained down upon both worlds.

My hands begin to shake, and I hide them in my skirts.

"I have served you well, my lord," Shin says, lowering his sword. "I have guarded your home. I have guarded your person—"

"And you have guarded my bride."

"—but I cannot serve you in this."

The Sea God's eyes flash in anger. "You would stand against me? I am a god!"

"As am I," Shin says fiercely.

Behind him the dragon takes a menacing step. My hand closes in a fist, and I wince in pain. I forgot I was holding my great-great-grandmother's knife. Blood trickles down my hand over the scar on my palm, so long hidden beneath the Red String of Fate. I made it when I swiped this same blade against my skin and pledged my life to the Sea God.

260

"Mina?" It takes me a moment to realize the Sea God is calling me.

Even though he appears grand in his magnificent robes, the palace behind him, the dragon before him, his eyes are as they were in the hall—full of a heartbreaking grief.

"Will you come with me now?" he asks softly. In the vastness of the boulevard, his voice is hardly a whisper. "Will you be my bride? I've done what you asked. I've ended the storms. I've taken my rightful place among the gods and my people. I've— I've woken."

He falters for a moment but then lifts his face. "I am the Sea God. And you are my bride. Come with me now, as you said you would. As you promised."

I look to Shin, and to the dragon, looming behind him. If I refuse the Sea God, will the dragon strike in anger? Silently it watches me, waiting.

"Mina," Shin says, a hint of panic in his voice. "You don't have to do this."

"You said it yourself, Shin," I whisper. "You know why I came here. It was always to protect my family." I look behind Shin and the dragon, to the city. The lanterns from the festival, which once shone so brightly, are now ripped and shredded. The people peek out from the wreckage of the buildings, watching me with wide eyes and soot-streaked faces. "I have to do this. Don't you see? I think . . . I think I *am* the Sea God's bride."

"Mina," Shin says, his voice hoarse. "Please don't."

"I'm sorry." I turn just as the tears start to fall, rush up the steps of the palace, and take the hand the Sea God holds out to me. He leads me up the stairs and across the threshold of the gate. The wind rises as the dragon lifts its great body into the air, gliding over the gate above our heads. My thoughts feel cloudy. My heart beats hollowly in my chest.

At the last moment, I look back.

Shin stands outside the gates of the Sea God's palace, his head lowered. He doesn't look up, even as the doors shut between us.

30

I follow the Sea God through the courtyard and into the hall. An eerie silence hangs over the palace, no evidence of guards or nobles or even servants. Reaching the dais, the Sea God hesitates before forgoing the cold throne and sitting on the steps. I join him, pulling my feet beneath my skirt.

The silence drags on. I study the boy-god, who appears ill-suited for his grand robes. He sits hunched over, his elbows balanced on his knees. I realize—I don't know his name. Immediately I feel guilty for having never asked. "What should I call you? What is your name?"

"You may call me Husband."

I blanch. "We are not . . . married, are we?"

"There must be a wedding first."

I sigh with relief.

"As for your second question, I don't have a name. Perhaps . . . you can give me one."

"What about . . ." I look past his shoulder to the mural of the dragon. "Yong?"

The Sea God grimaces. "If you must . . ."

He looks so appalled, I can't help but smile a little. "I won't call you a name that displeases you. For now, Sea God will do. I venture no one else in two worlds has a name like that."

"I do have a name. I just . . . I can't remember it. There are so many things I can't remember."

He peers down at his hands, and I'm reminded of what drew me to the Sea God in the first place. What must it be like, to be so alone? When I first saw him, I thought that I could protect him.

"When I sleep," he says softly, "I have the strangest dreams. There's a city of crimson and gold and a cliff and a dazzling light. And then there's pain, unbearable pain. But it's not in my bones—it's in my soul." He lifts his pale hands to his neck, as if the words in his throat hurt him. "And in all of my dreams, I'm drowning."

I move closer to him. He leans forward and places his head on my knees. "Mina," he whispers, "will you tell me one of your tales?"

I shouldn't be surprised. For the Sea God, stories are both an escape from the truths of the world and the only way to see them clearly.

My hand hovers above the Sea God and then comes down gently upon his soft hair. I lightly brush back the strands that have fallen across his forehead.

Joon's favorite stories were always the ones I seemed to pluck like a leaf from the air to best fit our moods, whether we wanted to laugh or cry, stories about love, about hate, about hope and despair—all the truths we needed to hear.

I would close my eyes, let my mind wander, and tell him—tell *us*—a story from the heart.

"In a village by the sea," I begin, "there lived a blind man named Shim Bongsa. He had nothing of material value, but he was content and happy, for he had his daughter, Shim Cheong, who he loved more than anything in the world. More than the warmth of a summer breeze, more than the sweet taste of honey in a cup of tea, more than the song of the sea as it kisses the shore. He was blind, but he saw the world, because the world to him was Shim Cheong.

"Now, in this village by the sea, there was a great storm. Many crops and livestock were swept away with the tide. The village elders gathered together and determined that the reason for the storm was because of the Sea God, who they say lived somewhere deep down in the great depths of the sea. In order to appease him, they decided to make a sacrifice.

"The previous day, Shim Bongsa had fallen into a ditch on his way home, and had broken his leg. Because of this, he could no longer work in the fields. Shim Cheong, hearing about the sacrifice the elders were preparing, volunteered. She would jump into the sea, if the village would provide rice for her father in her absence. The villagers quickly agreed, for Shim Cheong was kind and beautiful, a worthy sacrifice for a god.

"On the day of the sacrifice, she kissed her father on the cheek, and when she told him she loved him, she kept her voice steady so he wouldn't know that she was leaving him forever, and that she was afraid. The boatmen rowed Shim Cheong out to sea, and with one last prayer that her father live a long and prosperous life, she jumped.

"She went down, down into the dark depths. After a while, she didn't know whether she was dead or alive. Finally, her feet touched the bottom of the sea. Before her stood a magnificent palace. Coral formed the walls, and sea ivy grew up its grand towers. She stepped through the palace doors into a hall, catching sight of the Sea God sitting on a golden throne.

"He was a great sea dragon with a whiskered mouth and eyes so large and dark she felt they must hold all the wisdom of the world. Colorful fish of red, gold, and white floated all around him. Although fearful, Shim Cheong approached the throne, coming to stand before the Sea God with her chin held high.

"Shim Cheong would have been right in believing the Sea God was wise, for he could see all things. Looking into her heart, he said, 'Your love for your father is beautiful and good. Because of your sacrifice, I will honor you above all others.' He summoned dolphins to come and wrap Shim Cheong in a gown woven of the flowers of the sea, and he sent her back up to the surface inside a beautiful lotus blossom, which bloomed in the court of the emperor. The emperor, upon seeing Shim Cheong, fell in love with her, and she with him. And shortly afterward, they were married.

"Meanwhile, Shim Bongsa roamed the countryside, searching for his daughter. Even though the villagers offered to take care of him, he declined, for as you can imagine, he was bereft. To him, he had lost the world.

"He heard of a great feast the emperor was hosting for all the blind men, women, and children of the kingdom, in honor of his new bride. Shim Bongsa made his way to the capital. He entered the palace, drawn by the sounds of laughter and music. A hush fell across the hall, and the old man was curious as to what was happening. He heard the approach of light steps. The crowd gasped when the empress leaned down to embrace the old man.

"'I have found you,' Shim Cheong said to her father. 'You are home.'

"And Shim Bongsa, hearing the voice of his beloved daughter, wept tears of joy."

As I finish the story, a spell of sleep falls over me.

I wake to a strange tugging at my wrist. I look down only to sit up abruptly. *The Red String of Fate.*

Shin. I scramble to my feet. The ribbon leads me out the hall into the courtyard, where a figure stands alone, looking up at the starless sky. The Red String of Fate falters in the windless air. At the end of it is . . .

The Sea God.

31

Though the Sea God has claimed me as his bride, questions still plague me for the next few days as I wander the lonely halls of the palace. Lord Crane said that once the Red String of Fate formed between the Sea God and myself, I would know it was time to break the curse. Was he lying, or was there never a curse to begin with? A year seems too long a time to wait to see if the storms have stopped for good. And something within me feels restless, as if I'm peering at a scroll that remains unfinished.

I also worry for Namgi, wondering if Kirin pulled him from the river in time. Has Dai fully recovered? And Cheong. There must be a way to return her to the world above.

I thought Lotus House very large, but the entire grounds of that house could fit into one quadrant of the Sea God's palace. It takes me days to explore the eastern quadrant, where my room is located overlooking the garden. I never see anyone—no servants or guards—and yet the rooms are all swept clean, and the fires in their braziers blaze down every hall. I can't tell if the invisible beings that run the palace are ghostly servants or something else entirely. At all times of the day, the tables in the kitchen are laid with food, the dumplings steaming as if just cooked, the fruits and vegetables dewy as if picked and washed only a moment before. Elaborate dresses appear in my wardrobe overnight. And if I need anything, I only have to speak the words aloud for the object of my desire to appear—a warm bath or slippers for my feet.

On the morning of my thirtieth day in the Spirit Realm, I find the Sea God in the garden, where he spends most of his time, watching paper boats in the pond. Not for the first time, I peer at the pond to see if the paper boat carrying my wish floats between the reeds, but it's nowhere in sight. I wonder if the Goddess of Moon and Memory realizes that she owes me a debt. After all, though I relinquished my wish freely to her, she never fulfilled her part of the bargain.

"I have a request to make of you," I say, as I sit beside the Sea God on the grassy bank. "My sister, Cheong, came down during the last storm. I'd like to visit her to see how she's faring, but also speak with our ancestors, to discover if there's a way for her to return to the world above."

"In the last story you told, it was the Sea God who returned Shim Cheong to the world above. I'm afraid I don't have such power. Otherwise I would send her back, to be reunited with her father."

"And me? If I asked, would you return me to the world above?"

He says nothing, hunched over by the pond with his back to me. "I grant you permission to leave the palace. But you must return before sundown, at which time we *will* be wed. Otherwise you'll become a spirit and lose your soul."

I leave the pond, walking at first slowly through the garden, then faster, and faster still, until I'm running, up through the secret door, down the Sea God's hall, and across the many courtyards. The great doors to the gate—which had been shut upon my entering the palace—are open. I slip through, sprinting down the stairs and heading toward the river. To the south lies Lotus House, and though I long to go there, I know if I do, I might never leave.

The river is calm, peaceful. Still, I keep my eyes away from the water as I cross over the bridge.

Star House is a tiered temple located at the base of the eastern mountains. I arrive at the height of morning, the sun shining brightly over a meadow run wild with royal azaleas.

Black-robed servants greet me in the main courtyard of the mountain temple, men and women with their heads cleanly shaven. One woman bows to me, indicating for me to follow her. She leads me down halls cut deep into the side of the mountain and up a long flight of stairs. The air becomes thinner the higher we go, and we emerge onto a platform that overlooks the valley from high above. Cheong and another young woman are seated on woven mats, a small table laid with tea and fruits in delicate porcelain bowls between them.

The young woman turns at our approach. She's lovely, with a wide face, blushing cheeks, and bright eyes.

Hyeri.

She tilts her head to the side, studying me. "I know you."

"We've met once before," I say. "A year ago, the night you were to marry the Sea God."

"I remember now." She rises to her feet, coming to take my hands. Like Cheong, she's a head taller than me. Her voice is warm and inviting. "You were my handmaiden. You helped me dress and braided my hair. You listened on a night when I needed, more than anything else, for someone to hear me." She gently tugs me to the square table, pulling up a mat at the north side. "Come, please join us."

When I've seated myself, Hyeri pours me a cup of steaming tea. I bring it to my nose, inhaling the subtle scent of crushed chrysanthemums.

"I'm glad you're here, Mina," Cheong says shyly. I reach out and take her hand, squeezing tightly.

"You seem well, Cheong," I say, grateful to Hyeri. "I came here today not only to visit you, but also because I think there might be a way to return you to the world above."

Cheong widens her eyes. "Is it possible?"

"I have reason to believe it could be." I turn toward Hyeri. "What do you know of Spirit House?"

Hyeri sits back on her cushion, a thoughtful expression on

her face. "Out of all the houses, it is the largest. It lies at the bottom of the city, where the river begins. Spirits that manage to swim out of the river are brought to the house first, and then sent along, either to the home of their ancestors who are already living in the city, or to a guild master to seek employment. As it is, the best way to find your ancestors is to go to the house and present yourself to meet them." Hyeri turns to Cheong. "Have you relatives? Those who've passed before you?"

"I only have my father, and he is living still."

Hyeri sighs. "Well, not everything can work out perfectly."

I smile, amused at this strange perception of things.

"I was thinking," I say. "Perhaps my ancestors would help. After all, they are Cheong's ancestors, too. By marrying Joon, she's become a part of our family."

Hyeri sits forward excitedly. "That's right. Mina, you can go to Spirit House and arrange to meet with them. Ancestors are wise and have lived many years. Any knowledge they might share with you will be useful."

I nod, then turn to Cheong. "Since I don't know which of our ancestors will be at Spirit House, I think it best if I go alone. I'll speak with them, and then come get you."

"Thank you for this, Mina," Cheong says warmly. "Although . . ." Her smile falters. "What about you? If I'm to return to the world above, I mustn't go alone. You have to come with me. Your brothers are waiting for you, and your grandmother . . ."

My heart aches painfully at the thought of my family, our family. What I would give to see them all one last time. "I can't.

If I refuse to marry the Sea God and instead return to the world above, it's possible the storms will start again."

"Will you really marry him?" Cheong frowns. "But what about . . ." She never finishes her sentence, perhaps seeing the stricken look upon my face.

Hyeri and Cheong exchange a glance.

"I do find it odd," Hyeri says. "Everyone says the curse is broken, and yet the Sea God remains in his palace. Nothing has truly changed, besides the ending of the storms."

Hyeri is right, and it's also something I noticed in my time in the palace. Just as he was before he awoke, the Sea God is melancholic, preferring to be alone.

"Why was the Sea God cursed in the first place?" Hyeri continues, her questions stirring up something inside me. "And if he was cursed, who was the one who cursed him?"

There's a light knocking sound, and all three of us turn toward the entrance of the balcony where Shiki—god of death and Hyeri's husband—stands, dressed all in black like the first time I saw him.

Bowing, he says, "I apologize for the interruption—I know you'd wish to speak longer—but three visitors have arrived to see Lady Mina."

My heart stumbles in my chest.

I say my farewells to Cheong and Hyeri, and follow Shiki through the temple's halls, coming out to stand on the stairs that overlook the valley.

Three figures stand among the wild azaleas. Namgi. Kirin.

And Shin.

I approach the three of them across the field of pink and purple flowers.

"Mina, the Sea God's bride," Namgi calls softly.

A rush of relief envelops me. Last I saw him, Kirin was dragging his nearly lost soul from the river. "Just Mina," I say as Namgi reaches me, pulling me into a fierce embrace. I bask in his warmth. When his soul fled his body, he was so cold.

"Well, Just Mina," he says after releasing me, "how does it feel to be the chosen bride of the Sea God? Do you think at all of us, your not-so-illustrious friends?"

"It feels no different than before." I glance at Shin. He's held back from the rest. He doesn't look at me now, though I felt his eyes upon me as I walked through the field of azaleas.

"You look well," Kirin says, drawing my gaze. "Your clothing is very fine."

I peer down at myself. I'm wearing a simple pink-and-green dress, one of the many from my wardrobe. "Thank you," I say, blushing. "How is Dai?"

"He and the rest of your spirit friends left the house this morning after I deemed him fully recovered. Unlike Namgi, who is still too weak to be moving about."

Namgi grins. "I'm fine. Nothing could stop me from seeing Mina."

"You should be more careful," Kirin insists. "Not long ago, you were soulless."

"Not anymore, thanks to you!" Namgi attacks Kirin in a hug.

274

They go off into the flowers, arguing like they did when I first met them in the Sea God's hall—though I can see now how much they love and care for each other, their bickering turning soon to laughter.

I face Shin, my heart beating painfully in my chest. When I first met him, I thought his eyes did more to hide his thoughts than his mask did to hide his face. No longer.

He looks at me with such longing it breaks my heart.

"What are you doing here?" I ask softly.

"I said I would take you to your ancestors."

I almost fall apart then. Shin—tall, not very frightening, and honorable, who never goes back on his word, who always keeps his promises, even when he's hurting.

I swallow. "Then let's go together."

Spirit House is just as Hyeri described it, a gigantic building—shaped somewhat like a bathhouse—beside the River of Souls. It's at least five stories high and built in a square design. I can see the shapes of beings through the papered windows, feasting and dancing.

Shin leads us through the grand doors into the main room of the building, bypassing what looks like a huge line of very wet people.

Namgi leans down to whisper in my ear, "Recent arrivals."

The room is magnificent, a large enclosed courtyard, ranged on all sides with balconies on every level.

A portly man with round eyes and a mustache hurries to greet Shin. "Oh great and powerful lord of Lotus House—"

Kirin interrupts. "We need to arrange an ancestral meeting."

The man blinks rapidly. "Yes, of course!" He snaps his fingers, and a small, hunched grandmother hobbles over. She wears a mask depicting a youthful girl. Slowly, she hands the man a rolled-up scroll.

The man clears his throat. "Family name?"

"Song," I say.

"Village of origin."

"Beside-the-Sea."

"Are you the Songs of the Lower Mountains, the Farmlands, or the Riverside?"

"Lower Mountains." I grimace. We don't speak to the Songs of the Farmlands after their grandfather had a falling-out with my grandfather over a game of Go.

"Ah, here we are." The man's finger lands on the paper. "It looks like . . . both your great-great-grandmother and your grandfather are registered as Song ancestors in the city."

I can't breathe. Tears rush to my eyes. *Grandfather. My great-great-grandmother.*

"They are?" I whisper, overwhelmed. I turn to Shin. "They're here. I'm going to see them." I didn't know how much I needed to see them until this very moment.

"I'm glad for you, Mina," Shin says softly.

The grandmother coughs behind her mask. I turn from Shin and the others to follow her. We travel up five flights of stairs and down a hall with closed doors. She stops at the third door on the left and slides open the panel.

"Wait in here," she says.

I walk into the room, and she closes the door behind me. The room is small with low shelves filled with items, some of which I recognize from the ancestral rites my grandmother and I would conduct every year. There's the food we left out for my grandfather on his birthday the month before last. It hasn't spoiled. The bean rice and dried-pollock soup—his favorites— still steam from their bowls. Although I notice the amount in the bowls is less. There are the bright fruits my grandmother left for my grandfather, his favorites, and for *her* grandmother, the bouquet of fresh flowers picked from the garden—golden flowers and deep red hibiscus, as bright as the day we picked them.

My gaze falls on a cradle tucked in the corner of the room.

I suck in a harsh breath. It's the boat Joon carved, the one he labored over for weeks.

We were so excited when Sung, five years Joon's elder, told us he and Soojin were going to have a baby. Joon and I went out into the mountains so that I could make a prayer to the guardian of the forest while he cut down his favorite tree, the one he'd planted when he was only a boy himself. Out of the heart of the tree, he fashioned a cradle for the baby. He carved beautiful images into the wood of the bed—a crane in flight to guide the baby through her dreams, a rising tiger at the head to protect her from nightmares—and every night I stood over the unfinished bed and said a prayer to the Goddess of Women and Children, giving a kiss to the wood where the baby would one day rest her head.

When she was born, she took one breath and no more. We burned the bed outside in the garden, so that it might cradle her in another world.

I trace my fingers across the stripes of the tiger and the scratched feathers of the crane's wings.

Behind me, the door slides open, and my ancestors enter the room.

32

First, Mask steps through, then Dai with Miki, and even though I'm a little surprised, I'm not at all, because of course they're my family—they've been helping me this whole time.

Dai grins. "You cry too much, Mina."

Mask walks over, her elegant hands moving behind her head to untie the strings holding her mask in place. It falls to the floor. I look into Mask's face, and it's my own face looking back at me, except my face on her is far more beautiful. Or maybe that's just the love I feel for her reflecting back at me. She takes me into her arms.

I choke back a sob. "You're my great-great-grandmother, aren't you?" I can feel her nod against my shoulder. "When I was dying, you sang to me. I thought it was my voice, but it was yours."

"I sang to you, but it was your will to live that brought you back."

I turn to Dai. "And you . . . you're my grandfather."

Dai smiles.

"And Miki . . ." And now I'm sobbing. I can hardly get the words out. "Miki is my eldest brother's daughter." The little girl who never smiled that beautiful smile in my world but was given a second chance at life in another. Miki giggles from behind Dai's shoulder.

"Joon made a cradle for her," I say weakly.

"Yes," Dai says. "It was the boat that carried her. She would have fallen into the River of Souls if it weren't for that cradle. Something crafted with so much love could never sink."

Mask takes my hand. "Ask us what you need to know, Mina. We couldn't tell you before—spirits are forbidden to directly affect the actions of their descendants—but we can tell you now, in this most sacred of places."

I nod, brushing back tears. "I need to know how to return Shim Cheong to the world above."

Mask and Dai exchange a glance. "It's never been done," Mask says slowly. "But that doesn't mean it *can't* be done."

"What about going back up the river?" Dai says. "Shim Cheong is whole of body and soul. If she made it all the way up the river, perhaps she could pop back into the world above."

Mask shakes her head. "The current is too strong. And her body wouldn't survive the passage."

Seeing the expression on her face makes me wonder if I look like this when I'm thinking hard about something. I resist the urge to reach out and smooth the crease between her brows.

"In times of great peril," Mask says, "a wish can be made on the dragon's pearl."

I feel a strange stirring in my heart. "A wish?"

"That's right!" Dai shouts excitedly. "Now I remember. The pearl of a dragon is the source of its great power, and a wish upon one can make even the impossible come true."

I think back to all the times I've seen the dragon—on the boat and in the garden, as it flew through the sky, and ferocious outside the palace.

"I've never seen the dragon with a pearl," I say. Then I remember the mural on the wall of the Sea God's hall. In the painting the dragon was drawn chasing a pearl through the sky.

"It's possible the dragon lost its pearl," Mask says, "which might be tied to the curse."

"Or it was stolen," Dai says grimly.

In the Sea God's nightmare, he was wounded. Perhaps that was the moment the pearl was stolen.

"So if I retrieve the pearl and return it to the Sea God, the dragon will grant my wish?"

Dai and Mask exchange a glance.

"If it were so simple," Dai says, "most everyone would be looking for a chance to make a wish."

"Only someone the dragon loves very much can make a wish on the pearl," Mask explains.

"Someone the dragon . . . loves?"

Mask nods. "The dragon and the Sea God are one and the same. The dragon is the Sea God's soul. If the Sea God were to love another, that person would have the power to make a wish on the pearl. In the past, it was always the emperor who was beloved by the Sea God most of all. In times of great peril, it was said he could make a wish to change the world."

In the main room, I meet up with Namgi, Kirin, and Shin, and tell them what I learned from my ancestors. Kirin and Shin look unsurprised to find out the real identities of the spirits who've been helping me, but Namgi appears satisfyingly shocked.

"You must make apologies to your great-great-grandmother for me, Mina," he says sheepishly. "Tell her I didn't mean half the things I said."

"Namgi, aren't most of the spirits here ancestors to someone or another? Every spirit you flirt with could be a grandparent."

He groans. "Don't remind me."

With the knowledge from my ancestors, I know how to save Shim Cheong. Yet what seems simple is not at all, because however much I think the Sea God might honor me, he does not love me.

And Hyeri's questions about the curse have reminded me how I first felt when I entered the Sea God's palace, like I was missing the last part of a tale, the ending just beyond reach.

I flinch as a strange ache shivers through my heart. Out of the corner of my eye, I see the Red String of Fate pull taut in the air.

"Mina?" Shin steps forward. "What's wrong?"

The Red String of Fate gives another powerful tug, and I

groan. "It's the . . . it's the Red String of Fate . . ." Shin goes completely still. "Something's wrong."

There's another tug, and I collapse.

Shin catches me and lowers me to the floor.

"She's becoming a spirit." I can hear Kirin's voice above me. "It's been exactly a month since she entered the Spirit Realm."

I fight against the awful tugging pain; it feels as if my soul is being torn from my body.

"What do we do?" Namgi asks. "How can we help her?"

Kirin looks at Shin, who meets his gaze. "She needs to return to the Sea God."

Shin doesn't hesitate. In one fluid motion, he lifts me up off the floor, and I wrap my arms around his neck. With inhuman speed, he rushes from Spirit House, sprinting down streets and leaping across rooftops.

The pain lessens the closer we get to the palace. By the time we reach the courtyard outside the Sea God's hall, I'm strong enough to stand. Shin sets me down on the ground.

"Wait for me in the garden," I tell him before rushing into the Sea God's hall.

Like the first night, when the Red String of Fate led me to him, the Sea God is slumped upon the throne with his eyes closed.

Behind him, the setting sun paints the mural of the dragon in colors of orange and yellow, the pearl in burnished gold.

"Mina?" The Sea God's eyes flutter open.

I move to his side, and he looks up at me.

He's nothing like the Sea God in the last tale I told. That god was almighty and powerful. After all, in the end, he let Shim Cheong go home.

Looking at the Sea God now, I wonder, how can a god be so fragile? So human?

The pain from before has dulled to a low ache. Close as we are, the length of the ribbon is short, merely an arm's length. I close the distance, pressing my hand to his. His hand is cool and soft, while mine is warm and rough. Nothing startling happens. I'm not pulled into any dreams; there's no burst of light. When I move away, the Red String of Fate has disappeared.

"Mina." The Sea God sits up. "What happened? What did you do?"

"I am not your bride," I say gently. "Not truly. You don't love me, nor I you. We are fated, but not in this way."

I wonder if the Sea God will protest. His brows knit together and a look of genuine concern falls across his delicate features. "But you'll die, Mina. You'll become a spirit."

"Not if I can help it." I smile to reassure him. "You have to be strong, for just a little longer. Can you do that for me?"

"I— Yes. I think I can."

I turn from him and race out the door behind the throne, down the stone steps, and through the garden. The pain is gone, yet I know soon I'll become a spirit. And although I am afraid, hope rises within me.

I want to tell Shin everything—that I'm sorry for leaving him, that I felt at the time it was the only choice I could make. But I was wrong. There is always a choice.

I want to tell Shin that I choose him, always him.

I sprint through the garden, leaping over the stream and through the trees winking with the orange glow of sunset. I sweep past the meadow, across the bridge, coming out on the hill overlooking the pavilion where Shin stands.

Don't chase fate, Mina. Let fate chase you.

33

Shin is waiting inside the pavilion beside the Pond of Paper Boats. He turns at my approach up the steps, his eyes finding mine.

"Did you speak with the Sea God?" he asks softly, looking at me in that way that always makes it hard for me to breathe.

"Yes," I answer. "And I know what I must do."

Shin's gaze lingers on my hand, then shifts away toward the pond, but not before I see the look of acute pain that crosses his features. Tonight, the paper boats crowd the shore like a flock of ducks. It's as if at any moment they'll spread their wings and take flight.

"I won't ask anything of you," Shin says. "Whatever decision you make, I will abide by. If you marry the Sea God, I will protect and watch over you both. For all my life."

My heart fills with love for him. How good he is, how giving and kind.

"But I didn't want to hold back when it mattered . . . because I know you would never hold back, with your words or your actions." He smiles, and my heart flips over. "I may be soulless and haven't a Red String of Fate, but I don't need either to tell me that I love you."

"Shin," I say, breathless, "the Red String of Fate is gone."

He shakes his head. "I don't understand."

"The one between the Sea God and myself," I explain. "I pressed my hand to his, which, if you remember, I did with you when our fate first formed, though you insisted it wouldn't work.

"Well, it did," I say haughtily. "As I knew it would, because I don't love him. I love you, and I choose my own fate."

I lean forward, holding his shoulders for balance, and press a kiss to his lips.

Afterward, I take a step back, blushing, though determined to meet his gaze. He said, after all, that I don't hold back. Shin recovers quickly. Reaching out, he takes my hand, pulling me forward until I'm in his arms, and then he's kissing me. His heart beats fast against my own. I throw my arms around his neck, returning each of his kisses with equal fervor.

When finally we break apart, the love I see in his eyes steals my breath away.

"Lord Crane was mistaken," he says. "He said once the Red String of Fate was formed, you would know how to break the curse."

As I gaze at Shin, a knowing blooms within me.

"I don't think he was mistaken."

Shin frowns slightly. "What do you mean?"

"There's something I must do, somewhere I must go. Will you wait here? Do you trust me?"

He doesn't answer me at first, watching me with his sea-dark eyes. Then he smiles, a small quirk of the lips. "With my soul."

I run back through the garden, the hall, and the courtyards— the Sea God nowhere in sight—and down the great steps. My heart beats wildly in my chest. I feel as if all the answers to my questions are within reach.

I turn into the alley where I last saw the Goddess of Moon and Memory, her shrine tucked into the alcove. The bowl in front of the tablet is empty of offerings, so I place my great-great-grandmother's knife at the center. I then pick up the flint and strike it against the firestone, creating a spark that I catch with a piece of paper, bringing it up to light the incense sticks.

I step back and whisper a prayer. When I open my eyes, the Goddess of Moon and Memory is beside me.

She watches me through her candlelit eyes, though tonight, they appear dimmed. "Are you not afraid of me?" she asks, sounding more curious than angry.

"I am not," I say, and it's the truth.

"Are you afraid of nothing, then?"

"I'm afraid of forests."

She arches a brow, clearly thinking me facetious.

"When I was a child, I got lost in a forest," I explain. "I had been following my older brother when I caught sight of a fox and, chasing after it, lost my way. For the longest time, I couldn't remember how I got out of that forest. All I could remember was how fearful I was, the trees unfamiliar in the darkness."

The goddess closes her eyes, and I wonder if she's reliving this memory with me.

"I sat crying among the roots of a tree for hours. I was so afraid that no one would find me, that I would be alone in the darkness forever. But then I saw it—a light through the canopy. Moonlight slipped through the branches to light a path through the forest. It was the moonlight that led me home."

The goddess opens her eyes to watch me, the candles in them bright now.

"My grandmother always said that although the sun brings warmth and light, the symbol of our great emperor, it is the moon that guards women and the night. She is the mother that protects us all."

I take a steady breath. "We made a bargain, you and I. I shared a piece of my soul with you. It's only fair that you give me something in return."

"And what would that be?"

"A memory. Show me what happened a hundred years ago on a cliff by the sea. Show me what happened to make the Sea God lose all hope. Show me what happened to the emperor of my people."

The goddess pulls from her sleeve a very old paper boat, crumbling at the edges. It looks like a gust of wind could blow it apart. She holds it out to me.

I lift my hand and touch its papered wings.

I'm back on the cliffside of the Sea God's dream. But where then he was at the edge of the cliff, now he's nowhere in sight.

It's peaceful here. The wind sharp, but clear. The sun over-head shines down on the sparkling sea, where fishing boats are out on the early-morning waters.

I'm stepping closer to the edge, thinking to make out the faces on the boats, when the earth begins to shake beneath me, rocks tumbling from the cliff into the sea. A battalion of warriors on horseback approaches up the hill. At the head of the group—atop a magnificent warhorse—is the Sea God.

Yet, something's amiss. His golden armor is splattered with dirt and streaks of blood.

One man brings his horse alongside the Sea God's. He wears a chest plate with a seal depicting a rising tiger, denoting his rank as the general of the emperor's armies.

"Your Majesty!" the man shouts. "You must flee before it's too late."

The Sea God lifts the helmet off his head. The expression I'm familiar with—where he looks lost, hurt—is gone. He looks . . . fierce, like a leader. With a gaze steadied on the general, he drops his helmet to the ground. "I will not abandon my men. I will stay and fight."

"Your Majesty," the general growls, "you must live. You are more than one person. You are the hope of our people!"

The Sea God looks as if he will argue further, but then he curses. Abruptly he turns his horse.

But he's too late. The small group of men has lingered too long in the open. A greater enemy rides up the cliff, trapping the warriors against the edge.

The battle that ensues is bloody, terrible. The men form a

circle around the Sea God, but one by one, they fall. Soon it's only the boy and his general.

Realizing that defeat is upon them, the general raps his sword against the flank of the Sea God's horse. It screams, then gallops away from the battle.

Hope swells in my stomach, quickly plummeting when I see an enemy soldier rise from where he was hiding behind a large stone. He nocks an arrow to his bow, drawing the string back.

He releases the arrow. It flies curved through the air.

"Watch out!" I scream, but of course no one hears me. No one can see me. This is just a memory, of a time long ago.

The arrow pierces the Sea God's chest.

He slides from the horse, landing inches away from the edge of the cliff. The enemy falls back. They've accomplished what they set out to do. It's inevitable. A wound such as this is fatal.

I rush to the Sea God's side, hands hovering in the air above him. Even if I were to reach out, I wouldn't be able to touch him. We are separated by a hundred years. The arrowhead protrudes from his back, soaked in his blood. He's dying. The Sea God looks at me, and for a moment, it's as if he sees me. But then he turns his face away, his eyes searching. "Who are you?" he whispers.

I look up. On the other side of him crouches . . .

"Sh-Shin?" I say. "What are you doing here?"

He doesn't answer. Like the Sea God, he cannot see me.

The Sea God coughs, blood between his teeth. He looks young. Too young to die. "Why won't you answer me?" he cries. "Who are you?"

"Don't speak," Shin says, and his voice is quiet, soothing. "You've been shot through the lungs."

"Am I dying?"

"Yes."

The Sea God closes his eyes, a terrible sadness cloaking his features.

Shin watches the boy, and I watch him. He looks different in this memory. He wears long blue robes, similar to the one he wore at the festival. His hair is longer, held in a topknot. Softly, he murmurs, "You are afraid."

The boy opens his eyes, a furious, fierce expression taking over his features. But then he groans, the pain rising. His eyes cloud over. "I'm less afraid of dying than I am of leaving them all alone."

His words remind me of the nightmare. He said, *I've failed them. I've failed them all.*

Suddenly, the boy grabs Shin's sleeve. "My people. Who will look after them when I am gone? Who will make sure they are safe?" His words are desperate, his lips bubbling over with blood.

"I will."

"You . . ." The boy seems to deflate. "I know who you are. My father told me about you. He said you protect our people, that if I were ever in desperate need, you would help me. Will you help me now?"

There's a sound like stars sweeping through the sky. I look up to see the dragon above us, a massive pearl held in its left claw.

It's the dragon like I've never seen it before. Its scales are a vibrant, dazzling blue. Its whiskers are long, white. It even moves more freely through the air—buoyant, joyous. The dragon drops the pearl, and it explodes into light, re-forming as a magnificent pair of silver-blue wings, protruding from the back of Shin's shoulders.

The emperor looks at Shin, a look of pure wonder on his face. "Who are you?"

"I am the Sea God."

On a dragon's pearl, your wish will leap.

"Make a wish."

"I wish to live."

34

Back in the alley, the boat crumbles into dust, drifting from my hand in swirls.

"It is done," the goddess says. "By now, the Sea God and the emperor will have regained their memories, of who they were, of who they are, as well as the people caught in the power of the wish."

I can still feel the memory on my skin, the salt-kissed air, the sweep of the dragon through the sky, the Sea God. Shin. They are one and the same. In order to save the emperor's life, Shin gave the emperor his soul, the dragon. Now I understand how I could share a Red String of Fate with both the emperor and Shin, as for a hundred years, their soul was one.

"How did you know?" the goddess asks. "The memory only confirmed what you already suspected."

How did I know? I think of all the pieces I've gathered up until now—Shin, who lost his soul and his memories with it; the Sea God, who seemed less like a god and more like a boy caught in a terrible nightmare. But mostly I knew . . .

"Because I am the Sea God's bride, and Shin is the one I love."

After a pause, the goddess sighs. "Well, I can admit defeat when bested. But regardless of who bears the soul of the dragon, he can be overthrown. Hurry back to your Sea God, little bride. Let him know to expect a visit soon from the Goddess of Moon and Memory."

I study the goddess. Her face is flushed, her eyes bright with triumph. Yet, when I asked to see the memory, she'd already had it with her, waiting to be given. Somewhere in her heart, she had wanted me to see the memory. She had wanted me to discover the truth.

"If it's power you desire," I say, "then there's a better way to have it than battling the Sea God."

She arches a brow, her expression disbelieving. "And what way is that?"

"There is no goddess more beloved than the one who protects children." I think of the young mother who made the wish beside the stream, and the many before and after her who misplaced their hope in an indifferent goddess. "Yet I've met the Goddess of Women and Children . . . and I've never met a goddess more unsuitable for such an honored role."

"Are you saying that *I* should become the Goddess of Women and Children?"

"It would surely give you the power that you seek. For if it is true, and gods gain power through the love of their people, then you will have much, for the love given to and received from children is the most powerful love in the world."

The goddess watches me with a guarded expression. "But why do you think I would be suited for such a role?"

I think of my grandmother, who, after my parents and my grandfather passed on to the next life, raised my brothers and me on her own. I think of Mask, my fierce great-great-grandmother, who protected and guided me throughout my time in the Sea God's realm. I think of the goddess standing before me, who protected Dai from the Imugi, who shed tears for my sister-in-law and her child, who sent the moonlight to guide me home.

"Because, like the women in my family, you have the wisdom of a crane, the heart of a tiger, and the goodness and love that only a goddess who treasures children can have. It's a heavy burden to be a goddess so beloved, but I believe you of all can bear it."

The goddess quirks a brow, a subtle movement, but it's there. "Your belief is strong. You make it difficult to deny your words."

"I'll make it easy for you," I say, already turning to leave, shouting over my shoulder. "Just believe in it, too!"

It's quiet in the city, the atmosphere similar to how it was the first time I entered the Spirit Realm, but without the fog. Magic hangs thickly in the air. It's as if the city and all its wondrous inhabitants are holding their collective breath. I wipe the back of my arm against my eyes, dislodging the tears gathered there. They started when I left the goddess and haven't stopped since. But I have to stop them now. I need to be strong, stronger than I've ever been before.

I follow no Red String of Fate. The path I take is the one I know.

I know this city, and I know its many streets—its gardens, its canals, its alleys, its people. The main boulevard leading to the Sea God's palace is empty. The gates are flung wide. For the last time, I climb the steps and walk through the doors.

I run into Namgi and Kirin in the first courtyard.

"Mina!" Namgi races up to me, grabbing me in a strong embrace. I hug him back just as fiercely.

"You're here!" I shout. "I was so afraid I wouldn't see you before—"

"Mina, something extraordinary happened!" Namgi says. He leans back, and I get a good look at his face. There's joy there, and wonder. "We know *everything*, about the emperor, about the Sea God. *Shin* is the Sea God! Can you believe it?"

"Where is he?" I ask.

"In the hall. We arrived right before you."

Kirin approaches from behind Namgi, his always astute eyes watching me carefully. "What were you saying, Mina? That you wouldn't see us before . . . ?"

I release Namgi, stepping back. "We might have regained our memories, but the effects of the emperor's wish are still upon us. For a hundred years my people have suffered from the storms—this is true. But also, because of the absence of the emperor, our country has been embroiled in constant wars. In order to have lasting peace, we need both the emperor and the Sea God returned to us, and there's only one way that can happen."

297

Kirin catches on quickly. "You have to make a wish."

"But . . ." Namgi glances between us. "A wish like that is just as powerful as the emperor's. Anything could happen. Should you make a wish to send the Sea God and the emperor back to where they belong, it's possible that not only Shim Cheong, but *you* will also be sent back, as neither of you have become spirits yet."

"It's the only way," I say softly. "Namgi, you once asked if I was a bird or a bride. I think I am both and more. Though to you, I'd like to believe I am a friend."

"The very best," Namgi says, choking back tears.

"And, Kirin." I turn to the silver-eyed warrior, so steady and loyal. "I don't have faith in anyone as much as I do you when it comes to Shin's safety and well-being. You are the most trustworthy of companions."

"You honor me," Kirin says quietly.

Before I break down entirely, I turn from them, fleeing through the next set of doors. In the courtyard before the Sea God's hall, I find the dragon. It fills the entirety of the large space, its restless body beating against the walls. At the sight of me, the dragon goes still.

I step forward, locking gazes with the great beast. Its sea-dark eyes seem familiar to me, and I'm enveloped in a feeling of safety and warmth. Stepping between its feet, I pass beneath its massive jaw. The heat of the dragon's breath warms the top of my head.

Once past, I turn back, and hold out my hand. The dragon lifts one of its claws and places the pearl gently into my palm. It's the size of a pebble. Curling my hand around it, I hurry up the short steps into the Sea God's hall.

"Shin!"

He's slumped on the floor halfway down the hall. I rush forward and fall to my knees beside him.

"You know the truth now," he says, "of who I am, of what I've done. I am the Sea God. I am the one who takes and never gives." His voice is filled with a bitter agony.

My heart aches for him. For a hundred years, his people have suffered, the people he was sworn to protect. For Shin—stalwart, loyal, devoted—it must feel like the greatest betrayal of his soul.

"No," I say firmly. "You're the one who saved the emperor. You gave your soul to him when he was dying, the soul of a god. You knew only that amount of power could save him."

"I remember," he whispers, turning to me. "On a cliff by the sea, he made a wish to live." He gazes at me with such vulnerability and wonder, and I realize, as much faith as I have in him, he has in me. "What happens now, Mina?"

I lift my hand between us, opening it slowly to reveal the pearl inside. "I make a wish, and restore you and the emperor to your rightful places."

"And you?" he asks quietly. "In the story of the woodcutter and the heavenly maiden, she was sent back to the place where she longed to be, to her family. Is that what you want?"

My heart is breaking. Because his words call to a longing inside me. I want to see my family, my grandmother and brothers, to know they're all right, to give a proper farewell. I want to work alongside the villagers in sowing new life into the fields, in building homes that last. I want to see the trees grow tall. I want to see my sister-in-law give birth to a healthy child. But just as much as I want all these things, I want Shin all the more.

I love him.

"A year," I say. "Come to me in a year and ask me the same question."

Shin's gaze returns to me, and I see in his eyes all the words that he can't say—that he loves me, that he wants me to stay, but that he's just gotten back his soul, and he needs to discover who he is as the Sea God, for himself.

"Wait for me," he says, "where the land meets the sea."

The pearl begins to glow in my palm, warm to the touch. Shin covers my hand with his, gripping tight.

"I wish for the world to be as it should be," I whisper, "the emperor restored to his rightful place, and Shin to be as he once was, the Sea God and protector of our people."

The last thing I hear is Shin's voice, calling out to me.

I love you. Wait for me, where the land meets the sea.

35

I wake to sunlight in my eyes. I'm lying at the edge of the pond in my family's garden, with Shim Cheong beside me. Everything appears as it was a month ago. The earthenware pots line the back of the garden, packed with soybeans fermenting for the winter. The nesting ducks squawk from the reeds. Across the garden is my home, with its thatched roof and wooden walls.

The back door slides open.

"Mina!" My grandmother races across the lawn, Joon close behind her. I scramble to my feet in time to catch her as she throws her arms around me. "Oh, Mina, my love, my beloved granddaughter."

I hold her close, my tears flowing freely. Beside us, Joon gathers Cheong to him, kissing her soundly.

From around the house run Sung and Soojin. My grandmother lets go of me, and I'm caught up in my eldest brother's embrace. Then Soojin gently hugs me, smelling like hibiscus and the pears she must have peeled only minutes before. And then I'm in Joon's arms, and maybe it's all the memories of when he used to comfort me when I was little, when I scraped my knee, when the other village children teased me for my uncouth ways, but I start to cry great hiccuping sobs.

I'm just so *relieved* that they're safe.

Later, I'll tell them what happened in the Spirit Realm, how I jumped into the sea, and how I woke to a world of fog and magic.

I'll tell my grandmother that I met *her* grandmother, who called herself Mask and hid her face from me, because she knew if I looked upon her, I would know who she was. And I'll tell all of them about Grandfather, how he protects Miki, barely letting her out of his sight. I'll describe to Soojin and Sung how happy Miki is, and how she has Sung's joyful personality and Soojin's wits and beauty.

I'll tell them of Namgi, Kirin, and Nari, Shiki, and Hyeri . . .

And of Shin. How tall, not very frightening, and honorable he is. How he saved me over and over again, as himself, and as the dragon. And how much I love him.

But right now, I say none of these things.

After a while, we break apart, only for Cheong to gasp, "Mina, look!"

Blossoming pink and gold across the pond, like great stars fallen to earth, are a thousand lotus flowers in full bloom.

I thought the changes would come gradually, but in the weeks following my return, the effects of my wish echo across the land.

In places where the storms uprooted trees, saplings sprout overnight. Farther inland, where the droughts dried up the streams and rivers, water appears to fill the empty channels, soon teeming with fish and fowl. And even more wondrous, rumors sprinkle from the war-torn north that any weapon raised with the intent to harm crumbles into dust.

And then there are the small miracles. Neighbors working side by side to restore the land, planting crops and sharing time and labor. Small children in my village assisting the elderly to rest beneath the shade of the great pine trees as they play by the sparkling brook. Every week, I lead a band of women into the forest to dig for roots and gather berries and herbs. Sometimes we're so long in the forest that night falls, but we're never afraid, for always a path of moonlight appears to lead us back home.

Yet the most extraordinary miracle I only hear about a month after my return. A royal messenger arrives from the capital. Standing atop a barrel by the village well, he delivers a message that is more like a remarkable tale than a proclamation: The emperor who vanished a hundred years ago has appeared by magic on the steps of the palace, having not aged a day.

"Where has he been all this time?" the village elder asks, voicing all our surprise.

"He has no memories of where he was," the messenger replies. "But many believe he was in the Spirit Realm, protected for a hundred years by the Sea God himself!"

The villagers gasp, their eyes naturally turning to Cheong and myself, where we stand at the back of the crowd. I wonder what it must be like for the emperor, to have woken from an enchanted sleep after a hundred years, remembering nothing of the time he spent as the Sea God. For someone who loved stories so much, he now plays a part in one of the greatest of all.

"He's won back his palace with the help of the great-grandsons of his former followers," the messenger continues, "and is working to restore peace and order to the land as we speak."

A cheer goes up at this wondrous news.

After the messenger's proclamation, many villagers approach Cheong to thank her for her great deed, and she glances at me with a look of resignation. I shrug, smiling at her.

We noticed it a few days after our return, that most of the villagers believed it was Shim Cheong who ended the curse upon the Sea God, as she was the last bride to be sent down—and the only one, besides me, to have returned. At first horrified, she tried to correct the many well-wishers, but I told her that I didn't mind. And I don't mind, truly. After all, in the last story I told the Sea God, Shim Cheong *was* the Sea God's bride.

Seasons pass, and come spring, Sung and Soojin welcome a child into the world. Her great-grandmother names her Mirae, in honor of her bright future.

As spring blends into summer, I start to make the walk down to the beach. My family notices and, guessing the reason, makes preparations for my departure. My grandmother and sisters sew me a beautiful dress with fabric procured from their own gowns, both to honor me and to remember them by. My brothers fashion me a dagger—Joon carves a magpie into the hilt—to join my great-great-grandmother's knife.

Exactly one year after I arrived back in the world above, I'm waiting on the beach, my family surrounding me, when the sun sets and the moon rises. Shin doesn't appear. The next day we return to the beach, and then the next, and the next, until it's only me who waits every day by the sea as summer turns to fall.

First confusion clouds my thoughts, then doubt that he ever loved me, then understanding. Because if the emperor lost his memory when his soul was returned to him, then likely Shin did as well.

Fall turns to winter, and the following spring the same messenger comes back, surprising us all by declaring that the emperor has plans to travel to our small village in order to celebrate the anniversary of his miraculous return. A festival to honor the Sea God is to take place, first in the village and then on the cliffs by the sea, and the villagers rejoice.

Soon caravans arrive from the capital, bringing with them noblemen and court ladies whose servants pitch elaborate tents in the fields, exciting the children and setting the elders to grumbling.

For weeks, the whole village prepares for the emperor's arrival, stringing up lanterns in the eaves of the buildings in the village square and between the branches of the trees that line the pathway up to the cliffs.

Cooking fires blaze far into the night, and the loud banging of iron against wood can be heard from sunup to sundown as roofs are repaired and new buildings constructed to accommodate the hundreds of merchants and craftsmen who flock to our village in hopes of enticing the nobles.

The seaside temple dedicated to the Sea God is restored to its former glory, and an artisan is commissioned by the village to paint a mural of the dragon on the wall, surrounded by ninety-eight lotus flowers, to honor every bride sacrificed to save our people.

The hard work makes me wistful for the magic of the Spirit Realm, but it's also a welcome distraction from when my thoughts turn heavy, the longing I feel like a splinter in my heart.

The morning before the festival day, there's a loud commotion outside our home. Cheong and I look up from where we sit by the hearth, picking the tails off bean sprouts.

"What's that?" Cheong says.

I listen carefully. "Circus performers?"

"Maybe it's the eldest Kim son again," Cheong teases. "He is quite determined to claim your favor."

I fling a bean sprout in her direction. "I'm only eighteen. I won't get married for another ten years, at the least!"

The door slides open, and Joon rushes in. We watch as he leans against the doorway, panting. He opens his mouth, closes it. Opens it again. No words come out.

"Joon, my love," Cheong says patiently. "Who has come to visit, making all that ruckus? Are those drums I hear?"

"The emperor," Joon says, breathless. "The emperor has come."

Cheong stands abruptly, eyes widening. "To the village?"

"*To our home!* He's right outside the gate."

Time seems to slow. Cheong's and Joon's excited voices become incoherent murmurs. Cheong rushes to tell my grandmother and

Soojin, while Joon runs into the garden to get Sung. I look down to see the bean sprout I've been holding is now crushed in the palm of my hand.

We gather in the small courtyard of our house. Sung and Soojin holding Mirae at the head, then Joon and Cheong, then my grandmother, and, lastly, me.

Our servant, an elderly woman we hired after Mirae was born, opens the doors. The emperor strides through our small wooden gate. I try to see the Sea God in him, that scared, sorrowful boy, but he's no longer there. This man with his straight back and proud stance is like the young man from the memory, the one who faced death on a desolate cliffside and made a wish to live. He sweeps his gaze over us. His eyes meet mine, and I immediately lower my head.

I hear Sung approach him. "Your Majesty. You honor us with your presence."

When the emperor doesn't speak, Sung says tentatively, "May I offer you some refreshment?"

"No," the emperor says, and even his voice sounds different, deeper and more commanding. "Please introduce me to your family."

Sung hesitates for only a moment. "This is my wife, and my daughter."

I can hear the tread of their boots. "My brother and his wife, Shim Cheong. You might have heard—"

The emperor must make a sign of impatience because they move down the line. "My grandmother," Sung says.

They stop before me. "And my sister."

I look down at the emperor's shoes.

"What is your name?"

I swallow thickly. Why is he here? He should have no memories of me. I am a stranger to him. His hand takes my chin and lifts my face.

"Your Majesty," I say. "My name is Mina. I am the daughter of the Song family."

"Mina," the emperor says, in that deep, unfamiliar voice. "Will you walk with me? Perhaps, in your garden?"

I look to my family, who all stare at me with wide eyes. "Of course, Your Majesty."

We head into the garden, his back to me. He's different from my Sea God. He has broader shoulders and a warrior's height. He wears a sword at his side, and his hair is longer. A strange longing for my Sea God builds inside me. I realize—he no longer exists. The thought brings me to tears.

The emperor turns. He's silent as he watches me cry. I expect to see confusion, or perhaps disgust, on his features. But he looks . . . almost relieved, as if my tears prove to him a doubt in his mind.

"Mina, I apologize for coming to you like this. I realize this must be very . . . unexpected. I just—I needed to see you. The truth is . . ." I can see the apple in his throat moving. He's nervous. "The truth is that I dream of you."

I blink. "You . . . what?"

"I have nightmares. A memory of . . . of loneliness. Of a terrible helplessness against an overwhelming fate. The only constant is you. You're in all my dreams. Showing me the way out of the darkness."

The emperor takes my hand and lifts it to his mouth. His lips are warm against my skin. His eyes, when they find mine, are like the Sea God's. Like my Sea God, that lost boy, who until this moment, I didn't know I missed so powerfully. "Will you marry me, Mina? Will you be my bride?"

Later in the evening, Joon and I walk through the garden. In the past year, we haven't had much time to spend together, just the two of us. Joon has a family now, with Shim Cheong, and her father, and someday children, if they're so blessed. And although I will always be in his heart, he must think of them first. As he should.

Joon sighs. "I can't believe the emperor is here. In our *house*. And that he wants to *marry* you."

"It is . . . quite unbelievable," I say.

He nudges me with his shoulder. "And you told him, 'Let me have the night to consider.' My sister, telling the emperor of our country that she will *consider* his proposal."

Joon chuckles, adding beneath his breath, "I will admit, though. I feel bad for the eldest Kim boy."

We head to the pond, leisurely walking around the border. We're both quiet, lost in our thoughts. The ducks swim lazily in circles. When a cloud passes over the moon, I yawn. "Let's go inside."

"Wait," Joon says, calling me back. There's a troubled expression on his face.

"Don't worry," I say. "I won't make any rash decisions. I will either choose to marry the emperor, or I won't. Nothing or no one can force me."

He shakes his head. "No, it's not that . . ." He looks at the ducks on the pond. "I guess most brothers would be happy to have an empress for a sister. And I am happy for you. Or at least, I would be if . . ." He turns from the pond to look at me, his eyes searching.

"What are you saying, Joon?"

"This past year, ever since . . ."

I look away, and he doesn't finish the sentence.

"You try to hide it," he says softly, "but it's as if you're drifting away from us. Mina, I just . . . I want you to be happy. Will he make you happy?"

"You make me happy. The ducks in the pond make me happy. The clear skies, the calm sea, the lasting peace. All of this makes me happy."

"If you're happy, then why are you crying?"

I press my hands to my eyes, and they come away wet. "I don't know. I cry a lot, I think. I have weak eyes."

My brother wraps his arms around me. "Or a strong heart."

I bury my face against his shoulder, the tears endless, the pain unbearable.

Late at night, I make my way to the beach. There are dark clouds over the water. A storm far out at sea. In the past year, there have been numerous storms, each as harmless as the last. They bring rainfall for the crops and keep our rivers and streambeds filled. And the gods are thanked and loved by the people, the Sea God most of all.

Wait for me, he said, *where the land meets the sea.*

But I have waited for you, every day for a year, and you haven't come. What am I to do? How can I go on, waiting like this, when I know you will never come?

We are separated by distance, by *worlds*. By memory.

"Shin." His name is a prayer, a plea.

I turn from the sea and retrace the steps back home, where I lie on my pallet with tears in my eyes, only to wake hours later to the clanking of drums and the whistling of a bamboo flute. The Sea God's festival has begun.

36

In the morning, the children rush to the village stream, placing their boats upon the water. Then comes a full day of festival games, music, food, and laughter. Cheong and I stop to watch a talented performer sing the story of "The Sea God's Bride" to a rapt audience, accompanied by a skilled drummer. I'm surprised to find that the story she tells shares many similarities to the one I told the Sea God in the hall, which makes me wonder how much of storytelling is embedded in the land and its people, a consciousness that we all believe in and share.

Cheong and I explore the merchant stalls, where she purchases a block of honey on a stick for Mirae and roasted chestnuts to split between us. After some time, however, I start to notice something peculiar. For once the people we pass on the streets, even the elegant and aloof nobles, seem to overlook Shim Cheong entirely. Instead, they all seem to be staring—quite openly—at *me*.

Cheong stops one of the village children. Immediately I recognize her as Nari's young cousin, Mari.

"What's going on?" she demands. "Why is everyone staring at Mina? Tell us quick!"

Mari grins conspiratorially, looking so much like her older cousin in that moment that my heart lurches. "They say the emperor asked for Mina's hand in marriage. Yesterday, when he paid a visit to your house. Well, is it true?"

"Even if it were true, it's not respectable to spread rumors. Here, buy yourself a treat." Cheong flips her a coin.

"It's not a rumor if it's the truth," Mari says cheekily, pocketing the coin, though she doesn't forget to bow to both of us before rushing off to join her friends.

Cheong watches me carefully. None of my family members have asked me what my response to the emperor's proposal will be, though Grandmother claims I would never accept such an unequal match: *He is but an emperor; Mina has been bound to a god.* And Soojin quietly says in her kind, unobtrusive way, *But wouldn't it be nice for Mina to have a family of her own? And maybe he might help her move on . . .*

In the late morning, the festivalgoers return to their homes to prepare for the ceremony that will culminate the festival, when the whole of the village, including the visiting nobles and the emperor, will make their slow way up to the cliffs that overlook the sea. There the emperor will pay obeisance to the Sea God, asking him to protect his land and people for another year.

I'm already wearing the dress my grandmother and sisters have sewn for me, the skirt a bright yellow and the jacket pink like the petals of a lotus. Strapping my last gift—my dagger—to my waist, I wander out to the garden to wait. In the shallow waters of the pond, little tadpoles linger over the pebbles.

When Joon and I were children, we used to catch tadpoles in the stream beside our house with a small wooden bucket. We would catch them and put our fingers in the water to feel their smooth, slippery bodies. We'd release them shortly after catching them. Joon—always gentle, always kind—never could keep them for long.

There's a soft tread of footsteps. My brother, coming to fetch me.

"Joon," I say, turning, "is it time . . . ?" I trail off.

Standing before me is the Goddess of Moon and Memory.

I gape. "What are you doing here?"

She's dressed in white robes and a loose red jacket, her hair in a simple knot at the nape of her neck. She watches me with her candlelit eyes that before used to fill me with such terror. Now I feel only a steady warmth.

"Shin came to see me," she says.

I jerk back. "Wh-what?"

"It's strange," the goddess continues, either unaware or unmerciful of my wildly beating heart. "He should have no memories of you, and yet, he walks his palace in silence. He finds happiness in nothing, and his soul weeps. He's worse than when the emperor was the Sea God. Nothing can console him."

My heart is breaking. "Why are you telling me this?"

"Because, as you suggested, I've taken on the role of the Goddess of Women and Children. Do you know what that means?"

I shake my head.

"It means that everyone who once feared me now loves me. Even Shin, my greatest enemy, *loves* me. He knows me now as a goddess of motherhood and children. He knows me as a goddess who is loving and kind and giving. Tell me, Mina, how could I be cruel to someone who loves me?"

"I don't know. Can you?"

"It's . . . strange. When I was feared, I hated everything and everyone. But now that I'm loved, I can't stand to see those who love me suffer one moment of pain. I blame you, Mina. You've turned me into a kindhearted goddess."

I look at her, my heart in my throat. "What did you do?"

"Have you forgotten? I may be the Goddess of Women and Children, but I am also the Goddess of Moon and *Memory*."

A gust of wind picks up the petals of the pear tree that have fallen on the ground. They begin to swirl around the goddess.

I stumble forward. "Wait!"

In a moment, she's gone.

"Mina?" Cheong comes out from the house, peering around the garden. "Are you all right? I heard voices."

"Cheong, I—"

Behind her, Sung and Soojin rush into the garden.

"Mina, Cheong!" he calls, breathless. "The emperor has already arrived at the top of the cliffs. We must hurry or we'll be late!"

Cheong looks as if she wishes to speak with me more, but Mirae, strapped to Soojin's back, begins to cry, and Cheong hurries over to soothe the child, presenting to her with a flourish the honey block she purchased at the market.

My family hurries to join the last group of villagers, Sung and Soojin with Mirae, Grandmother, Cheong and Joon, making their way up to the cliffs.

At first I keep up with them, but after a while my steps grow slow, my thoughts distracted by the breeze sweeping through the trees, and soon I'm alone on the path.

It's a familiar climb, one I used to make often when I was younger. I remember racing up to the top, breathless with both exertion and anticipation. There's a point where the path grows steep, and it's a bit of a struggle to take the last few steps, but it's worth it, because once I come up over the rise, it's there, waiting for me.

The sea. The water stretches out to the horizon, its beauty unparalleled, filling my heart with a joy that is boundless, that both grounds me to this moment and spirits me away, to a world far beyond this one, to the place where I long to be.

I'm so wrapped up in the spell of it that I almost miss the watchful faces of the people lining the path, nobles and villagers alike. They stand on either side of a grassy carpet, at the end of which waits the emperor.

I'm reminded of my first night in the Spirit Realm, when the Red String of Fate led me to the Sea God. And I realize, like then, I'm meant to walk down the path to him.

The villagers look at me curiously, the nobles with expressions of confusion. They must think the emperor has made a mistake, asking some girl from a backwater village by the sea to marry him.

In the last story I told the Sea God, what did Shim Cheong

think when she came up in the lotus blossom and married the emperor? She went from peasant girl to ruler of the land.

The truth is, she didn't jump into the sea to become an empress. She jumped into the sea because she loved her father. What else could she do? Nothing extraordinary is ever done out of reason or logic, but because it's the only way for your soul to breathe.

There are many pathways destiny can take. For instance, the path ahead of me leads to the emperor. I can take his hand, and I can become his bride. Or I can follow the path back to my village, to the place where the land meets the sea, where I know now my heart is waiting for me.

Which destiny belongs to me? Which destiny will I grasp on to with both hands and never, never let go?

The emperor must sense my indecision, because he takes a step forward.

Something large passes overhead, casting a great shadow over the cliff. The crowd erupts in screams and chaos, as everywhere courtiers and villagers scramble back, falling down in their haste.

The dragon drops from the sky, landing on the grass. Immediately it begins to glow with a radiant light, heavy wind gusting out from its body.

My braid comes loose, my hair whipping wildly around my face.

The glow from the dragon disperses. Where once was the dragon, now stands . . .

The Sea God.

He looks magnificent, in light blue robes with the emblem of the dragon stitched silver upon his chest. He looks every part the Sea God, the powerful dragon of the East Sea, just as he looks every part Lord Shin of Lotus House, who accepted a pebble for a soul.

"Mina," he says, in a voice filled with longing, hope, and love. "The Sea God's bride."

And I laugh, remembering the first time we met, how he called me the Sea God's bride even then.

"No, Sea God," a voice says from behind us. "She is my bride."

I turn to face the emperor of my people, noticing as I have before the changes in him—not just in his bearing and confidence, but the small changes of having been awake for two years after sleeping for a hundred. He's no longer a boy, but a young man. Though still, I notice how the sword trembles in his grasp. After all, to the emperor, the Sea God is not only a god, but the protector of his people. A tenderness rises up within me. He would protect me, even against the god whom he loves most in the world.

As for Shin, he really must remember me, because he steps aside, knowing the one to answer our emperor will be me.

"Your Majesty," I say, pressing my hand to his as I did that last night in the hall of the Sea God's palace, when the Red String of Fate dissolved between us, a fate neither of us had chosen. "Your dreams are real. They are the memories of the time we spent together in the Sea God's realm, where you were the Sea God, and there was no emperor. Do you remember?"

He lowers his sword. "I . . ." A look of wonder passes across his face. "I remember."

"If you remember anything, remember this. I saved you."

Tears begin to slip down his face. "I remember. I was lost, for a long time. You found me. I owe you my life, Mina. I owe you everything."

I shake my head. "You owe me nothing. Only perhaps, this moment. You don't need me anymore. It's time to let me go."

A pained expression falls across the emperor's features. I think, perhaps, there will always be a connection between us. Our stories have become inextricably entwined. And even though I belong to myself, I *want* him to choose this, too. Only then can his story truly begin.

He's silent for a moment, his gaze steady on me. Finally, he whispers, "Thank you."

It is enough.

"Years from now," he says quietly, "I will tell my grandchildren how, a long time ago, I was saved by a goddess."

"A goddess?" I laugh. "A girl, maybe."

Placing his hands on his stomach, the emperor of my people bows to me. Then he bows again, to the Sea God, and, with one last lingering look, walks down the great grassy carpet, toward his own destiny.

Turning, I rush into Shin's arms. My tears are flowing now. "This is less where the land meets the sea and more where the mountain meets the sky."

His arms tighten around me. "Wherever you are, I'll find you."

"I'll make it easy for you. Because I'll be right here. With you."

"That does make things easier." He laughs, his breath tickling my ear. Then softly he says, his voice hesitant, "Will you be content, being the bride of a god?" His question brings back the memories from two years ago, when he worried that I wouldn't be happy, separated from my family, living a strange and immortal life in the Sea God's realm.

I lean back to meet his gaze. "I take back what I said earlier." He frowns, his arms tensing around me. "We'll have to be apart sometimes. After all, I'll want to visit Hyeri and go on walks with Nari in the city. And it's not healthy for your other friendships if we're together all the time. What about Kirin and Namgi?" A thought occurs to me. "Did they lose their memories as well?"

"They didn't," Shin says, "but were afraid that telling me of you would reverse the effects of the wish."

"Thank goodness for the goddess, then. She's afraid of nothing!"

Shin wraps me in his arms, his heart beating fast. "Mina, I've missed you so much."

He pulls back only to lean forward for a kiss. There's a loud cough behind us.

I hunch my shoulders, turning to face my whole family, standing only a few feet away with huge smiles on their faces.

Joon is the first to approach, taking me into his arms. I close my eyes, trying to burn this memory into my mind, this feeling of being in his arms one last time.

"To think," he whispers, "this all began because you were chasing me. I will miss you, Mina, my favorite sister."

I scoff. "You only have one sister."

"Yes, and she is the bravest person I know."

Then, one by one, I say farewell to my family. Sung, Soojin, and Mirae. Grandmother. I hold her the longest. This will be the last time I see them, maybe forever. Even when they pass on, many years from now, they might go up the river into heaven. They might take the river into another life.

Shim Cheong is last. She sweeps me into her arms. "Mina," she says. "Thank you. Thank you for everything."

"No," I say. "The truth is, you're the one that I am most thankful for." She starts to protest, but I hold her close. "Your story has been told over and over again, by everyone but you. I might have jumped into the sea to save Joon, but it was your hesitation that gave me the courage. With everyone and everything pushing you toward the Sea God and a fate not of your choosing, you looked back to what you wanted. And because of that, to me, *you* are the Sea God's bride. The girl who, by saving herself, saves the world."

I hold Cheong for a moment longer, then step back.

"Mina." Shin waits, holding one hand out toward me.

I take it, and with a smile, I tell him, "Let's go home."

Acknowledgments

The Girl Who Fell Beneath the Sea is truly the book of my heart, and I am so grateful to everyone who has come along with me on this long and most rewarding of journeys. To my agent, Patricia Nelson, whose unwavering belief in Mina's story gave me the courage to see through the hard times and to truly appreciate the good times. To my editor, Emily Settle, never in my wildest dreams could I imagine a more perfect editor for *Girl* than you.

To my genius cover designer, Rich Deas, and wildly talented artist, Kuri Huang—thank you for creating the most beautiful cover an author could ask for.

To the team at Feiwel and Friends, especially Starr Baer, Dawn Ryan, Michelle Gengaro, and Kim Waymer: It's an absolute dream come true to work with all of you. And to the team at Hodder, thank you for welcoming my book with such warm enthusiasm.

I finished the first draft of *The Girl Who Fell Beneath the Sea* while attending Lesley University's MFA program, and an unforgettable moment for me was reading aloud the first chapter at graduation with all my mentors, family, and friends in the audience. Thank you to the incredible faculty at Lesley, particularly Susan Goodman, Tracey Baptiste, Michelle Knudsen, Jason Reynolds, and David Elliott, as well as my extraordinarily talented and hilarious cohort: Stephanie Willing, Devon Van Essen, Candice Iloh, Michelle Calero, and Gaby Brabazon.

To the readers who gave feedback early on, I am forever grateful: Cynthia Mun, Ellen Oh, Nafiza Azad, Amanda Foody, Amanda Haas, and Ashley Burdin. This book would not be what it is today if not for you. To my critique partners: Janella Angeles, Alex Castellanos, Maddy Colis, Mara Fitzgerald, Christine Lynn Herman, Erin Rose Kim, Claribel Ortega, Katy Rose Pool, Akshaya Raman, Meg RK, Tara Sim, and Melody Simpson. I'm in awe of all your talent and so honored to be a part of this group of writers! And to my dear friends: Karuna Riazi, David Slayton, Michelle Thinh Santiago, Veeda Bybee, Sonja Swanson, Lauren Rha, and Ashley and Michelle Kim—your support has meant the world to me.

The Girl Who Fell Beneath the Sea is about a lot of things, but to me, it's first and foremost about family. To mine: the AZ Chos, Como Helen, Uncle Doosang, Adam, Sara, Wyatt, Alexander, Saqi, Noah, Ellie, and Zak; the FL Chos, Como Katie, Uncle Dave, Katherine, Jennifer, Jim, and Lucy; the DePopes, Como Sara, Uncle Warren, Christine, Kevin, and Scott; the Goldsteins, Como Mary, Uncle Barry, Bryan, and Josh; Heegum Samchon and 외숙모; Heemong Samchon, Aunt Haewon, Wusung, Bosung, Minnie, Josiah, and Ellie; Heesung Samchon, 외숙모, Boosung, Susie, and Sandy; Emo, Emo Boo, Chuljoong Oppa, Nahyun, Bokyung Eonni, and Seojun. And to Toro, the best boy! I love you all so much.

To my brother, Jason. There's a reason Mina's story began with her chasing after her brother. Because he was her whole world. I love you, and I miss you.

To my paternal grandparents, 오창열 and 오금환, and my maternal grandparents, 김중업 and 김병례—thank you for showing me by example that there are no limits to what I can achieve.

To Mom, Dad, and Camille: Thank you for being the best, most supportive, and loving family.

To my readers, new and old—this one's for you!

Beneath the sea, the dragon sleeps
What is he dreaming of?

Beneath the sea, the dragon sleeps
When will he wake?

On a dragon's pearl,
your wish will leap.

On a dragon's pearl,
your wish will leap.